# We Were Young

*Also by Niamh Campbell*

This Happy

# We Were Young

## Niamh Campbell

WEIDENFELD & NICOLSON

First published in Great Britain in 2022 by Weidenfeld & Nicolson
an imprint of The Orion Publishing Group Ltd
Carmelite House, 50 Victoria Embankment
London EC4Y 0DZ

An Hachette UK Company

1 3 5 7 9 10 8 6 4 2

A CIP catalogue record for this book is
available from the British Library.

ISBN (Hardback) 978 1 4746 1170 1
ISBN (Export Trade Paperback) 978 1 4746 1171 8
ISBN (eBook) 978 1 4746 1173 2
ISBN (Audio) 978 1 4091 8862 9

Typeset by Input Data Services Ltd, Somerset

Printed in Great Britain by Clays Ltd, Elcograf S.p.A.

www.weidenfeldandnicolson.co.uk
www.orionbooks.co.uk

*For my family*

GIRL ANGEL/SATAN:
There is only one woman in the world.

*The Last Temptation of Christ*, dir. Martin Scorsese, 1988/
Nikos Kazantzakis, 1955

In a bare room with a sacred heart, a tin tub full of water issues steam, gingerly, under hanging lamps. Cormac can see other people lined along the walls, pressing back against cement, and hear at intervals the shuffle of their feet.

There is a thin chair with a backrest like a fan. Cormac watches his friend and, latterly, colleague Alice sit in this: the gesture marks her as involved. A girl – an actress or an artist – enters from behind a partition. She wears a white gown. It seems more of an aesthetic choice than a concession to historical accuracy. The girl walks slowly and stiffly and her face is closed in pain.

On reaching the bath, the girl begins to undo the gown, to pluck at buttons, and in the time this takes, its excruciation, Cormac detaches to check out the set-up and the props. He notices an incongruously modern light switch by the door. Rain rushes over one of the long, deep windowpanes and leaks, arching, through apertures. Someone – a middle-aged woman – moves closer to the bath; she crouches down.

All wait.

Cormac is thirty-seven and has been moving in art circles

for a long time. He sees himself watching and watching the watching and still feels awkward about it.

The actress, naked, steps into the bath. Her stomach is soft and she has no pubic hair. Tan lines mime a swimsuit, which seems decadent in November. Cormac feels aroused and panics slightly. Why did they have to choose an actress with a taut, sexy body? Is that really necessary? Are you supposed to ignore that?

Please, the girl says, can you pass me the soap?

A bar of soap, dry and sharp-cornered like a block of white cheese, sits in a dish. The middle-aged woman springs from her hunkers and hands the soap to the girl. Alice does not, however, stir; she watches intently as the girl begins to lather, shivering; as the girl begins to keen softly, wincing and gasping just. The pain is centred on her breasts. She moves as though her breasts are agonising. She has pop-up, youthful breasts, which are nice to look at. Cormac tries not to look.

Someone is singing somewhere – upstairs – voices – and it is, of course, *Ave Maria, gratia plena*.

Sitting forward in the water, the girl whispers to them, Do you know where my baby is? She asks, Do you know when my father is coming for me? It was two months ago I was left here. I think.

The women shake their heads, no.

Do you, the girl looks at Alice, do you know where my baby is?

I don't, Alice replies. She clears her throat. Cormac cannot see her face now, only the carved black bob of her hair. The mention of a baby is painful and he doesn't want to think about it. Some more people have entered this phase of the show, so he moves away from the wall and

2

leaves: he takes the opportunity of folding himself into a group shuffling out.

In the next room, there stands a coffin on wheels and stems; two girls keeping watch in aprons and smocks; a hush, a peephole in the wall, a grille; the face of a woman glaring back at them.

This room is worse, he thinks.

All coffins take him back to the first coffin of life. That coffin on its stems, indenting a marshy rug before the fireplace, still tips into his dreams sometimes to roll idly down inclines like a child's disaster pram.

Impishly, Cormac figures, I'll say this to Alice. I was *triggered*.

Alice, unbelievably, is still in the previous section. The sequence, he guesses, has one or two more instalments. A door to the side of his eye discloses frantic movement in a small adjacent room. Cormac thinks: It's so small, if I move in there someone will implicate me and I'll have to go along with it.

Better stay put.

A young woman has approached the coffin and is reading the nameplate. Her red hair is caught at the back, half-knotted in a scarf, and by the low lights her complexion is peaches and cream. She does not have the face of a model, but the rosy distribution of her features could be made to look achingly noble, achingly delicate. As he thinks this, she becomes conscious of his attention and looks up, alarmed. Cormac turns away to face a blacked-out window with despair.

Alice has progressed: she is sliding into an alcove in a corner of the room. Cormac wonders if, at this point, Alice is tormenting him, if it has started to become comical to her. Watching her now he can see she is absorbed. She was not afraid of the naked actress.

What? asks the woman by the coffin suddenly.

Cormac starts. The room has been so quiet but for 'Ave Maria' upstairs, the muffled sounds of action in the small adjacent room. Now everyone, the audience against the walls, is looking at him.

What? repeats the girl.

She is glaring at Cormac. He cannot tell if she is an actress or a member of the audience. Has he been staring at her? No. She is an actress, or unhinged. He looks back and shakes his head. Don't bring me into this.

What?

Oh god, is she an actress or not?

The women in smocks, sitting in chairs, do not look up. She has to be an actress then. And yet she wears a raincoat, a pashmina scarf. Facing him, her cheeks are high and flush with body heat.

I – don't know what you mean, Cormac says weakly.

From her alcove, Alice leans forward. She is smiling ever so slightly at him. She is watching with everyone else.

Do you know the way out? the girl asks him now.

Cormac's heart sinks. No, he says.

The audience, blissfully left out of this shit, continues to watch him with interest.

You must know, the girl insists.

Well, I mean, there's a door downstairs, Cormac says. He hears a rustle of laughter and feels emboldened a little by this.

The girl does not respond.

Cormac jumps when a hand sneaks onto his shoulder.

It's another actress – demonstrably in a smock this time – and she whispers, Come with me.

This new actress leads him back the way they came, but instead of turning into the room, she pushes a fire escape and reveals a staircase to the street. Cormac feels the blast of the evening, sees the greasy glint of rain. The actress says, Run!

And then, as he advances towards the stairs: Come back through the front if you like.

The steps lead to a side street of sack-like cottages, where the rain has stopped and it's peaceful, with windows of television tumult and lamplight. He turns and sees the wide gap of Dorset Street. A kebab shop flashes green and yellow neon palm trees: yellow, green.

Behind, the fire-door smashes shut.

Oh thank god, Cormac says out loud, laughing.

On the pavement, as people are exiting the building in pairs, Alice pulls on her gloves.

What did you think of that? she asks.

Intense, Cormac decides. Really intense.

But in the bar he asks her, Do you think that was a bit simplistic, overly simplistic, or anything like that?

Not sure what you mean, she says.

There is a crowd in. They sit in one of the battered booths with menus in English and Korean, confident they don't need to look for anyone they know – it's Friday, their colleagues will be ranting over rounds in the place opposite the depressing Tesco on Bolton Street.

The pub, on the Northside, was a dive bar all its life until a strip of Asian restaurants absorbed it. The new owners left the place intact but started serving bibimbap

5

and fitted banquettes where the function room had been. It's still popular with whiskered men from the flats but also with art kids and organised anarchists, Spanish mullets and keffiyehs, girls with jags of crimson lipstick crossing and crunching together in kaleidoscope.

Cormac remembers Worker Party meetings when he was at college, which were composed of whiskered men with border convictions muttering internecine oaths in an upper room of the Teachers' Club. He would join the six or seven students pressing arselessly to a radiator at the back. They used to meet the Irish conversation class coming down the stairs.

Alice removes her coat now to reveal a panel of charcoal silk.

I like your gúna, Cormac says.

It's a skirt and top. She holds her arms up in an antique attitude. Her own lipstick is vampy and her movements ever slow and ironic.

She came to him that afternoon as he was trying to turn off a projection screen. If you didn't shut the system down correctly the next user might see your search history or otherwise trespass on prehensile impulses created by the internet. It's in Devices, she explained. The lecture hall was hot, windowless, artificially lit. He sweated distressingly under the lights. More and more, the rooms he teaches in look and feel like interfaces – nexuses of raw, unshaded, stage effects – instead of real places.

Just fix it for me, will you?

As she did she said, If you're free tonight I have tickets to a thing.

He was pleased. He likes it when she asks him to accompany her because this suggests she holds his opinion

6

in some esteem. He looks at her now, and looks at her often, but retains a more vivid and representative image – a summer evening, years ago – of Alice at an anniversary Mass for Thomas in a tube of snagged sateen, a pork-pie hat. She was back from Berlin and staying with him, sleeping with him, and that night they hitched to Sutton beach for a rave.

You think – simple? she prompts now, in the booth, of the show.

Maybe that's not the right word. I mean, he winces, there's this idea of virtue behind it, right? Of righting wrongs.

Not righting wrongs but bearing witness.

Yeah but, he smiles at her, you know what I mean.

Culture doing what politics won't, she supplies.

He is surprised and encouraged by how developed this opinion seems, implying the integrity of a system of ideas he could slot his own irritation into. He agrees.

He says, I suppose so – but I mean it gives this. He pauses now. It gives this *eternal subject*, always right-on and virtuous. Nobody can argue with it.

You want, Alice asks, to dispute the wrongness of locking up unwed mothers in workhouses?

Of course not.

The wrongness, then, of representing it?

No – no. No, I mean, there's a whole historical *complexity* and the issue, say, of incarceration, of class.

Class?

A boy arrives to take their orders. When he asks if they want knives and forks, Cormac and Alice look aghast. In his wake Cormac fills their glasses and collects his thoughts, conscious of her attention and wishing to live up to it.

7

She looks at her phone a moment, but her facial expression is quietly canalled: she has a son – he is fifteen – named, phosphorescently, Ambrose.

Theatre is a middle-class thing, Cormac begins at last.

Not always.

Ali. He shakes his head as if disappointed. Pretty much always, he says.

Not inherently then. Now she is trying not to smile.

No. I suppose the Yiddish workman's theatre and Brecht and the supreme subaltern whatever. The Shannon Fisherman's Guild. By now both of them are laughing. I am sure such forms are inherently pure. But in Dublin only the middle class will ever go to the theatre.

How dare they, she says.

How dare they, he agrees.

Eat the rich. What happened to *eat the rich*?

We ate them.

We became rich!

Speak for yourself, Cormac says. Let me think about this and get back to you.

I'm all ears.

I can't say anything.

I wasn't aware you were saying anything.

But, a beat later: I think what you're trying to say, she concedes, is that it's not automatically morally superior to use these things for art.

He is gratified to feel she must agree. I wonder, he ventures, about it being self-congratulatory.

It lets, she admits, pretty actresses play distress.

Cormac nods mildly, still more pleased. You think?

You think, she accuses.

No. I didn't mean the actresses.

8

She laughs warmly then. Through the crush of the pub they see mullioned windows, a stained-glass crest, the calamitous flash of a passing ambulance. Here's our food, she says. The boy places down two plates of sushi, green squirts of mustard, chopsticks in paper sleeves.

I mean, Cormac continues, I don't think the acting was bad necessarily.

Well it's confrontational – it's supposed to make you feel uncomfortable.

They didn't make you feel uncomfortable.

I'm a woman, Alice explains simply. I don't need my dominance toppled.

And I do?

I don't think it would ever happen to you.

The food is good, and brief. When Cormac glances around for distraction some moments later, having finished his meal in a series of swipes, he sees Nina – sees her at once, across the room. She is sitting on a bar stool and talking animatedly. Her hands are raised and her eyes are rounded, earnest and alight. She sits in profile so a lamp behind shines pinkly on her piled-up reddish hair.

She's been there for a while, reports Alice.

And did she see us, do you think?

I don't know.

Cormac suspects that she, Alice, does know, and he feels sunned by fortune suddenly. He waits until Nina turns, suspiciously casual, before saluting her – she sees him and breaks into a grin, her dimples even from here in steep relief.

She has an opening soon, he tells Alice.

She never turned in anything that time.

Did you want something from her? For the magazine?

9

Yes, a review, ages ago. Alice speaks in a cooler tone. It was nothing. You want to say hi?

I'll ask for the bill while I'm up, Cormac says. He crosses the bar in the echo of this abruptness. It is petulance. What she said about dominance: *I don't think it would ever happen to you.* He does not scrutinise or sift these feelings, however, but melts into the heat of Nina's greeting, her novelty.

Where have you been lately? the girl shouts, with mischief, over the noise of the bar. You haven't been seen. There's a bounty on your head.

All lies. He holds up both his hands.

Dead or alive. The genius Cormac. Always lovely to see you. She is chanting and turning from him. She is with friends.

It's after eleven when Cormac walks home. He takes the route from North to Southside: follows the tramline down Abbey Street, under the sad yellow sign for a mid-century employment agency, to turn at the Gin Palace and cross the Ha'penny Bridge. Some of these outlines or the script of vestigial shop signs make him remember colophons, bosses, met in earliest life.

He has thought before of a fantastic walking tour that would cause holograms of intimate inscription to pop up over corners and buildings, like a computer; so instead of the Google logo, you might have the state publisher *An Gúm* – detail from an illustration glimpsed in a textbook, nineteen-eighty-seven – or the emboss of a scout medal for bike repair, *bi ullamh*; do you see? A button click would cause the past to cascade as contextless images, flat: time itself revealed to be circular after all.

This would be clever, but you worry that other people don't experience the environment in the same way. That it wouldn't resonate.

It's getting late now and the streets are loosening. On the bridge, a man in a blanket breaks into action and holds out a cup that is bitten at the edges like a lip.

Spare change for a hostel, he calls.

Do you want, Cormac asks, something in the shop? He nods towards the Centra blazing like a shrine on Merchant's Quay.

The man considers it, then says, Not really to be honest now.

Cormac enters the dazzle of the shop and dials for a twenty from the ATM and, as he waits, thinks, I hope it has twenties left. There were years – years ago – when everything was fifty notes only, idiot agape of the city's cash machines. He breaks the twenty up and crosses the bridge again, jiggering with chill by now, to poke a folded note into the cup.

Ah, says the man. Good man.

He does this periodically. Say every six weeks. It buys karma and some distance; it measures time. Two years in the city centre now. Did not expect to stay this long.

Cormac continues along the quay, the suicide strip of low wall and the light on the river ribbing and recomposing. The quaint boxy burgher building on the corner of Essex Street. Crowds.

At first, he thinks there's another homeless person crouched in the doorway to his building, then wonders if it's one of the loiterers who routinely pretend to be lost as they pace before the laneway to the gay sauna. Up close, though, he realises it is Patrick, sitting on the step.

Heya, Cormac hails.

His older brother slides to his feet with great reluctance, as if in pain. Even out of his work suits, Patrick always looks formal and handsome and funereal; he holds himself languidly, stooping from the spine.

What's up? Cormac asks.

No less than three lads, Patrick drawls, in the last half-hour have asked if I want to go into that fucking sauna.

Did you consider it? Cormac puts his key into the lock.

I was starting to think that at least I'd be warm. I was wondering where you were. I've been ringing you.

My battery died. Cormac pushes the door to. The windowless hallway smells of trapped air and, on the floor, a layer of news-sheets and menus have become coloured mulch. Were you out in town? He asks this without looking at Patrick.

I went to Brogan's for a while. Where were you?

Theatre. Alice.

I see. *Theatre*, Patrick says.

Cormac knows by his mood that Patrick has been put out by his wife again and decides to be gracious.

You should try it sometime, you might get civilised.

I'll have you know, says Patrick, standing now by the barricade of bicycles, Deloitte have been sponsoring shit for years and given us tickets many times. I will have you know I am not unfamiliar with the theatre.

He asks, What floor are you again?

Three, Cormac reminds him. Very top.

The men begin to climb, and as they do, the building stretches and tightens around them audibly. The steps are hollow and the walls hollow. A child, perhaps, has dragged a pencil against the paint, consistently, a faint fault-line.

12

Their bodies trip the sensors so the lights wake up, wetly, like eyes.

I'll have you know, Patrick continues, that I saw *Anna Karenina* in the summer and it was like looking into a fucking mirror, let me tell you, of my life.

Cormac lets them into the flat, where a window slightly open in the kitchen-living room spreads the sound of the street. The air smells fresh from rain, and potent in its coolness, like a wild thing. It's November, but the *Weltgeist* since September has been climate-catastrophe mild. The apartment looks onto a square of slippery paving slabs and benches, in the shadow of City Hall. In daylight, tourists and addicts sit on the benches; by night, revellers expelled by Dame Lane pause there to fraternise or hail taxis or buy pills from a well-dressed, banker-looking guy who always meets with a rougher man for the midnight rush. The banker is the face of the operation and the rough one takes a seat, on a news-sheet spread with care, in front of the Castle gates.

Patrick slaps the switch, but Cormac reverses this and turns on table lamps. The place feels welcoming now, even though the kitchen chairs are broken and the recycle bin overflowing. Patrick looks around for something to comment on and then, inspired, asks, How's Alice?

Good I think, Cormac says. He raises the blind of the opposite window, closes the open window, and dims the more vigorous lamp.

Still getting divorced?

I presume. Cormac pauses to judge the atmosphere, the angle of coffee table and irascible shag, the ceiling with its bulb like a drop of ice.

What is the husband like again?

Garrett – oh, he's just a prick really. Beat up his own hole.

Aren't you all?

Well yes, but this one more so, Cormac says. The thing is, he explains, Garrett and Alice edit this journal together, they run it, you know about that? They've been doing it for years. They are still business partners.

Nightmare. Patrick has lost interest.

Last year, when an edition of the journal came out without any of the visuals Cormac supplied, Garrett sent him an email from the editorial account that read: Dear FILL, thank you for your interest. While we liked your work we have not found a place for it this time. Please feel free to submit again in future.

The sound of the street, now, is the sound of the ocean or a storm outside. Patrick sits on the sofa, on the morass of throws preserving the sofa, and sinks into it quickly; annoyed, he hauls himself to the harder edge. Can I smoke? he asks through a cigarette.

Cormac reaches for the plastic ashtray that he keeps on top of a press. Putting it before Patrick, he says, So, wine or something? Whiskey?

What do you have?

Just that.

Whiskey then. No beer?

Hang on. No, no beer.

The Jameson is Senan's and the flat is Senan's too, although Cormac has been renting it so long ownership has become, intuitively if not legally, muddled. Senan, a composer, is either on tour or on residency or in Berlin. Sometimes he stays with his parents outside Edenderry, recording samples and playing piano in a soundproofed cowshed. Cormac has not seen him since June, when he came by one weekend and stayed, picking guitar and leaving a half-read novel open everywhere – the couch, the table, the toilet – like a witless hint.

Senan bought the apartment with his brothers. There are five of them altogether. Senan is last and *the shakings of the bag*: he is slight and precise, tow-headed into adulthood, darting through a crowd in an auditorium or lobby or party or street always, hood up, head down, onto something or out to meet someone. Even now he comes and goes with little warning. He took Cormac out to Edenderry once: in the bedroom that had been Senan's, there hung equestrian rosettes faded by sunlight and a framed picture of Snoopy the Dog. The place was a self-built bungalow and about the melancholiest thing Cormac had ever seen. His mother was small like Senan and placed her hands on her son's shoulders as if blessing him, or compressing him, singing, My little pal he was, my little pal!

Whiskey can make a man mean, Patrick remarks, looking at the bottle.

There's always tea.

I'll put water in it. Patrick stands and sees to himself at the sink. The kitchen is a strip of linoleum in country dun. Each of the glasses has a county crest on it. They remind Cormac of holidays to the north-west in childhood, of turf-smell and ginger ale, a bath of well-water drawn for him in a house on sand and gravel overlooking the lough. This was their cousins' house, the farm with its sunken and guttered pigpen, the bath of yellow well-water without bubbles or foam.

He, Cormac, at four or five years old, backed up crying out and refused: What is that, what is it, what?

15

He remembers Thomas sitting in the bath, leaning out – Thomas's face, at nine or ten, intact.

Cormac's glass, in his hand, wears the crest of Tipperary. He thinks, I know absolutely nothing about Tipperary. I couldn't even place it on a map.

The well-water looked dirty: he had not wanted to get into it. The well-water had been the colour of beer.

When Patrick returns to the sofa he smokes for a moment before saying, So, tell me all your news. Cormac laughs, as he knows he is expected to.

How's Ursula? he parries back. Patrick reacts with a private twitch of the eyes.

I'm lying low, he says, tonight.

Well, I didn't think you were here for the craic.

Patrick looks sharply at him. Yeah, no, he says, I can just go, Cormac, like, I'll find somewhere else, OK?

Cormac swallows a mouthful of the Jameson and shakes his head. Not, he coughs, what I mean.

It's not a problem, right? I can go to Kehoe's.

Don't be stupid, stay.

Cormac thinks: And anyway, seriously, Kehoe? But then he feels sorrow on Patrick's behalf – a surge of loving dread – which becomes pity, and thrilling.

And how are – the kids?

They're asleep, Patrick answers gruffly.

How much calmer he felt, Cormac thinks, with Alice, just a small time ago. How calm in her company. And how he had shone in the ten-minute attention of Nina, who was tipsy but also chaperoned by some guy and dipped in queenly conspiracy to Cormac, whispering fiercely, It's been so long since we hung out! How happy, he thinks, I was. A mere hour ago.

It's lively out there, Patrick says.

Friday night.

What play? Patrick asks suddenly, fixing his eyes in a resting gaze on the pane. What theatre?

Cormac frowns. He must feign a degree of simplicity to avoid making Patrick feel stupid. It was – you know, immersive?

Huh?

You go into the play, like; you are part of it.

Oh right.

It was about Magdalene laundries, he explains.

Patrick looks taken aback at this, but then smiles with faint wickedness. Oh, he says.

So it was dark.

What, did you, like, have to wash sheets or something?

Just watch mostly. But, Cormac sits up and twists towards Patrick in his chair. Get this, at one point I'm just standing or whatever, in this room, with a coffin.

What? Patrick barks. A coffin? With a body?

No. I mean, I presume not. It was shut. It was a prop. So anyway, I am just standing there and this girl comes in, dressed normally – like, the actors and actresses are all in either this, period costume, or nude. But she wasn't. I thought she was a member of the audience.

She was a plant.

Cormac begins to nod vigorously. Yes! he says. A plant!

Did she talk to you?

She starts saying, *What, what, what?* Like, as if I'd been staring at her.

Were you?

I don't think so.

Was she hot?

17

Cormac feels a flutter of shame but answers anyway, Little bit.

Sounds stressful, Patrick commiserates.

You know what? It was very fucking stressful.

Stay away from them theatres. Patrick shakes his empty glass. Stay away from them *actresses*.

Help yourself.

Patrick pours another whiskey and lights another cigarette. He does not dilute the drink this time.

So you went to a play with a naked woman in it? When Cormac nods, Patrick asks, And where can this play be witnessed?

It's an old bank. Not a theatre. They had it set up inside – Cormac shapes this with his hands – like a bar and a parlour and then cells or something. It's empty. It's been boarded up. Probably the National Assets Agency, like, owns it now.

Patrick smokes thoughtfully for a moment and then says, We're backing a data analysis intervention, with academics, on vacant properties in Dublin. He refers to Deloitte. Making a database, he continues, to categorise them as derelict, habitable, private, probate, protected, things like that. So it's humanitarian. He speaks this technical language fluently. It is one of his registers: the others are bawdy, boyish and profound.

Humanitarian?

It's towards solution-based approaches to the housing crisis. It's, you know, co-funded by UCD.

As opposed to what, destruction-based approaches?

To what? Oh, right. Patrick says: As opposed to nothing at all. It gets results.

It gets profit, I'm sure.

Same thing, darling, Patrick says. But, you know, your shtick is always cute.

My shtick?

Noble. He drains his glass. *Beautiful soul.*

This makes Cormac laugh. Fuck you, he says. He stands up, feigning casualness, and continues, I'm going to have tea and I'll make you one.

No tea for me, Patrick objects, but when Cormac places the mug before him he picks it up and sniffs.

What's on in the window? he asks. He raises a hand and points to it. It's like a TV, that window. Especially since you don't actually have a TV. Every time Patrick comes into the apartment he makes this point as if he has only just thought of it.

I can stream on the laptop, Cormac drills.

Both rise, bored, and move to the window and watch the street. The crowd has diminished and everyone is wasted now; two men hanging onto each other try to hail a cab but are distracted by women with heels in their hands walking zombie-awkward down Dame Street. A road-sweeper grinds along the kerb, grazing the pavement with its brushes. These buff the shoes of the men and cause the men to leap back, shouting abuse.

You want to go to bed?

Yeah, but I'll shower, Patrick says.

When Cormac lies down, Patrick lies next to him, smelling wet, and passes into sleep immediately.

Cormac watches headlamps calculate across the ceiling, preoccupied by the constipated awkwardness of sharing a bed with someone who is not a lover. He has known Patrick for longer, of course, than any lover – he has known Patrick all his life – but time and ascension into identities have made them strange. Patrick will not sleep on the couch. Cormac suggested it once and Patrick laughed. This is because he is tall: tall and an arsehole. Cormac knows that to sleep in the living room himself would be a sin of capitulation and so when this happens, and it happens lately with more frequency, they lie side-by-side like boys again.

The room is greyly basic, books crushed into corners and firmed like mud, and there have never been curtains or blinds. In here the ceiling is also high, the bulb he doesn't use dropped low in compensation, and plastered in scalloped motions which comb it in total harmony, each wave building to be broken on the next.

He remembers the dead mobile phone and realises that not only will it chronicle calls from Patrick, but many missed calls from Ursula, as well as messages in her tautly melodious tone. He will be summoned. There may even be lunch in a café of women in pastels, the bubble and squeak of engagement diamonds table-to-table, scent of lemongrass cologne.

Can you pass me the soap?

Do you know the way out?

You have to know.


When he first moved back to the city, two years before, Alice phoned out of nowhere and asked, Is this your number, this is still your number, yes?

No, it's someone else.

Would you like a gig?

Depends.

Rehearsal shots for *An Triail*.

It's in Irish.

The photographs will not be in Irish, she said. But if you don't want money, that's fine. If you want to starve and stay in your mother's box room, that's fine.

I'm not in a box room. But he was laughing. I have a place in town.

He took the commission and cycled to one of the Georgian buildings on Parnell Square. It had been the council chambers for Fingal and Cormac said, on learning this, Oh wow, I'm from Fingal. No one responded to this or asked him anything: Alice only introduced the actors and left. The building was being restored – downstairs, corridors were diffused by pale terrazzo and smelled of Dettol, flower water, candle wax, smelled like primary school, and spindly stairs turned beneath a carriage clock. On the first floor, a huge room lined with mahogany was fitted with ancient benches and stalls, a table inlaid with leather at the centre, everything shining in ghoulish puce. It looked like a nightmare from the eighteenth century. It looked like a ghost story by Sheridan Le Fanu.

It's incredible, isn't it? the actors cooed.

Every chair in the place was mighty and spiked, every surface was polished but dark as wine, finished with shamrocks and sigils and unicorns. The ambience was red – of redwood, cabernet, oxblood – so that it pulsed or ached an auric, hellish red. Cormac had a sense that every lacquered dresser, every holy parlour, of his life had been aspiring to look like this nightmare room.

A pale girl sat in the dock for her photographs and gazed at a velvet curtain; the actor playing the cad posed in a judge's throne with a halo of carvings above his head. He looked insouciantly up. He looked, when Cormac was reloading, between Cormac's legs.

21

Cormac remembers it partly because the commission led to work and further work, it was the first move he made towards staying in Dublin, but mostly because of the crush of the room. The shock of its age enclosed him with intimacy, aching with an opulence he found freakish and stimulating. It comes down to atmospheres – trying to decant and describe atmospheres. This is life. As he took more pictures, just of the room this time, the actors chattered and dispersed. The air of sexual intrigue about them was more boring than they knew. Pretty soon he was by himself, looking down at the mundanity of Parnell Street from a window with panes that felt cold and friable, like slate.

Happy, or at least awake. It had been some time.

Alice arrived at five and there was hope in her eyes, a surprising openness. He thought of this as her mother-look, even though it predated her becoming a mother, which she had at twenty-five. He told her, It's absolutely beautiful upstairs, come and see.

I've seen it before.

It's for hanging judges, he said. The four horsemen. Landlords shot with muskets on the way back from a league meeting. All of history.

He said, It reminds me of my old school.

There's a lot of history to it, yes. Alice was smiling at him. Weakly or lovingly now. His enthusiasm. He could have reached out and touched her cheek, she might have responded erotically.

If you stay, she promised, you will be working almost all the time. Your reputation is sound and I have a lot of contacts I can share.

Aw shucks.

Whatever you like, she said. Ungrateful runt.

He dreamt of it, the chamber of wine-coloured shadow, regularly. Somewhere between kidney stones and a poem. Wakes in the darkness with a white shoulder turned away, his brother's shoulder, thinking of the Old English word *uhtcaera*, or dawn-sorrow, not only because of the blue hour in the two chastely separate panes but because he learned *uhtcaera* from a theatre director after the opening night of *An Triail*. It was at the Pavilion. Alice introduced them, gathered with others in a restaurant of deal tables scrubbed to the colour of buttermilk and three options only on the menu: clams, haddock, hake.

Do you smoke? the director asked, leaning back on the communal bench to shout around the narrow shoulders of the *Times* editor between them.

No, Cormac apologised. Well, if I'm drunk.

Well, drink up and come out, the director said.

They stood by a halogen lamp on the street. It was dark and growing turbulent at sea, with wind ripping over the pier and shaking rigging audibly – gory locks, he thought randomly, weirdly: *shake your gory locks at me* – and this wind also pulled at the awning of the restaurant. It made noises: noises everywhere. People still promenaded with umbrellas bent against it in the dark. The director was Cormac's own age and dark-haired, broad but of average height, impatient with the play and with the insincere talk inside.

Nobody speaks the language, he complained.

Ah, but the *libretto*.

Fuck it. It just gets funded, the director laughed, to write in Irish, he said. The *Times* guy is over from London. No, not for this – just generally. I know him. Do you know him? The director dropped a name.

Oh sort of, vaguely, Cormac realised. I went out with one of his sisters.

You did?

Long time ago. Art school.

Funny, the director squinted. Alice said . . .

Oh both ways, Cormac assured him chipperly. His voice sounded over-earnest, but he had been back a mere matter of weeks and it was lonely.

The director had spoken at length, over haddock and/or clams, about a fascist countess you could stay with in Spain, the widow of a Francoist with a grand house that she rented for residencies. He'd spoken with so much ire Cormac knew he was nervous. Little leather florets on her shoes, the director insisted: little leathery florets. He half goose-stepped beneath the table angrily. His sneering was ugly but also touchingly adolescent. Now, standing outside, he stooped somewhat to smoke hungrily. When Cormac said *both ways,* the director burst into surprised laughter and said, Tonight I have to travel all the way back to Louth. I am staying in this place. He bowed and turned away and looked fretfully towards the harbour, the pier, the promenade. Clanging, ringing, carried everywhere. It was strange.

Cormac felt sadistically confident. Can I come? he asked.

No, the director snapped. More gently, then: Not tonight.

It had been some time.

Cormac set out the following evening. The director picked him up in a stale, unwieldy car, smoking once more, fresh smoke spicy in the gloom of older, layered smoke, at Dundalk train station.

This place is pretty strange, he warned. I'm minding it. I'm a kind, he continued, of ornamental hermit. He was stooping again, his hair extremely black and his clothes more casually aristocratic this time – a linen shirt loose, pale slacks. He was big-eared and heavy-lidded and sexy, and there was something rustic to his looks at odds with the bohemian dress, the obvious stress and impatience with which he floored it through back roads and narrow lanes, the fey gesture with which he held up an eternal cigarette.

I am on an adventure, Cormac thought.

Why haven't we already met?

I've been away, Cormac said. And anyway, I'm hardly on the scene, these days.

You are pals with Alice though?

A long time. You know – art school.

A great woman. She told me to take you out. She said you're sad.

Cormac absorbed the lie with new solicitude; the man was nervous again. She's right, he said. I'm very sad. He asked, Where are you from?

Durham. Now, the man barked. Here we are.

They turned into a long drive, lined with darkening trees, that wound superciliously around a large landscaped green and opened before a turreted country house. It looked vacant and foreboding, or demented, as all ascendancy architecture ends up appearing. The turrets were kind of insane.

Wow, Cormac contributed.

I'm in the stables. Yes, for real. The owner is a tech guy from California. He likes opera. I'm going to write about it, the place, I mean.

The director parked the car before a stable-house with stalls taken out and smoothed over: it was smaller than the big house, but still elegantly unusual, yellow light trumpeting out of a large window over the double doors with certain luxury. After the engine it was quiet but, as they stepped out into the still evening, Cormac heard, all around, the menacing and collective kvetching of rooks.

Spooky, he offered this time, stupidly.

Oh you get used to it, the director said.

The director's cock kinked upwards and tasted of soap scum. His body was formed solidly, not in a way that suggested labour but rather some inborn earthiness or genetic eloquence: this kind of body was rare and, to Cormac, fascinating. It was a big-brother, older-boy body, a father-body, thatched with black hair, nipples spaced apart crazily. There was a huge half-moon outside the window as they fucked. Afterwards the director lay smoking and gestured to the remote rafters overhead, gaping and accumulating shade, like the ceiling of a cathedral.

I dream I hear horses, he told Cormac, and smell horses. I think it's haunted by horses. Do you want to sleep?

Yes, Cormac sighed. He pushed the heels of his hands into his eye sockets and yawned. It's been some time.

Me too, the director said quietly.

In the blue hour, the first light, they were woken by cold and the pallet bed was fragrantly close to the floor, like a planter or something more notionally ghoulish – a grave – and, feeling him stir, the director spooned him from behind in a gesture of surprising affection or predation spoiled by the whisper of, Are you sad, are you feeling sad? It was so absurd, Cormac didn't reply. He wondered why he was being mocked when they were both here, both awake, on the floor of a stable behind one of the many grand houses a person working in a provincial art scene tends to encounter, the ancestral homes and piles and fantastic albatrosses of directionless heiresses and tech guys from California. Of the patron class.

Cormac had watched people injure themselves by falling off garden statues after midnight in midsummer, seen handbag designers streak hysterically through a butty garden maze, cycled for champagne and DMT up the drive of a horn-rimmed country house outside which someone had graffitied ROBBER BARONS – really, literally that – so that the squire son had left it there out of mirth and complex, gilded Leftism.

If being mocked was a prelude to sex it felt depressingly like something a girl would go through.

But the director said, with sudden kindness in Cormac's ear, At this time of day you wake up lonely because it's instinctive. There is even an Old English word for it – *Uhtcaera*. It means dawn-sorrow. I remember it because of u-h-t *uht*. Like UHT milk. Like milk-sorrow. Because I think dawn and milk go together.

It sounded prepared but it was beautiful. Say again, Cormac said.

*Uhtcaera.*

Milk and dawn.

Don't know where I get that from.

Cows and dawn and farms, I suppose, Cormac said. The director struck him as tenderly English in that minute, English like the foolish-seeming flatness of farmland when you leave St Pancras, in a northerly direction, by train; English like *all shall be well and all shall be well*; English like a chapel in Surrey he saw with wooden saints remaining but their eyes, which had been pearls, were jimmied out; English like a saint named Pancras.

Cormac experienced an expansive sense of political empathy and rolled over to take the kinked, solid quality of the cock in his hand, kiss lips roughened by a night of side-by-side dehydration. Felt a jaw pressing back too passionately out of advantage in the way people do when they know that they might not see you again. This made Cormac feel superior in the instant because he understood himself as genial company, as relatively effervescent, as capable – these days – of living in a city and tolerating people, not hacking out to the countryside for elegance and misery. The first months after Alva, the months spent panicking in his mother's house, were fading now.

Oh yes – it was possible. All manner of things could be well. He wanted to leave shortly after, and though he did not say so, the director knew. Cormac felt the shaming vibrations of the other man's awkwardness. Extending empathy once again, he asked, Can you show me the house, or will they not be awake?

They won't be awake but I'll show you, the director said.

Together they entered by a back door accessed through a kitchen garden, which was frozen and close to the earth – slight green florets frosted and wadded resiliently: Cormac thought, *little leathery florets*, of the fascist countess with her veal strips and boiling broth, her pendulous flesh, her spiteful conversation, so real to them all as it was sketched over clams and/or hake: flies buzzing brutally in the backdrop of her *fucking galería* – because the door was left unlocked. The little bloom of cruelty made him feel bad by association. He put a hand on the director's arm

28

and squeezed it as they came into a large, brassy kitchen, suggestive of the kitchen in a hotel, with copper pots hanging on the walls like a brass section.

The odour of freon and drainwater made Cormac think, always, of his adolescent stint as kitchen porter, restoring history to him in a single insubstantial strobe.

They padded around the ground floor with creaturely care so as not to disturb anyone, passing through a morning room and a dark library and a reception hall with a flowing staircase and brass rods anchoring a thick carpet. In the suspenseful silence, it felt like Christmas morning, everything enchanted.


Patrick disturbs him in the morning with a shudder of the bed. He is dressed and smoking obnoxiously, smoothing hair in the tile of mirror.

I'm off, he says.

Are you sure?

Listen, if she calls, don't say anything.

There's nothing to say, Cormac reminds him. You didn't do anything.

Patrick laughs. No, he says, I didn't do nothing. Stay in bed, it's grand. I have to go: remember, all right. If she phones. I was good.

I'm not lying to your wife, Cormac calls.

After this he switches on the shower and stands under a hitched pitchfork of water – thinned by limescale: *need to treat* – enjoying a suspension of critical thought. A fossilised cobweb quivers in one of the high corners of the ceiling, its spider twisting idly like a bead, as Cormac thinks complacently, I wonder how long it will stay that way. You never see a spider decay.

At first it was hard, even painful, to live alone, and even now the physicality of the place can overwhelm him; it is grey and large and lumpenly present, established in its identity rather than yielding to him. He lives with it more than in it. Just now he steps into the front room, where the radiator has turned the air clingy with heat, and rolls out the foam mat to meditate. Sits cross-legged.

Ordinary, orderly thoughts wisp by the mind inconsequentially, undisruptive: with kindness, a kindred organising conscious watches them.

How good at this I've gotten, Cormac thinks.

Long ago: the mock-fort opposite the Saint Vincent de Paul children's home. Off-season with the long grass wet and blue. Mock-fort sprayed with an obscene fleet of Pacman heads and smelling, within, of piss. Memory of this. Memory of the kitchen garden, the countess.

Memory of a girl in a circle, Hamburg, tilting her head forward into the hit for a moment before launching back, throwing her wide eyes over them. She said, with horror or dissatisfaction, I've seen infinity, that was it.

These thoughts pass always, only pass, specific but nodal or closed. If discomfort comes it is physical and exact, it is the crunch of spinal discs where these meet the base of his back; it is the organs pressing wetly between bones. This creates a carsickness or sensation of weight. It's distracting, but no position that isn't flat relieves it, and lying flat feels like cheating.

Cormac speaks to this discomfort, or tries to, by a method of echolocation that sounds out symbolic resonances. He learned this from Sadbh, who he met again shortly after London. He met her at some opening and she was dressed as a woman named Sadbh should be dressed: draped like a hodegetria in cheesecloth and hiding a child behind the sublimated column of a leg. She'd had a shaved head at art school but now her hair was grey-blonde in abundance. At art school she had been a gifted typist and Cormac told her: I remember you typing my essays for me.

I was a giver, Sadbh agreed.

She then embraced him robustly, without warning, before stepping back to take him in. People look at Cormac a lot because Cormac is good-looking but, at this point, shortly after the shoot for *An Triail*, and on account of the break-up that had sent him home – the break-up with Alva – quite a few people were not speaking to him. They glided by with bared teeth or buffed against that ring of enchantment a community places around one lately returned from abroad. Even if you'd slept with a person once, they might act like they're not sure who you are, although sometimes this is down to a husband in the background now, or a wife.

Sadbh's exuberance was a faintly destabilising tonic, then, at this opening of long portraits, huge windows, a drunk breathing onto a pane outside with bitter mischief, especially when she invited him out to her house in Bray that weekend. She was edging into Wicklow proper at the time. Alice said, Be careful, she'll send you away with a love potion.

I wouldn't mind one, Cormac replied.

This was ungenerous of Alice. What Sadbh had was a cabin at the end of her garden, a massage table, a bundle of burning sage. That huge chiropractical poster of chakras or chi-lines you see everywhere. She placed him naked on the table and lined crystals on his spine. His penis was slack with terror the entire time; there was nothing inappropriate, he'd agreed to the naked table, and it felt unnerving not because it was invasive but because it was all-embracing, motherly.

After the naked crystals, Sadbh sat next to him on a camping chair and nodded as he started to explain about Alva in the well-rehearsed terms he used for everyone but found the voice telling the tale detaching from him, speaking like a radio, giving way to acid flatness, stopping in his throat. He began to weep without feeling and she watched him through owlish glasses. She said, No need to apologise. As he dressed afterwards, she continued, There is a lot of blockage at your waist.

Cormac tried to joke. He said, Well I haven't had the ride in a while. As he said it, the crudity made him wince, but she didn't flinch.

She answered almost wonderingly, Oh no, that's not what it is at all. Come back, she told him, whenever you like.

Cormac sees the actress who harassed him at the play later that morning, waiting in a queue.

This is Beatyard, which is closing down, and early enough in the day that there is space and light around coffee and salad concessions; around picnic tables, hoardings, kids with beards and block fringes. The actress is queuing for coffee and Cormac is queuing too. He recognises the actress immediately as she stands staring into the middle distance.

Hey, says Cormac on a whim. She looks at him. I saw your play last night, he explains.

Did you? Cute creases flicker and melt on her forehead. Oh right! I was mean to you. Was that you?

Yeah, you were horrible.

Did you like it? She asks this earnestly.

Of course, Cormac lies.

That's good, because I was a late addition. My part, I mean. They weren't sure about including someone in, like, normal clothes? So that's good. Well. She picks up her cup and raises it. Nice talking to you!

You too! Cormac says.

He brings two coffees to the table where Alice sits with a notebook and, suddenly, her son Ambrose. The kid was not there when Cormac set off to buy coffees. His abrupt apparition makes Cormac start.

Ambie! What's the craic?

The boy lifts his face and smiles doggishly as if this is a joke. He has his father's features − dishwater blond but with curtains, girlishly angular − but not, so far, any pronounced personality, or rather a speculative gap where once-and-future selfhood might reside.

You've got tall, Cormac adds. The kid still stares.

Ambie's doing *Frankenstein*, Alice says as she smiles on her son.

The boy raises a paperback ruefully. He's enrolled at an intensely academic school but bowing and shy. Or at least Cormac thinks. It's been a while since he's seen the boy, who is frequently sent on enriching missions to stay with country and continental relatives. Just now he is also giving off a disquieting *Death in Venice* pang that is new − clear-skinned, slight-wristed, devoid of any apparent artfulness − and probably accidental.

The kid, his gaze unbrokenly levelled at Cormac, speaks at last and says, Mum and I are going to the dead zoo after this. You know, like.

33

The Natural History Museum. Can I come?

Cormac does not want to come.

No, says Alice.

The day is still mild but everyone is banked behind coloured scarves. Cormac, detaching from Ambie, catches sight of the actress as she weaves between bodies and seems to greet someone by the entrance to the yard. The space has a provisional feel, a clearing in urban decay, with breeze blocks and lumber and the red cladding of mansions backing shabbily onto it. A sash over the vegan fish wagon reads *Closing! Thanks to all of our customers!* Cormac points at this and says, Looks like they're saying: closing because of our customers.

Hmmm? Alice looks up. Thank you, she says to the coffee cup. Ambie has returned to *Frankenstein*.

That.

Oh yes. Alice squints behind her sunglasses.

Closing. Thanks to you bastards. Cormac sips his coffee, which is not very hot. I just saw the actress from the show last night, he says casually. You know, the one who asked me, *What?*

Caroline Brabazon.

Do you know her? He also says, Jesus, what a name.

Just of her. She's a dancer or a maker or something. Alva would know.

Cormac often guffaws at the word *maker* because he feels it is affectedly inclusive nuspeak for rich kids who collaborate adenoidally, but not this time. Alva is his ex-girlfriend, a choreographer on a scene with a maximum of four credibly employed choreographers orbiting like terrible emperors at any time. He clears his throat.

34

Ah right, he says. She's younger than Alva.

Alice looks again and smirks. She says, There he is, and Cormac follows her nod. Ambie turns his mild face in the same direction with interest.

A tall, gaunt man of late middle age is crossing the yard and scanning it purposefully, looking intensely out of place in a tattered Chaplinesque suit. When he sees them, the man ducks towards them and begins speaking long before he is close. His speech is a vowel-blown monologue without context or address.

Alice stands deferentially and extends a hand to shake, saying, Laz, thanks for meeting us. Cormac notices her accent sliding down a few scales and returns a version of her smirk.

So in the fifties, the man is droning, this place was a small breakers yard, then a petrol station, and these – he points army-style, aiming, at the dull mansions behind – would have been tenements, crowded tenements, right before the great movement, the great displacement, of all the tenement people to suburbs like Tallaght and Cabra and Crumlin: these places – he looks severely at Cormac now – were country villages or wasteland before that, you understand. *Tallaght* means plague grave, *Cabra* from *cabrach* or bad land. They took the people out of the tenements, out of these communities where they might have been poor but there was a strong sense of togetherness, they took the people out of the tenements and transposed them to these places on the outskirts which had been the sticks before that. Those lucky enough to get into the Iveagh Trust flats were different, the Iveagh flats were sought after, they were the Holy Grail, but since they were for Guinness employees first and foremost, there

35

was no permission to join a union – no unions allowed at Guinness; did you know that?

I didn't, Cormac replies. Alice is looking on with anxiousness, having removed her glasses and pawed with sudden clumsiness at the recorder. Ambie has, apparently amiably, returned to *Frankenstein*.

The man sits down on the edge of the slat where Alice sits. He stretches his long legs in the suit, his arms, before crashing a heavy elbow down on the tabletop.

I'm grateful, she starts to say.

This is still a populated area. People forget about that, but it's still a populated area. The Christian Brothers is still there – the man points again – and the Carmelite Friary would have been a central focus at one time. There's a population here and it's very mixed, but what they have in common – and thirty years I'm community organising here – what they have is a need for safety and quiet, for a quiet place to live. There are people, the man continues, looking now at Alice, who think Dublin is a theme park and forget that it's a populated area, it's been populated for two millennia.

To their untrusting astonishment, the man stops. He seems to be done.

Well, right, says Alice.

I'm Cormac, by the way.

Lazarian, says the man. As if used to bemusement he adds, dryly, Liberties in the fifties was a great place for names.

Beatyard have had their licence revoked, Alice explains at last. They'll be closing – she reads from the notebook – at the end of the month. The place is not zoned for housing.

Here? Lazarian chucks his head back.

Here, yes. Not zoned for housing.

Not suitable.

Yes, but without being zoned for housing, Alice presses, it will probably become another hotel.

Lazarian does not respond for a moment. Head back, the fleshless nostrils flare; when he swings forward again, he leans to look around the place, at the coffee queue and the young people dressed as if it were the nineties, a kind of styled congelation of how the world looked in a decade Cormac remembers. They wear those barbed wire chokers schoolgirls snapped distractedly in the cinema queue. A slipway at the Drogheda Omniplex.

Beatyard have been refused the licence, Lazarian explains at last, because of antisocial behaviour.

Antisocial behaviour emanating, definitely, from here? Alice has replaced her sunglasses.

Where else? The man shrugs, betraying a hint of bleak frustration that might in other contexts, Cormac thinks, give way to rage.

Canal drinkers, Alice says.

Lazarian lifts his weight from the table and causes it to clap.

So locals, you mean? So homeless?

Cormac is slightly frightened for Alice until the strange man shakes his head and smiles.

Hipsters, he says, all these hipsters think the closing of a business is the worst thing that can happen. The way they are talking about the space, you'd swear it was a kibbutz. Lazarian laughs. Where are these people when the corporation is selling off public land?

There's a whole agitation against that, Alice replies dully.

She has met the dualish darkening of atmosphere by remaining still, unreactive. We carried an article about it in July, she adds.

Lazarian holds up his hands.

This is a populated area, he says. All this hoo-ha about the licence being revoked, but has anyone asked the local people what they think? Antisocial behaviour at all hours – people drinking in the street, fighting.

But is that because of Beatyard? Alice persists.

You don't think so?

I'd say the proximity of the canal, she speaks steadily, has an effect. She puts down her pen. You have an interest, she praises, in landscape and zoning, and protecting Dublin. Leaving space for creative quarters and not only hotels.

I'm not much interested, Lazarian says, in creative quarters.

Arguably – and this is not necessarily my argument, but arguably – something like Beatyard, which hosts events and start-ups, is doing something useful with this space. Arguably, it's not possible for the centre of a city to be quiet at night. I also think a lot of the people living around here are paying high rents to live in the centre, and it's a contradiction to then try to make it as quiet as a suburb.

Well actually, Cormac finds himself interjecting, the South Circular is basically tenements again. Migrant workers. Ten-to-a-room and all that.

Alice looks at him vapidly. Ambie laughs.

People, Lazarian says, can't be dealing with antisocial behaviour where they live. As he speaks, he keeps his eyes, not unkindly, on the boy.

That's fair enough, says Alice.

It's very much a stereotype, Lazarian continues, to say that homeless people are causing it.

I'm not, protests Alice.

To me, Lazarian says, that's dodging the question. That's tarring people with the same brush. This kind of thing, this kind of thing you have always seen in this country – the poor are scapegoated. You think, he raises his voice, a hipster pub is the victim here; I say this kind of interest in a commercial enterprise is typical of people, the kind of people who want artisanal everything and will fight for that but not for the selling-off of council property, the selling-out of people at the bottom of the ladder, the lifeblood of this city, which is akin to murder of a whole, living culture in this city.

He concludes. He has pronounced it *artis-eeh-nal*.

All right, says Alice. That is your stance. She says, Can we get you anything? Cormac is going to take the photographs.

No, I have to get on. Lazarian looks at his watch. So you may as well get the photos going now.

Because he will not stop talking during the session Cormac catches the man open-mouthed and dark-eyed, like a prophet, with his strong face and powerful body hard against a blur of beards and block fringes.

When he has shaken their hands and left, Cormac packs up the Nikon and tells Alice, I don't really think he was listening to you.

Oh no, he was, Ambie disputes.

You were no help, she tells Cormac.

I'm sorry, I couldn't really think, like – I have no opinion, Cormac says, on the fight between hipsters and sans-culottes.

It's hipsters versus international hotel chains. It's hipsters versus fucking Condé Nast.

In many ways, he tells her sagely, these are the same thing.

Just you wait until you are gentrified out of Essex Street.

And put out to seed, he agrees. Will you want the photos straight away?

As soon as you can, but thank you for now. You're dismissed for the day. She stands up. Ambie follows, lapels on a smoking jacket hanging open like a broken bird. He wears a T-shirt underneath with what looks like the logo of a video game. Cormac feels a fatherly rush of approval towards Ambie, and is relieved.

I have no plans, he objects.

He wonders, wincingly, about the dead zoo.

Well we do, Alice says. Do some work, do some art.

Boring.

Do you have a girlfriend? Ambie asks, then, unprovoked. He stands looking at Cormac with less innocence but still in the benign shade of his mother, where all is excused.

None of your business, child, Cormac says. Stick to your books.

Alice asks, swinging a bag onto her shoulder, Are you leaving now? They might walk with him, they might escort him awkwardly back into town.

I'm going to have something else here first, Cormac says, looking around for the actress again.

Because the actress does not materialise, he drinks more coffee and sends a message to Nina.

She is in her studio, she says, on Railway Street, and he is welcome to drop by.

Maybe I'll see you tonight? he suggests.

Excuse me what, she says.

Cormac tells her he is coming right away, that he is on the way now. He adds a string of puckish emojis.

He sets off down Aungier Street, edging along a pasteboarded hoarding behind which something old has been reduced to a squalor of rubble and hawsers. Two men, slumped in the uncanny pose that follows injection, tip forward side-by-side from a step. It is so clear and still a day that he almost sweats.

He thinks of photographing it, the wreck of the building: he thinks of coming back later, when it is dark. The weird marionette-like misery of the slumping addicts is impossible to express. He looks at them and feels culpable – he imagines a lens raised, the smash of an old-fashioned bulb, just to test or exercise his own callousness.

He said to Sadbh once: Do you know that film, *Man with a Movie Camera*?

Of course, she said.

I feel that way sometimes. I feel, he held up his arms and clawed his hands, I feel like a – dead thing, a frame, recording things.

You feel passive?

Yes. Exactly.

She said, Take my hands. Lemon oil like cough drops smoking from a salver on the sill.

When Cormac first came back things were starting again: building, selling, work. He'd left, as he liked to tell people, a dole queue doubled around the block; left to read gnashing accounts of bailouts from abroad, and expected

41

to stay away, perhaps, forever – at least consciously, at least insomuch as he talked about it – but came back anyway, defeated.

He and Alva had, in London, broken up. Patrick and Ursula were newly wed and their happiness, it seemed, was solidified as singular and durable for the same reason Cormac returned: the death of his father, of his and Patrick's father, suddenly. It was springtime when he flew out of Heathrow at the first news of the stroke. The sky was bare and the sea a curdle of commas beneath him, coming inland, coming over the green glow of Howth. On the airport roundabout there was a ring of daffodils. Low cliffs of coming rain. It smelled, after the fried-doughnut dryness of London, like chemical fertiliser.

Travelling the rest of the way by coach, Cormac became aware of the end of something, or of something passing by definitively: not the life of his father but an epiphenomenal privacy of his own, of Cormac's own. The privacy of his love for his father, an intensity, which would now be taken out and cooled and passed around with funeral food. That would become an object.

He knew this because he had gone through the same thing when Thomas died. He was at school then, the need for privacy was ferocious; those years were too painful even now to contemplate. Facing this, on the coach from the airport to the North County, he felt shame.

Unpacking a suitcase on the bed of his childhood, more shame. His clothes and books, the snarled but gummy mass of cords and wires linking chargers, headphones, earbuds, all this was embarrassingly meagre, like vanity.

His mother was sitting in a downstairs chair, and said, You made it, at least, in decent time.

And actually it was about that time the old man died, in the Saint Francis Hospice, before Cormac had a chance to wash and change and visit him. Patrick was there. Ursula drove them back and stood in the hallway, looking thin, worrying the long strands of her hair between her fingers and lingering. He remembered this reticence afterwards, how young she seemed.

Well, you were here too late, Patrick brayed.

Patrick, their mother warned.

Patrick, said Ursula softly.

Are you all right? Cormac asked.

No. Patrick left, stormed into town, came back sober – to their great surprise – sometime later and told them he had walked along the beach, the coast, up by the bandstand and the tower and the collapsed kelp-collectors' cottages, to the rubble pier and the yellow headland. There were seals surfacing and slipping out of sight, and seagulls sliding on the wind, and the lush crunch of winkles underfoot.

I would have gone with you, Cormac complained.

You were never here, Patrick shot, although this had nothing to do with anything.

Days after the funeral, when the house had not returned to normal, Cormac came back from one of the many walks he'd been taking around the town – banally sunny but sharply shaded by the old market house, the old courthouse, the old commercial hotel, the old barracks – to meet his mother in the hallway as she hissed, There's a friend here to visit you, a boy from school. I remember him. In the front room.

Senan sat by the mantelpiece and Cormac's mother's pale collection of ornaments, bits of bog oak and a copperwork Brigid's cross, with one of the creamy mugs that

43

belonged to her seventies crockery set. The room was so clean, the phrase *spick and span* pricking into Cormac's head mindlessly, it still seemed to expect something, the coffin or the guests. Senan's hair was short and spiked, soft potato blond, and he was dressed in black, not like a mourner but with style. Cormac's eyes fell on the long white fingers around the mug.

Hey, man, said Senan, standing up.

Great to see you.

I was at the funeral.

I didn't notice, I'm sorry.

I know, you didn't see me. Senan spoke quietly. I was with the gang from school. I talked to Patrick.

I'm sorry, he never said.

It's no big deal at all.

The men sat. The feminine formality of the room, which had always been Cormac's mother's room, felt intrusive. There was a reproduction of a big-eyed char-girl over the fireplace. She wore a maid's cap and looked afraid. As a child, Cormac had believed the picture to be haunted, its eyes searching him out as they watched television or when he lay, bleating and blanketed, on the settee during sick days with a glass of 7UP.

If we stay here my mother will interrogate you, he warned. This was not in fact likely.

I wouldn't mind. But Senan laughed with him. They stepped into the street. Cormac didn't know where they were going or what this visit meant. Senan said, I've the car, if you like we could go for a drive.

With relief, Cormac nodded: Cool.

They drove to Skerries, then through it. They drove through Loughshinny and the Black Hills, lanes lined

44

with shattering red-berried hedges and auto-body yards. They drove the route of the motorbike race in childhood: memory of standing back from the road in a field behind pasting tables of minerals and candyfloss in polythene. The drone of engines when the race began was a dirge beyond the trees – death by decapitation every few years – and child-Cormac put his hands over his face.

Smell of motor oil and candyfloss and rapeseed. It was a strange thing, he thought, for his father to take them to; his father who had been such a gentle man.

I've been taking time off to write, Senan explained as they drove. I have a place in the city now. A flat.

Good for you.

Well, the bottom fell out of it. Senan squinted over the steering wheel, ever weak-eyed but averse to wearing glasses, even at school. Cormac was amused then disturbed by the intimacy with which he remembered this. The market, Senan continued. Bottom fell out of the market for a while. He was apologising, in his way, for being successful enough to own a flat.

Where do you want to go? he asked. I'm lost. He switched on the American satnav. It could not pronounce the little townlands: Clogheder, Ballyboughal, Courtlough. I tell you what, Senan now began to laugh, we can go and visit the school. He pulled up along a hedgerow to put information into the satnav.

You know the Franciscans had to give it up? Cormac said.

I didn't. Jesus. Why?

Funds, I guess. Too expensive.

What are they, getting sued? Senan was leaning over the thing now, hanging from the wheel by one white hand.

45

The engine fell quiet and they could hear the crows in the haws overhead. Senan was squinting again. What does that say?

Don't you have your glasses?

They're filthy.

Take this road, Cormac told him smoothly. Go straight. I'll direct you. I know where it is.

So are they getting sued? Senan asked on the road. Have they been getting *handsy* with the boys?

You tell me, man, Cormac said.

Nobody laid a hand on me anyway. Brother Corbie only liked to look. Imitating the monk's sibilant snarl, Senan cried, Only flip-flops in the showers, boys!

The boys were busy enough themselves, Cormac said.

We certainly were.

Cormac felt himself redden and regret.

You used to look out for me, Senan told him, suddenly and quietly, then. To Cormac a sense of disturbance returned, because this wasn't true.

When the silence had held for another moment, Senan continued. I was so sorry to hear about your da, who I remember, who was a lovely man. I was sad for you. I drove all the way out from town. I heard from Finn and Lawless on Facebook. I thought about you a lot. I think it's two years or something since I saw you though. In person.

I'm OK, Cormac said with difficulty.

Are you back for a bit? Will you stay?

I haven't decided yet.

There's the gate, Senan said.

It was open. They clanged over the cattle grid and parked by the willow tree, in the shade of the water tower and the brutal ball alley. The school buildings, seventies pebble-dash, stood empty. They talked, remembering together and for one another about the castle where the brothers lived, where a landing with a sampler reading *Make me a channel of your peace* had been defaced to read *penis*. Where the taxidermy fox and owl, both frozen in action poses, rotted movingly in a glass cabinet. Maybe, they agreed, it was different now.

You broke your foot, Senan told him then, jumping off the ball alley.

That wasn't me.

It was! I remember it. You were dared or something.

That wasn't me, Cormac insisted.

Was it not? Senan stared at the tree. The tree had been there, always. Islanded by tight little tiles just like the tiles of the swimming pool. It was an old tree, so familiar, seeming abject and abundant as a crone.

I'll drop you back, Senan said at last, but you should come into town sometime, I am playing a lot of things. He named some bands he would be playing with or subbing in.

I'll see, Cormac told him warily.

There are people who want to see you. Lots of people are coming back now.

Are they working?

Does it matter? There's always something to do.


Cormac crosses the river: buses on the quays loll under wheels of seabirds and the channel running by the Abbey is, as ever, scaldy with the smell of weed. In an old trade yard off Railway Street, high-alloy doors are shoved back on their runners so two cats can caper in and out of

47

the sheds. A rockery prettifies a hill of surplus earth and there are shells set into this – razors, winkle shells.

From the sheds comes the squeal of a saw, but a sculptor, leaning over prongs of steel, switches this off and lifts his visor rakishly as Cormac enters.

Howiya, says Cormac, recognising the man but not recalling a name. I'm looking for Nina?

The man points to the far end of the shed. There are workbenches, partitions, ordering it. Somewhere a radio plays and the saw begins again, this urgent noise becoming less distracting as Cormac progresses into the dim space with its earth floor. He sees Nina on her knees in jeans and a roll-neck, hair clasped fetchingly at the top of her head. She is looking into a kind of igloo, the outline of an igloo, traced three-dimensionally in wire mesh. Bales of mesh – dangerous stuff, he thinks – have been pushed under her bench.

Hey, Cormac says, finding his voice watery against the wall of noise. Sculptors' studios always make him feel exposed and unmanned. He prefers, lately, the hierarchical classroom and the intimate darkroom.

Oh Cormac! she greets.

Careful with the wire mesh. He cannot stop himself. I know a guy who got sepsis from that once.

She is still hunkered, looking up at him.

I mean, it was years ago, he qualifies.

How are you? Her tone is warm.

I'm good. Can I take you for a walk? Give you a break? He sees, only then, that she is wearing gardening gloves. Those are a good idea, he says.

We can sit in the kitchen, it's warmer in there.

Now the saw has been switched off and set down on

the concrete floor. The sawing man is in the kitchen, a sun-trapping annexe on a mezzanine, boiling the kettle and browsing a cupboard full of the kind of things artists drink – matcha, chicory, Barleycup – in search, it turns out, of an aggressively pedestrian brand of instant coffee. Nina greets him and sits at the kitchen table.

Anyone for coffee? the sculptor asks.

Yes please. Nina answers for them both. Are there biscuits?

Good question. The sculptor begins to open other cupboards, each emitting notes of ginger, masala and cardamom. Toothpastey peppermint tea. Makes you think of Everton mints and cold community halls. Cormac wonders if this break is going to be taken with the sculptor, whom Nina seems familiarly fond of, encouraging him with the cupboards, saying: Steal something expensive.

I'm all right for coffee, Cormac says, deciding to be a dick. He is standing against the window with his back to the sill. The window looks onto a street where, Nina has told him, they see stop-and-search altercations and muted gang assaults so often they have stopped looking out of this particular window.

No coffee, are you sure? Nina turns. All right. She doesn't move from the table. The sculptor has found a half-eaten baton of digestives.

These have, the sculptor explains, taken on the taint of the room. They taste like mould, most delicately. He holds up a biscuit with a baby-finger kinked, an old maid's high-pitched voice: *Eau* de passive-aggression, don't you know?

I like them like that, Nina says. I had a dream about you last night, she tells Cormac next, pivoting not untypically.

49

What did I do? he banters back.

Stood me up!

The sculptor hisses. Bad form, man, he says.

My apologies. I've been a bit absent lately.

I saw you on culture night, she reminds him. At IMMA.

That was a weird crowd, Cormac recalls.

Yes, it was all the sponsors. Men with Botox.

Is that what that was?

Cormac is pleased because the sculptor, who was evidently not at IMMA on culture night, now stands awkwardly, holding his coffee cup.

Stepping into this advantage, Cormac adds, They make you feel poor. A peasant. You are the entertainment, or the help.

I've had some things acquired by the Arts Council, Nina says.

Congratulations!

They have works by you.

They have a few.

They have three: pieces from *Father of my Children*, *Sutton Woo!* and *Corn Princess*. He does not say this, as he is sure Nina knows. It pains him a little to think the sculptor may not know.

Nina is smiling on him secretively now.

You have an opening coming up, he reminds her.

Another ordeal, she says, but she is smiling still. OK, she concedes finally, let's go for a walk outside.

So I'll get to that welding for you really soon, the sculptor says.

No hurry! Nina drifts a coat from the back of a chair and throws it on, beginning to wind a scarf around her neck. We're making good time, she says.

50

Cormac picks up a biscuit from the table and nods sportingly at the sculptor.

See you soon, man. Thanks for that.

As they walk into the street Nina resumes her theme. In my dream, she says, when you stood me up, I was alone on a piazza, a square, and it was bucketing with rain. I was watching people coming towards me with umbrellas.

Nina can be eccentric. Her intelligence is what Cormac prefers. It is this intelligence, but also her generosity in receiving, meditating upon, and describing the scope of Cormac's own intelligence back to him or to other people, which he has come to enjoy. It is the mood he hopes to induce, against her discussion of a dream, by asking, What are you working on? What's the igloo about?

It's a cell, she says. It's the sketch of a monk's cell on Skellig Michael. Ned and I were there.

I've stayed down there.

I know, you told me.

Skellig Michael is a big birdy rock of an island in the Atlantic. He didn't know she'd been. There's an artists' colony nearby, or a few – holiday homes and austere farmhouses smoked out with Palo Santo, produce cooperatives. Alice spent a week there last winter and wrote: I am going to throw myself into the sea.

Who is this Ned character anyway?

He has the new residency, Nina explains, looking ahead as they cross the junction before Connolly Station. A cyclist whips by Cormac's shoulder, close and dangerous, calling a warning too late. The figure is pious and bug-eyed behind sunglasses. That residency, Nina continues, it has been funded for another year.

Well, I hope his intentions are honourable.

51

Nina now laughs loudly as they ring through the door of the Christian book and coffee shop.

It is partly a joke and partly an indulgence of curiosity to come, as they often do, to the Christian book and coffee shop. Nina likes the reproductions of Harry Clarke on the walls but dislikes the zoomorphic retellings of Bible tales. She searches each time for a recording of the song she learned at school – about unicorns, unicorns too daft and distracted to remember to get to the ark, unicorns who drowned at the end of the song and never, she says, left her thoughts – before they find a table underneath a hot little sconce.

Tell me more about the igloo, he demands.

I don't want to talk about it yet, she says. I am up to here with this show. I had a studio visit and everything yesterday, and you know how you worry for days before a studio visit and waste all this time even in advance.

I haven't had one for years. I'm above it, or past it, one of those things.

What, she asks, did you think of the laundry show?

When Cormac pulls a face Nina says, Yeah, very worthy, I know.

Alice liked it.

I was going to write about that show, she tells him now, and see about reviewing it.

I'm sure Alice would be delighted to print a review from you in *Lux*.

Ha! Nina says.

Cormac pardons himself to use the bathroom. He has drunk too much coffee and passes a stingingly liquid stool. He returns to the table feeling light-headedly refreshed.

After this, you know, she raises her coffee cup to her lips, I will have to get back to work.

I have no plans tonight. You should come over.

Oh yeah? she teases. And what if I have plans?

Cancel them. No – not really. If you have plans, come over afterwards.

I'll have to see, she says.

Tell me about the igloo, he persists. Is it all about monks?

Well, she says. Does it look like a playhouse to you?

A little bit.

*Genius is the recovery of childhood at will.*

Very nice, he says.

Rimbaud, Nina says.

So it is about childhood? Monks and cells? He thinks of Ambie for some reason, and the dead zoo, and the seedy indie-cinema bang of that entire enterprise.

Monks and cells and childhood, she says, because Skellig Michael and the monks are childhood. The childhood of the island. Genius of the land: recovery of childhood at will. Didn't you have to learn about monasteries in school? And fairy forts?

And crayon it all in.

Childhood of the island. She is tracing a circle on the tabletop. Religion. She gestures about them. Illuminations, she adds. Illuminated manuscript.

Intriguing, he says.

So what are you working on?

Teaching – teaching takes over these days. I'll have more time soon.

You've been saying that for ages, she says.

Come with me to the Institute then, and I'll show you some stuff. That'll shut you up.

I have to work.

No you don't, Nina.


She was one of his first students. This is why he tries to explain things to her.

When I was starting out, he tries to explain, beauty was the enemy: beauty was bourgeois. We were all about the ugly and in-your-face.

Did it have its own kind of beauty? she asks.

Now you go into a fancy restaurant and the pipes are all exposed.

I know what you mean.

When I was a kid, he continues, the town hall in my home town smelled of vomit. A very specific quality of vomit – the smell of vomited *chickatees*, corn snacks. Do you remember chickatees?

I think it is pronounced chickadees.

No, these were ten-penny corn snacks. They were chickatees. Trust me and shut up and listen, OK?

Nina laughs.

Anyway, that smell was so distinct I can think of it now, I can remember it. That was fine ugliness. Fine, artful ugliness. I had this idea of reproducing it and bottling it. But the town hall was demolished years ago. They built over the square. The town square was originally a – kind of – *warren*, of public toilets. Now that the toilets are gone, I imagine there must be some kind of queer, you know, history associated with them.

The toilets were stinking, lurking blue bulb-light. He never went further than the top of the stairs.

I came to art school, he continues, and all this ugliness was in. I felt like, somehow, I was in. But only in reified form, you understand.

We should record this conversation, she says, and publish it. Imagine posterity missing out.

They leave the Christian book and coffee shop to walk into the city centre. This is the era: it's not strange that doorways are wadded with sleeping bags and bodies that may or may not be dead; even this has become normal; men and women, propped up underneath the hoarding of another demolition site, look ruddy, only lately brutalised. Their numbers grow like an army in the opening weeks of a war from the last century. It is too fast to cogitate, or perhaps this thought is a defence against thought.

Cormac and Nina take the tram. They travel to Grange-gorman. Blunt sun bores into everything, frigidly, burning off shadow. There is hardly anyone in Grangegorman – a few bodies dotted on the green slopes, walking dogs, and crows clacking from the peaked roof of the old chapel of rest – and the grounds are scraped clean with new trees tied to posts, peaceful and elegant.

It's nice, this new campus, Nina agrees. I was only ever on Kevin Street.

Do you know what was here before?

Yes: the Richmond lunatic asylum.

I'm in the studios, he tells her, pointing, which were the women's wards. I'll show you.

The walls within the nineteenth-century building are whitewashed and the stairs a suntrap corkscrewing upwards from the floor. As they pass through a corridor, Cormac presses his hand to the wall, tracing a gentle curve, and says, The walls are rounded because they had to push the beds through them. He shapes the wide wheeled beds by throwing out his arms. Now the effect is like a lighthouse, he explains.

Windows glow harshly in a room with a high ceiling. Dividers divvy the space into workstations where beds would once have been, suggesting the adjacent set-pieces of an Ikea showroom. Everything is white and spacious and paint-smelling. In one workstation a girl is crouched, absorbedly painting something into the seam between two dividers. The other stations are abandoned but untidy with tools and wire and canvasses; each one different, separate, bespeaking personality.

It's a bit of a dreary place, Cormac apologises insincerely.

It's gorgeous!

She says, There was a man who was Superintendent here, in the hospital, in the sixties. I saw a programme about him and he says about it – about this ward, I think – *all the mothers of Dublin were there*, numbed. Looking out the windows on the city lights at night.

From the windows you can see the mountains too, and at night there are lights on the mountainside.

Does he? Cormac is moving a canvas aside.

Yes, meaning the heyday of the hospital. All the mothers of Dublin, out of sight.

My mother was one of them once.

She was?

Not here. In John of God's. He does not expand upon this. He takes out a galvanised bucket of sponges and white spirit. I love this bucket, he says. It's the chicest thing I own.

Nina begins to laugh, repeating, Chic!

You can help me, he says, scrub this mounting wall – I'm going to paint it and use it again. But you'll need to wear gloves or else your hands will peel away.

I can help you?

Be a friend. It's quality time.

And what will you do for me?

Entertain you. The famous Cormac.

Get to fuck. But she begins to help anyway.

As they work, he tells Nina the story of the sectioning. We had a haunting in our house, he explains, when I was really small, only two or three. It was a specific kind of haunting. Something left footprints, tiny footprints, and spilled soil on the stairs.

What? She stops scrubbing.

That's the story. You see, nobody ever told me this, or I can't remember them telling me – it was just there, we always knew it, this episode of footprints on the stairs. Maybe the sound of something running up and down the stairs, and then the soil. Soil and little footprints. That's the story: we were sent, my brothers and I, to my grand-parents, I think, and a priest blessed the house and so on. You know my father was a Christian Brother? For six months, out of school.

I'd get a priest in, Nina agrees, if I had ghost feet from the grave on my carpet, yes.

After that, she went into John of God's for weeks. She never spoke about it, she never speaks about it.

Are these things connected?

They have to be.

It's a metaphor. Nina squeezes a sponge of turpentine. It drops into the bucket and darkens like a leaf.

You think?

A metaphor for miscarriage. She says this softly. She is crouching. I suspect, she says.

Maybe. Cormac cocks his head. Very good, he says. Very clever.

When they have finished, Cormac locks his camera with the memory card from Lazarian's shoot in the locker beneath his desk. It's coming into evening and growing gloomy. Let's head on, he says. Good work, comrade.

As they cross the dimmer campus now, he beckons to the slope and the walls below, the green space lit by huge hood-eyed floodlights. There were more walls, he explains. There were layers of walls around the asylum. The whole place was so hidden, people could live beside it for years and never go in, or even know it was here.

They emerge through a gap onto Prussia Street. Nina looks around sharply. Hold on, she says.

I know.

I've lost my orientation completely. Where are we?

Behind Tesco. It's like a secret. Anyway. He nods toward the road. Lead the way.

As they walk she says, Hold on, what is it you are working on?

The asylum! Cormac says.


Later: they are walking together up the steep and thinly pavemented incline of Kilmainham Lane. It is Saturday evening now and they are going to the Old Royal Oak. They can hear a bodhran from here and Cormac says, Diddle-i-di music, what's that about? Do the musicians just break into session spontaneously? Into *seshoon*?

People enjoy it. We might dance, Nina ribs.

Irish dance you do straight: every slat of the spine

stacked, hands by sides and knees lifting brusquely and apparently rationally. He has heard the idea is to appear static from the waist up, which is to say at the level of the window, in case the English pass by. This doesn't sound likely to be true, but maybe it's true after all.

We'll go into the snug, Nina says.

But now, look up – coming down the hill, freewheeling in unhurried flow with the shape of the road, the sky a silver glaze – a shape on a bike that they know. An angular man with a moustache. He raises a hand in unhurried greeting. His air of authority suggests he has fully expected to meet them here on the road.

That's Garrett, Nina says. He must be coming from the Museum.

Alice's husband sees them too; his brakes shriek almost endearingly as he draws up before the kerb. Anyone else would allow the brakes to shriek in slapstick and graze to a stop in the role of village idiot. But Garrett is not funny.

Howiya, Cormac says.

Garrett asks, Have you heard the news about JP Devlin?

No, what?

He died.

What? How old was he, fifty-something?

Garrett shrugs. Maybe. Anyway.

Was he sick?

No, I think it was an accident. I think he fell.

Nina asks quietly, With drink?

Cormac is surprised.

Did you know JP?

No, but of him, Nina says. He edited so many things.

Did he fall somewhere, drunk?

I don't know the full story, Garrett says. He leans like a

59

gossip over the handlebars of the bike. I don't think he was found straight away either.

His wife.

They were long split up. It wasn't good. We're waiting for more, and the funeral details.

This is terrible, Cormac says. Have you, he asks carefully, told Alice?

No, but I'm on my way to meet her.

Garrett is still married to Alice.

Garrett says, I'm going to have to go. He says this as if they have been detaining him. He is father to Ambie: it never seems natural to think. He resumes his freewheel now, sinking out of sight towards the bridge over the thin but diligent Camac.

Cormac feels the stillness of the evening and the world transformed, slightly but uncompromisingly, by this quiet loss. There is something careless to a person disappearing from the margins of your life: you feel at fault.

He and Nina walk to the pub in thought. They sit in the snug with the little stove and order hot whiskeys. It feels fully like midwinter suddenly.

He was, Nina says eventually, so handsome. JP.

Cormac remembers. In his memory he climbs a narrows staircase in sour light, the light of unloved, interim spaces, past a freight lift with a folded rubber stopper like a squeeze box. He enters the semi-derelict space overlooking Charlemont Street where JP Delvin, young and looking like a cartoon Etonian, explains to everyone – journalists with arms banded across their chests, girls in pop-coloured tights sitting sassily on the edge of a desk, art-school kids – that the entire issue, the very first issue, will be funded only by a seat-of-your-jocks loan, so they'd better not fuck it up, and of course they won't since they have been chosen, he says, for their *hunger and originality*. It's not possible to tell if he's joking and it doesn't really matter anyway.

I remember, Nina says. Vaguely.

He remembers the room above Charlemont Street and he remembers the girls. At that time girls had sunbursts of blonde hair and cuffs of fake tan at the ankles and wrists. Cormac, twenty-one, was working as a gallery technician and had, that day, a throbbing gash above one eyebrow, badly bandaged by Alva. JP pointed across the room and said, You, what's happening there? He gestured to his own forehead for reference.

It's nothing, Cormac said. The room was looking at him. I was mounting a big crucifix, and it fell on me. No stitches. It's all good.

Giggles frilled the air a moment, lifting and falling with musical agency from the tanned anorexics, but JP simply said, Well work hard and find distinction and you can pay someone else to mount your crucifixes.

Find distinction, he repeats to Nina now. He always had these phrases. I was an artist – that's how I saw myself – and I made sure my work for him was dirty, you know? I did a lot of street photography. I can still hear him. Cormac laughs. *This is not fuckin Britpop, Mulvey: this is not Les fuckin Miserabilus.* We painted, Cormac continues, a girl gold and had her posing at the fireplace of a tenement. They were completely empty then, those buildings on Henrietta Street; they hadn't been rediscovered. There were needles everywhere. We were not in the least bit subtle. Nothing was subtle. It was fun. I can still see him.

You're getting upset, Nina says gently.

I am, amn't I. But it's a shock. I hadn't thought of him in so long. He invested in these restaurants and they all went bust. Everything folded in the end. A lot of things did, like, in twenty-ten.

Perhaps he was quite alone.

Or always troubled. Someone who is that energetic and eccentric, it can be too much. Very gentle though. He was a gentleman.

Cormac thinks of other deaths. Heroin overdose in a suite of a mid-range hotel. Hanged man off the viaduct at home. Two falls down stairs: fine old houses with narrow, nervous stairs. Bankruptcy suicides, naturally. Into the path of a truck on an orbital road; jump from an overpass. Fall or jump. Thomas.

OK, no more whiskey. Nina rubs her eyes. It's dark out, she says. Let's go.

They were students – Cormac and Garrett – when they met. On Achill in fact, at the Elvis café. That summer, Alice had a car: she and Cormac drove across the country and it took three hours, not five, shorter than the cross-country trips of childhood, and Cormac felt cheated, and reminisced.

There were people leasing a farmhouse for the summer in a field packed by silver cloud and backing onto the silver sea. The weather was heavy with diffused light. Every room was red or aubergine – they were like multiple organs – and in the evenings they sat at a picnic table out the back. Someone's passionate dachshund squeezed between calves and ran to the edge of the garden to cry at them all for a reason that seemed meaningful but was not received.

Cormac can remember, every evening, someone saying, *Come on, dope,* at which point the dog spurted into alertness and ran to rest its chin on a knee. Cormac had been nervous of dogs all his life. He noticed the narrow mouth of teeth like that of a mounted pike. He avoided the dog. They worked in the morning and, in the afternoons, he and Alice crossed sloblands to the café named Graceland. Garrett arrived late and they found him there one day, drinking coffee.

He remembers that Alice brightened immediately, saying, This is Garrett! The man looked up from a table – glow of confetti behind him, must have been pale Formica – without rising and pointed to the things he'd already bought in the gift shop: worry-stones, fridge magnets with An Irish Blessing, tin whistle.

I got all the required crap, he announced, and Cormac thought instantly, This man is an arsehole. He did not see the melancholy in the raw little island as a sounding-post for rootlessness and homesickness. Even at twenty, Cormac possessed enough tact to be tolerant, but Garrett only processed life unkindly and then said things everyone already knew, like: This is brand Ireland.

When they went to a quieter beach to sunbathe, Garrett kept snarling, *Oh he is gone from me, gone from me surely!* Cormac said: Wrong island, man, wrong play. The sand was littered with curls of dried seaweed. A helicopter tilted on the horizon throughout – its clatter carrying like the sounds of a building site – and that night a woman bent up the driveway avidly to find them at the back.

Two men are drowned, she said bluntly. Men off Doohoma Head. Other side of the island. So ye are welcome to the Stations.

They went to the concrete church, almost all of the gang; they wanted to go because they saw potential in the story and the surreal ritual of incantation, of a group of people circling the church and pausing to genuflect, of a single sprout of grass growing from the wand-like cross at the top. They, the students, must have looked like shiftless idiots, hung-over and underfed. Another apple-cheeked woman approached them at the end to say, Ye're welcome, and nobody thinks ye are strange.

I want to go back, Cormac said the next day.

No one's leaving yet, said Alice. She seemed hurt but he couldn't explain to her why he needed to leave. It was because the praying had disinterred something, pulled it to the surface by an iron cord, and if he tried to explain, he would feel the deadweight at the end of the cord. He went to the twiggy beach by himself with a sketchpad instead. Garrett came to swim, ignoring him, running into the waves and standing waist-high in the water to jump with the rolls of the tide. Wading inland at last, he belly-flopped onto the towel next to Cormac and remarked flatly, I never learned to swim.

You should not go in then, Cormac said. That's dangerous.

Alice tells me you had a brother who died. Did he drown?

No.

Is that why you want to go home?

He didn't drown.

If it upset you, you know, you didn't have to go to the church thing. I didn't, I stayed at the house. You could have stayed with me.

I didn't mind.

64

It's understandable. But after this Garrett fell silent. Waves took hoarse runs at the shore. It was hot and hanging and the dunes were prickly.

There are buses, Garrett concluded at last, if you want to leave. A moment later: A friend of mine drowned off Rosslare a year ago. He drowned himself.

He was laid on his back now and Cormac looked. He sensed Garrett wanted to be looked at, naked but for sodden Speedos, white and bony and defined and, he thought, half-erect, like a dog – like the dachshund – cocking its head. This wasn't what Cormac expected, but he thought suddenly of being fucked with full-stomached anticipation. They could go to the half-smashed baths, over cutting shingle, to a blowhole where the water sneezed and slapped against stone. There was a place like that at home: it was known as Isaac's Hide. The myth was a man named Isaac went insane and killed his family by dashing them on the rocks.

Garrett got up and walked back to the farmhouse then, and Cormac stayed in Achill, after all, for the rest of the week.

Nina sleeps at the edge of the mattress, a pillow clenched in her arms, with her back to him and her spine a sleek sign for privacy. This is one of the things Cormac likes about her: after sex she ruffles his hair and rolls away, to be alone.

It is Sunday, now, at his. He rises before her and makes tea to drink in the chair by the sash window. The street below gleams blamelessly.

All Sunday mornings start with the smoke-smudged, watery skies of Cormac's childhood, when their father would take Cormac, Patrick, Thomas and the dog to the demesne or the Back Strand, to the ruined church and tower at Balrothery, while their mother made dinner and sang to the radio. On these Sundays, they would climb the wet hill to the tower, tailing Shep, and hear the ravens conspiring or clapping, agitated, rising together.

At the demesne, the boys might look into the bared teeth of the icehouse, the subterranean tunnel running to the cellar of the big house; Thomas or Patrick shouting into it, telling Cormac, There are bodies in the icehouse, there's an *oubliette*, prisoners dropped onto a bed of spikes. They would make the sounds of bodies impaled on spikes, blowing raspberries. The ghosts came up for Cormac dragging chains. Salt-and-ice pack the bodies: mummies, crystals, forming in the icehouse.

Their father said, *Oubliette*, French for *forget*.

There is a wedding in City Hall now, this morning. Cormac watches a car with ribbons draw up and secrete a pot-bellied man, a thirty-something bride straightening her veil as a wind whipping down the steep street disturbs her white skirt. She wears a stole against the cold. She turns, then, to the steps of City Hall, with her chin tilted and her shoulders straight, embarking on this solemn stage of life while being undermined, really, by a kind of pigtail-pulling breeze. The pot-bellied man is her father. He looks around with dazed delight as taxis raise a drone of salutation with their horns.

The bride ignores it. She stands waiting in contrapposto, holding down the errant veil. They climb the steps and are gone and that is all.

Oh lovely, Nina says from the doorway.

Good morning. Would you like tea?

66

Please.

She crosses the room and ruffles his hair once more. He turns his face to her with a squint. So brown, she tells him again. My hair is greyer than yours and you're older than me.

I sold my soul, he says, you see. He rises and darts past her freshly, avoiding any kiss. While he fills the kettle again, she sits in the chair by the window with her hands folded on her lap as neat as a cat's. She wears one of his Aran jumpers and her own candy-pink underwear. Her toenails are polished but chipped. Last night he opened her legs rather dutifully and dabbed with his tongue. She smelled of marzipan and curled her toes with pleasure or distaste.

What are you doing today? she asks.

Family. Mother, brother, sister-in-law, Cormac says. Oh, and kids. Niece and nephew. I'll go out to Fingal, and I'll stay. He wonders why he feels as though he is lying when it is all true; something about her blasé tone but interrogatory undertow. She tends to wait cannily, in the morning, to ask what you are doing that day. She never volunteers her own plans first.

How about you? he asks.

Welding! I guess. Supervising welding. You look so young, or youthful. She resumes her theme as he places a mug before her. And especially because your hair is so dark, until you emote.

Emote?

Nina pulls a severe expression, like a bird of prey. Suspect or grimace or, like, smile too much, she explains.

All right then. Cormac perches on the sill. I'll be all self-conscious about that from now on.

You should wear sun cream, she advises.

I am young, you know.

You're almost forty.

I'm a long way from forty. A few years yet.

The conversation is becoming harsh. Sensing this, Nina asks evenly, How are your nephew and niece?

They're great, Cormac tells her. They're the best kids.

Can I use your shower?

Of course! Here. He moves from the sill to the toppling clothes horse. There's a clean towel for you. He waits for her, feeling uneasy and hoping she will leave shortly. He does not enjoy feeling diminished, ever, in her eyes or anyone's. Although he knows she takes pleasure in teasing him, at times there is an edge to everything that could catch, and cut, or merely fray.

Cormac sees his phone flashing silently with Ursula's name. He feels a flood of pleasant dread and obligation, safe as formal clothes or a sovereign law. He's had no word from Patrick since Saturday morning, and the messages Ursula sent him on Friday night – *I suppose he is with you?* – were relatively restrained.

Yo Urse, he greets her now.

Yo, she shoots acidly back. Still good for today?

Absolutely, what time?

As they are talking, Nina emerges. She drips about the kitchen-living room in the towel, apparently hunting out bits of jewellery and items of clothing, pausing to dress openly in the doorway to the hall. There is really no need and her eyes remain emptily trained on thin air throughout as if she is simply performing a series of exercises.

Nonetheless, and as she has intended, Cormac finds himself distracted by the dip of her hip and the kidney-shaped portion of buttocks cheeks exposed by little wavering underpants. She has no waist but an exceptionally pert backside. He has come to suspect her of knowing this, in spite of the chasteness of her movements by daylight – of the cat-hands, the smiles that are as earnest and alarming as a sob.

When he gets off the phone to Ursula, Nina asks immediately, Was that your brother?

Ursula actually.

Such a name, she says. But I liked her so much that time, Ursula. OK. She stands before him as if for inspection. I'll go? She steps forward then and kisses him on the lips, as she always does before she leaves. She makes a valiant point of it. It is quite Girl Scout.

Have a nice day, she says, but at the door she turns around.

OK, she laughs.

Everything all right? Cormac asks.

All right, so just sit down a moment. Nina tucks some hair behind her ears. She has tiny, hardly visible ears.

Because Cormac is already sitting, he waits for her to take a place on the couch in an atmosphere of new silence.

All right, she repeats carefully. So, do you remember a few weeks ago, we spent the night at your place and then we walked as far as the tram stop on Westmorland?

I think so, he says, sitting up.

You told me you weren't one hundred per cent sure that you'd used the condom right.

Cormac feels a ghostly blow to the back of the head.

Did I?

Yes, you said you would feel better if I took the morning-after pill to be safe.

Cormac feels a density at the base of his skull.

I remember, he says.

You said this right before you got on the tram. Like, the very moment before. And I did take it – the pill. Don't worry, this isn't a big reveal. At this Nina leans forward to scratch the bulb of her anklebone, looking away.

Cormac turns dizzy with relief.

I just wondered, she says, if you realise that the morning-after pill can cost fifty quid.

I didn't; I'm sorry, I should have given you money.

It's not that. She has straightened up, but stares at her feet and the floor. Well, it's not only that.

I can pay you back now.

No. She waves a hand, looking at him at last, smiling weakly. I had the money, it's OK. It's just that I was hurt, when you said it. That you were cavalier. But – she raises her hand again, against his interjection this time – I know I have no right to be offended because you're not my boyfriend.

It's just, she says, that I was.

OK, he says.

She looks at him as if taken aback at *OK*.

I was pregnant before, she tells him. There is a slide towards vehemence, now, in her tone.

I found out when I was five weeks, and I had to have an abortion, and it broke my heart. She is looking him in the eyes. I couldn't get past it for so long. Nobody tells you how devastated you feel. My feet – she points to her feet – went up an entire shoe size and never went down. After only five weeks. This was ages ago. It wasn't legal then. I had to buy pills on the internet.

70

My hair fell out, she continues cruelly. For weeks after-wards. It was always coming out in the shower.

Cormac feels quietly tortured and cornered, but also deeply melancholy for her in this moment.

She holds out a hand and says with wonder, insular in herself a millisecond, I would run my fingers through my hair in the shower and it would come out in clumps.

How are you, he asks, these days?

It's OK. She smiles sadly then, at last, changing without warning. He feels there is a brittle lability to the moods of women and it functions defensively. Behind a sudden brightness, they sit watchful as a creature in a shell.

Cormac knows that Nina understands her own sad smile, however, as resilient.

But I realised, she continues now, the other week, when you said that to me, about taking the pill, I realised that once it was a small thing to me. It was an abstract thing to me once. And now it's not.

She stands up and begins to comb her fingers through her fringe. If I get pregnant again, she says to the floor, to the shagpile, I have no doubt about it now, and no matter what, I will keep it.

Right.

I want you to know that. I'm not trying, obviously, to get pregnant or anything, but this is all. I don't know. She drops her hands and looks at him in appeal, as if she wants to hear his opinion.

He has none. She seems to have forgotten that she's told him about this before.

I want these things, she says at last. I want what every-body wants. The alien aura of her demeanour softens and passes. That's all I wanted to say.

71

When she leaves, he does not stand at the window and watch her reach the street but enters fully into the demands of the day, pulling out clothes and changing his mind about them, laying out more clothes. Showering carefully in the damp of her earlier shower. Making more tea and packing his messenger bag. No time, and indeed no inclination, today, to meditate.

It is Patrick who phones after ten and says, We're on the quays.

Which quay? Cormac swings the bag onto his shoulder and feels for his coat in the gloom of the hall.

Actually we're caught up and we'll have to circle again and come back around for you – eh, yeah. We're outside something called Tattoo Rink?

I know it, I know it.

It has a skating theme. Or a snowing theme. There is a north pole – I believe – in the logo.

Know it well.

A polar-themed tattoo parlour, Patrick continues blandly, where one can order mochaccino.

Nobody drinks mochaccino. It's black now. No lactose and no fat.

I don't care for my coffee's sexual preference, Patrick replies. This is one of his favourite jokes. Sometimes it is: I don't care about my coffee's gender identity.

Cormac hurries out of the building and into the street. He regrets forgetting to grab a scarf. There is a red one Alice gave him, expensive, which Ursula admires. He thinks about going back, jogging up the angsty stairs, thinks of the flat freshly deserted: decides not.

In the lean light of Sunday afternoon, when the meal has

been eaten and cleared away, Ursula stands in the hallway with Maude and Jake.

The hallway is carpeted with brown villi, like mincemeat, and its walls are woodchip. Ursula is bargaining. She is using two small packets of sliced fruit in her bargaining. Jake loses interest and totters away. Maude, six, fixes her gaze on her mother and contemplates, sucking in the flesh of her bottom lip. Cormac can't say what it's about. He wishes only to soak through it and mount the stairs onto the landing where the wall curls in cold sun like enamel: like a mollusc. Like a lighthouse or the women's ward actually.

So are we finished here? Ursula asks. She adds, Now don't be bold in front of Uncle Cormac.

His mother sits on her bed with boxes spread about. I thought, she says, Ursula was going to help me.

I am! Her daughter-in-law pipes. Hold on a moment, Joy.

Cormac leans on the door frame, soft with standing damp, and smiles. I remember that, he says, pointing to a long gown with a painterly pattern in green and grey. And I know what that's called, he further says.

A Juliet cap. Joy turns the bracket of fabric in her hands.

Put it on, he suggests.

Not at all. Not now. She sets it aside, looking at it anxiously. Not this time. She becomes preoccupied, her face cloudy with thought.

Cormac picks up a wide-brimmed panama hat and pops it onto his head.

Gaum you, his mother says. Her fond word for fool.

Ursula appears. She is a tall woman with dark hair and a high-quality bone structure. Her narrow eyes make her

73

look mischievous, as if on the verge of playful laughter all the time, which is strange because Ursula is not mischievous; her humour remains managed and compact, diplomatic and collegiate, until she loses patience. She is gracefully *together* and Patrick admires her for it, dramatically, especially if sentimental with drink, because her poise is bulletproof: there is no one, he often insists grandly, I trust more than her.

Patrick is outside, now, rooting around for something in the shed. Relations between Patrick and Ursula would appear to be fine.

It unnerves Cormac to realise how much the house has forgotten them. It's so cold and ill-insulated it often feels like a coppice or a grove: something growing, something rinsed by elements. Over the years, it has gone from being the unthought exoskeleton of them to a chillily withholding thing, blanched and bleached but scented with dampness and growth under ghost food, drying clothes, potpourri. There are whole rooms it seems their mother doesn't enter any more. Doors blunted with draughtblockers and louvered presses stocked with bed linen in vacuum bags, photographs in boxes sealed by masking tape. To the back room have been banished all religious effigies – sacred hearts with snuffed-out lamps, Martin de Porres, a statue that looks like it's breaking bad news – so that this resembles a shrine or a sickroom even though no one has slept in it, probably, since the early noughties.

Now, Ursula commands, you wanted to wear something simple, Joy, didn't you?

Well, Joy lifts her hands and gestures about her, somewhat weakly, I don't know. Is this simple?

With no jewellery, perhaps, Ursula says.

Oh, but I always wear my opal. Joy becomes fretful again. The occasion is a wedding she resents being invited to. She is going anyway, with complaint. This helplessness is an affectation of age. Once she was the kind of mother who said, smelling already of outdoors, I can't kiss you with this lipstick, go to bed.

Cormac passes into the bathroom and pisses as delicately as he can muscularly manage on the porcelain, aware of women's voices nearby. When he returns downstairs, Patrick is dragging a dinged suitcase across the kitchen floor.

Maude beckons with her little hands to the dining room and cries, In here, Daddy, in here!

Patrick grunts in response, as if the suitcase is too heavy. Ah jaysus, he whines, sure I'm dead entirely!

Here, Daddy. What's in it?

A corpse.

What's a corpse?

Patrick kneels before the undulating dresser, glass-fronted cabinets of plates, by the volcanic four-foot vase filled with ornamental grass. It has always been there: the dresser, the volcanic vase, these have always been there. But only in adulthood have they begun to strike out of context with all the callous lambency of a hangover.

He photographed parts of it, years ago, for a show. His father was alive and sat warily in a shaft of sunlight: scanty viscose on the picture window, narrow knees. His thick glasses made him look uncannily young, like a blinking schoolboy waiting for the master to leather him. He, Cormac, did not use the photograph in the end because it was far too humanising and he was going at that time for an artless working-class animus vibe.

Ah here, Patrick complains. The suitcase is closed with an old-fashioned combination, buttons from which braille-raised numerals have been grazed away. Ask Nannie, he instructs Maude, if she can remember the suitcase code. Ask Nannie what the numbers are.

They listen to the child's feet on the stairs, to Ursula's call of Don't run, Maude, and Cormac sits down in their father's old armchair. The chair looks startled or outraged: its back curves inward and its arms kink to the ceiling hysterically.

You could just try a screwdriver in it, he suggests.

You're welcome, says Patrick, to give it a go.

There might be stuff in that, you know.

Yes, I imagine there is.

Things, I mean, of Thomas's. It could upset her.

There will be all kinds of things, Patrick says cryptically. Maude has returned.

Nineteen-hundred-seventy-nine, she says.

Jesus, well done, Patrick laughs.

The combination doesn't work. He tries again. Maude stoops, frowning.

Try my year of birth, Cormac says. Patrick tries it, and Thomas's. What year, he asks, was the old man born? And Joy?

Maybe it's me, suggests Maude.

This was locked long before you were thought of, baby, Patrick says. You were sitting on a fence in heaven. You were a twinkle in your daddy's eye.

Prompted by this, she comes behind him and puts her arms around his neck, wrapping her legs and digging her shoes into his ribs.

Patrick grunts again and then says, Cormac, find a screwdriver. Try a few. There's loads out there.

Cormac walks through the kitchen and the petrol-smelling alleyway, coming out in the shadows of the fir screen at the foot of the garden. These trees smell rich and Christmassy, splaying roots into a rockery of hydrangeas and terracotta cuffs from chimney pots. His mother's garden. An estate agent once regarded these, the trees, with an empty smile, saying, Oh what a feature, yes, that's a plus, privacy. Patrick laughed. First people in here, he said, will cut them down. And then Joy decided that she didn't want to move anyway.

Cormac's father told them often that his family's farm in Leitrim – the old place, long gone, townlands over from the bungalow of yellow bathwater – was turned into a plantation. Thousands of trees from Finland suck the salt and the rot and the goodness from the poor north-western soil: the county has been depopulated for trees. And here in Dublin, bending over the grass and picture window like sponsors, are the trees, a piece of Leitrim really. A piece of troubled eternity.

He enters the shed. He meets with a mangle of bikes and boxes and garden implements made morose and unsettling by the fact that he cannot remember them. The tough, stunned-seeming skull-shape of a bike saddle; whose was that? How old is that? Sultry with spiderwebs. Odour of sawdust and soil. The box the dog slept in decades ago. He discovers a toolbox of drivers and washers and bolts.

At college Cormac made small sculptures from dowels and sprockets and, where possible, fluting animal bones – bits of deer, bits of fox, the eerie pin-skulls of birds – foraged for in the mountains, along with liberty caps, under the guidance of classmates from the Southside. The shed still contains three or four sculptures. They blend into the debris around them and yet remain distinct. He feels they are still elegant in their articulations: they embody a logic growing autonomously: this hollow hammered into that egress and everything ultimately tapering at the top like a candlestick.

I used to love making those, he thinks. He wants to say aloud, but there is no one else in the shed.

At art school he would find the materials to make them himself. Around Kilmainham especially, walking home at night, gathering smashed headlamps and shrapnel from joyriding accidents in cul-de-sacs to put with animal bones and tree debris from the mountains. At that time he was renting a room in a terrace – moth-bothered lantern, porch of lozenge tiles – and returned there with harvests of hubcaps and kneecaps for gluing together into the night. Smoking joints and pissing out the window if he felt too stoned to navigate the stairs.

Young then. Before Alva and everything.

Cormac takes two screwdrivers back to the house. Patrick has opened the suitcase anyway. Came apart in my hands, he explains.

For all of his bravado, he is now hunkering over it awkwardly, hovering, reluctant to touch anything.

It's just books, cries Maude in disgust.

These are your Da's books, Patrick tells her, from way back. He lifts one, another. His eyes are fixed on them. The case gives off a vanilla tincture of decay. There are textbooks and eighties paperbacks, little black-clad books of school poetry, and a book about mental bicameralism Cormac ducks to pick up and examine.

78

Oh god, this was mine, he says. *The Bicameral Mind.*

Now, here, Patrick says.

What is it?

Collected Yeats.

I'm pretty sure, Cormac says, you could have just bought that one again. In Oxfam.

Not this copy, Patrick says.

Ursula enters with the baby in her arms, saying, Someone really wants to hang out with Daddy. Having handed him over to Patrick, she sweeps immediately out, returning with green fabric in clear plastic. I'll have it dry-cleaned, Joy, she calls as she bends to fold this into a shopping bag. But I probably won't get out to you until next week.

Look at this. Patrick has put the baby on the floor and is handing Ursula the book; handing it from his hunkered position, making Cormac think at once of the middle-aged woman, by the bathtub, holding soap. Ursula picks Jake up again instead.

Was that from the wedding? she asks.

What did we read at the wedding?

Something about sleepy – old, full of sleep.

'When You Are Old', Cormac softly says.

Funny title for a wedding, wasn't it?

My idea, Patrick remembers. When you are old and grey and full of sleep. Pick up this poem, something-something. He searches the book, still kneeling – clumsy in his outsized way, occupying all the floor – until he finds it and reads aloud.

Ursula tilts her head and echoes: Pilgrim soul.

Cormac travelled home for their wedding. He remembers it now in a sequence plotted by the layout of the house.

79

He remembers himself, his body, in the suit bitched about for not being fitted obsessively enough – he was not in Dublin, he would not come back at weekends the seven times Ursula asked – and loose at the shoulders, since the guy at Louis Copeland decided to guess in a generous direction. He remembers standing in the garden in the warmth of a summer morning and the perfume of the firs. Everything felt opulent. His mother in her dressing gown and three aunts in boxy lavender, sitting on deckchairs discussing the tumbling mallow bush and the leatherwood, drinking Nescafé not from mugs but from little white cups. His mother would not get dressed until the final moment and in her hair she wore foam rollers.

Moving into the kitchen, destabilised by sudden shade, and the ghost of Thomas shifting back and forth – back and forth, back and forth – and the table of forsaken fry, the white baguettes cut into slices and the rasher rind slimily pushed aside. The ghost of Thomas smoking on a wet evening: back and forth.

The scalloped blind over the sink a seashell shade of pink.

In the dining room, a large gang of town cousins in blue suits with tanned wives Ursula would try to keep out of photographs. They all had children who whooped and whined and had to be hoisted up and false-dropped and hushed up, and their children did not have names like the e-softened Maude and Jake; their children had names like Lee and Molly-Mae. They greeted Cormac with robustly hopeful friendliness. They wanted to include him, but he could not be included because he had never been someone anything could include and had never felt happy any-where, in childhood, except school and especially beneath the mansard roof of the room where Senan practised for piano exams.

The bedrooms were full of children. Unwatched by adults, they played complicated and coyly political games. Only Patrick was in the boys' old room, smelling of last night's whiskey and Taking a Moment of what Cormac presumed to be quiet horror or panic or perhaps even prayer. They'd both been devout at one time: after Thomas. Went through a phase of *folie à deux*.

And finally, in the front there stood his mild father, watching the street for the limousine. Cormac could still see his mild father's narrow head, the tuft of snowy hair, the placid and unknowable and priestly separateness of his standing in the street like this, on his own. Cormac watched him fondly in the memory and felt grief. Now the house was nothing like this.

In the dining room of now: All right, say goodbye to Nannie, Patrick suddenly, loudly and nasally commands.

Maude begins to complain. Taking her lead, baby Jake squawks in dissent. Their father hoists Maude onto a shoulder with a military briskness matched by utter nullity of facial expression; Ursula, searching for her car keys, visits every surface of the ground floor tranquilly until she has found them, raised and clicked them like maracas, transferred Jake to the other side of her sharp little hip.

Give us a hand with this will you, Patrick says.

You're going to take the whole case?

I'll sort through it at home. Don't worry, I'll hold onto anything that's yours.

Cormac and Patrick haul the case, between them, to the wide boot of the car. The junk in the boot – toys, a number of silk and woollen scarves, wellingtons, a bottle of cava, a bale of magazines – speaks to a life between glamour and haste Cormac privately considers proof of his brother's class traitorhood.

You're still OK to stay? Patrick asks.

Sure thing, it's mid-term, Cormac says.

He feels, however, something like loneliness as he watches their car sweep down the darkening street, head-lamps rolling, and the mitten of Maude waving madly from the rear window. When they have turned onto Main Street it falls quiet again.

All my life, he thinks with a certain banal romance, I have watched cars turn that corner and disappear. Cars I know and cars I don't.

Across the road, in rest, is the house of Mrs Darcy, who minded them as children until she got nerves; the house of the Byrnes with the son who is living, he's heard, openly gay somewhere in Dublin now; the house of the Finns, whose father worked nights but exploded out in daylight to rage at them; the house, at the end, of the wardrobe suicide with rope and roller skates.

In the hallway, underneath the glass-beaded electrolier, Joy bends to pick something of Maude's from the floor.

Just ourselves now then, she says.

But she has her coat on when he turns, after a half-hour, from washing delft. Patrick's suitcase has left a streak on the lino. Cormac spots this now and hopes she doesn't see. It looks like motor oil and you'll never get that out. I knock into Mrs O'Mara, she explains, on Sunday nights. Will you come?

Do you need me?

She'd like to see you, I'm sure. I'm always telling her about you.

As she locks the door behind them, he feels the street bearing down, chilly and odourless as ice.

The houses of the street are flush with the pavement, with deep-set windows and lintels of stone. They were built in the eighteen-hundreds for workers at the hosiery factory. There were other hauntings in the town, quite a few, when he was small: poltergeists in particular favoured the council estate on the hill. They, of course, had the soil on the stairs. A folktale tells of a caravan burning down on the hill, one hundred years ago, when it was still bare. People say the central headstone in the graveyard, a concrete rhomboid studded with seashells, is the grave of the traveller children who died in the fire. This grave is sealed with cement and illegible. The story functions as a foundation myth.

Following his mother makes Cormac feel sheepish and slightly absurd. She walks briskly on her small feet – she is lean, like him – and carries the poinsettia she is taking to gift. She will not let him carry this. It looks violent but elegant by streetlight. When she reaches the O'Maras', her son overtakes her and holds her by the shoulder, causing pause. He reaches out and strokes the brass doorknocker, which is shaped like a man.

What the hell, he breathes.

Yes, it's unusual, isn't it?

It's a man, a male figure, in profile pose. Its outline is instantly and acutely recognisable.

Oh my god. Cormac begins to hiss with laughter, pushing two hands to his face to contain it and shaking his head. It's Pearse, he says. It's Patrick Pearse.

83

Shush, says Joy.

It's the head of revolutionary martyr Patrick Pearse.

Cormac raises the knocker and lets it drop, just as his mother snaps, There's a bell, stop messing will you, Cormac.

Mrs O'Mara, her hair no longer permed but grey, answers by peering around the edge of the door and then crying, Oh Joy, it's yourself; she looks down at a frothing dog and holds it back with her leg. She wears slippers and the rubbery heat of the house meets them as they come in. There are in fact two dogs, yipping yellow-white shih tzus, and Mrs O'Mara squeaks, Quiet, quieten down! Now you, don't be bold! She puts her hands to Cormac's lapels. My god, she says. Who's this?

That's Cormac, the youngest one, Joy tells her. The lecturer.

She used to say *photographer*, and lecturer is an upgrade. She has never said artist because that is a term without a stable referent.

Cormac. Mrs O'Mara shakes her head. My god, she repeats, so handsome, Joy.

I love your doorknocker, Cormac grins.

There's a man makes them, the woman tells him, and sells them at the market in Ring Commons.

Is that still going?

Is what, the market? Oh yes. Mostly, you know, just selling those pirate D-V-Ds. Here, she says. Come into the front.

A fire burns in the grate and gives muggy heat to the upholstery, the velvet floor-to-ceiling curtains of an earlier age. The dogs resume their spot on the rug. Cormac's aesthetic eye, ruthless and practised, takes in the kitsch

84

richness. He has moved on from it, this world. He has moved on, but the street of his mother and Mrs O'Mara, where all their neighbours and childhood memories and dream landscapes reside, cannot be allowed to move on because he needs it: he demands of it a weight and density, an anchoring, ossified as habits of wallpaper and shepherd-esses of Lladró porcelain and bun-faced lapdogs, the ambient heavy-handedness of RTE, the glint of twisting firelight on GAA trophies.

Cormac sits now on the chintz settee.

You're too good, Mrs O'Mara is saying, accepting the poinsettia.

I know it's a Christmas plant, rattles Joy, but they go all year.

It will be Christmas before we know it anyway. It's sooner and sooner it starts.

When they are settled with tea and Christmas biscuits and the television on mute, Joy and the woman begin to talk about Patrick and Ursula, and more specifically about the house they have bought, a palatial new build at the end of an unfinished street between Raheny and Don-abate. Patrick and Ursula are pleased it remains unfinished because the builders' bankruptcy left fields of zoned and ferny stubble vacant, blank and stately, in prairie to the horizon and the sea.

These are the old lands of distressed demesne houses, the Portrane madhouse, and once-profitable arable farm-ing. They have ordered their driveway mosaicked with red-brick to accommodate cars, but the green stretching around seems to extend from the garden and softens an otherwise functional effect.

85

The house looks remote and exposed and hungry for burglary, but Joy, describing it to Mrs O'Mara now, warms to the tone of humble amazement she adopts to put it across. It's like a mansion, she insists.

Oh I'm sure she'd want only the best, Mrs O'Mara agrees.

Oh yes.

She'd be used to it.

She'd have you think that, Joy says.

Cormac pictures Ursula, again, as he saw her at the house-warming in May: standing at her patio with a champagne flute, a dress wilting from her shoulders, and staring at the acres of baize, the landscape rolling to the old coach road, to the remains of a mill race mincing over stones. To the large wheeled sign at the edge of the motorway reading COMING SOON.

They grew up here, in North County Dublin, Patrick and Cormac, but when Maude was born, Patrick bought online access to extensive census records from their father's homeplace near Ballinamore.

You can go to the National Library for free, Cormac had pointed out.

Who has time for that, seriously.

They were sitting on the patio behind the place they were then renting. He remembers Ursula in a deckchair, looking bloodless, her arms resting above her head in a pose of strange abandon. Nipples distractingly tenting the fabric of a different dress. She was trying to breastfeed with, he gathered, a stressful lack of success – he remembers the conversation on account of the nipples and remembers, also, a baby monitor between them, by the ashtray. Patrick was allowed to smoke outside. Another house on the street was being finished; there carried the grind and scrape of a bucket digger clearing chainies and screed.

Basically, Patrick said, there's a fuck-ton of Mulveys.

Funny to recall him in the heat there: *a fuck-ton of Mulveys*. They were odd names too, he explained, exotically Protestant – Golden, Coote. What he meant was that he could not dig through these Mulveys to find anything of interest, anything he might hold onto for Maude, and turned with reluctance to their mother's family instead. This was easier. There were two brothers, in nineteen-hundred, living in a laneway off the main street: two wives, two Margarets, ten children between them, all of whom could read and write (*R.C.*) but not in Irish, most of whom worked at the factory.

So there are your blood origins, Cormac said.

Ah here. Patrick dashed ash into the tray ostentatiously. No shame.

Are you disappointed, Ursula?

She had closed her eyes. Her arms were still folded above her head. She said, with a boldness that suggested she'd been paying more attention than he thought, We found my grandmother's house in Virginia and the artificial lake was not there yet. It said on the map, *land prone to flood*.

Oh yes?

My family have a country grudge with the neighbours that goes back a long time. They say the artificial lake causes flooding on their land. But there you go: land prone to flood, in nineteen-hundred.

Can't you show it to them?

Oh no. I danced with one of the sons at a disco and nearly got shunned. She laughed, then winced: Maude cried, appalled, through the monitor.

87

He did very well, Mrs O'Mara is saying, speaking of Patrick. And you, sir, she demands. Is this one the lothario?

I don't even know, Joy says. He doesn't tell me anything.

Nothing to tell, Cormac laughs. The chocolate biscuit in his hand is melting fast.

You're still young.

He is not, says Joy.


Cormac checks on his mother before bed.

She is sitting up, reading with half-moon spectacles, in the ring of light from her lamp. A battery of pills for her arthritis and bone density clutter a locker otherwise occupied by magazines and library paperbacks. There is a cosy smell like Vicks VapoRub in the room.

'Night, Ma, Cormac says.

Goodnight, chicken, she replies. Her warmth fills him with warmth and permission to relax: pleased, if sadly so, he pulls her door closed behind him. He thinks of the things they have put her through over the years, Thomas, Patrick, Cormac, their father, who is dead now too.

He often thinks this when he undergoes some gesture of finality with her lately: hanging up the phone, closing a door, signing off on a birthday card.

The known, shadowy contours of the landing strike him now as déjà vu. There is a kindly wash of rain on the roof. His most vividly nonsensical memories still exist in this place, but the stairs sink into darkness flatly now. Nothing is mysterious. How he used to imagine the place in darkness as he lay in bed and listened for wind and sprites and xylophones.

Odd thought. Is the guitar there? It is, behind the door in the box room. It's too late to touch or even contemplate.

Thomas would play it, but Cormac remembers above all his father singing 'Courting Blues', 'Reynardine', 'Wichita Lineman'.

There was one occasion, and only one, when their father reefed Thomas from the kitchen table by the collar; reefed and dragged from the room. Cormac can see the arched and doorless passageway from dining room to kitchen: he sees the two men – one spry but vigorous and the other a fleeting of fabric and long hair – passing through, frozen darkly against light like shadow-play. It's almost spooky. I am tired, he thinks grandly. I went out on Friday night and Saturday night – sex, Nina spiralling whitely in the space above him, turning around – and I'm tired now, though it puts a weekend around tidily, being popular.

He wants to chuckle, or flirt with someone. He moves from the well of the stairs to the box room.

The book – *The Bicameral Mind* – had been his, but it was from the seventies, so it predated him. It was a theory of primitive man being addressed by God, or gods, within his own head, like a psyche had chambers and anterooms and lecture halls. There was a picture in it of a mask, or maybe it was a sculpture, something very old, showing a face with a circular mouth. He picks it up from the dresser, now, but puts its down. Tender drumming of rain: light fingernails on the windowpane.

To the box room have been exiled an old Calor gas heater, lamps made from Chianti bottles, and a blown photograph of an empty crosswalk in West Hampstead Cormac gave her himself from his master's degree in London; this, framed, hangs next to the map with inaccurate Balkans that was Patrick's when he was at school. Cormac has searched here many times for his mother's old twin pierrots, their porcelain purity spiked with wabi-sabi, because he is taken with a memory of where they stood either side of a mirror on her dresser long ago. Vials of Lourdes water shaped like the Virgin too – he used to collect those, but they are harder and harder to come by these days. He should never have melted five of them down to form the base of an antic lamp included in his graduate show.

Against the window with its dust-catching pelmet there is a single bed. Cormac lies on this, scrolling through lighted lists of updates on his phone.

Nina has sent photographs of the completed cell structure, standing sparely against sawdust, with one of the studio cats sitting under its meshwork vault like a household god.

It still looks like an igloo, he types.

That's not, she says, politically correct.

What are you doing?

I'm still at the studio. Where are you?

In my mother's house.

Oh yeah, she says. Send nudes.

Midweek, this time.

A woman opens the door to the old building from within. She uses her foot to push a breeze block up against it, gravel growling on cement, and glances back into a darkness of incense and tar soap. Waiting for a cue. When it comes, she puts her finger to her lips. She tells them to be quiet in Irish.

In a bare room with a sacred heart, a tin tub full of water issues steam, gingerly, under hanging lamps. Cormac can see other people lined along the walls, pressing back against cement, and hear at intervals the shuffle of their feet. The difference this time is that the soap is not white but red, like flavoured gelatine.

Knowing what is about to happen makes the performance in the bath seem more contrived, such that his awareness becomes vertiginously meta, a watchful analysis of himself watching the watching and watching the watchfulness, watching the space in which the watching finds its presence, godawful.

For this reason he hurries to the coffin room. There, the actress–dancer Caroline Brabazon, who he's looked up online, prowls with an air of depressive passivity.

He progresses to the small adjacent room. A woman is trying to open a window. Do you know the way out? she hisses. You have to know.

Lights come up at the close of the hour. Audience members are ushered into the downstairs space, set up like a bar in a theatre stage set, for the post-show discussion. A sixties television, astonishingly small, plays soundless footage of the inaugural flight from the Mayo Marian shrine. Disgraced priests who have not yet been disgraced lift their smiles to the sky.

Looking at the stage, Cormac is reminded of an amdram production he saw, years ago, because Ursula was starring in it. She kept this hobby up until Jake was born. She played, this time, a young woman patiently imbibing ghost stories which folded into them beings and fairies reminiscent of the agents in DMT. The stage reminds him now, with such clarity, of this mild memory and of Ursula, her short but shifting haircut current at the time, her slightly squeaky intonations, basically just playing Ursula in a draught-threaded nineteenth-century schoolhouse in Skerries.

In the play, her character finally turned out a ghost story of her own, prosaic and understated, as if she were turning out the lining of a handbag to loosen lint and coins. It was the story of a drowned child making calls from the afterlife.

The director of the laundry piece is a woman whom everyone fears. She sits with folded arms on a chair before the crowd. Her interviewer gestures to the sound guy and asks, Are we rolling? He checks his apparatus, gives her a thumbs-up.

Excellent, says the interviewer, turning to the room. We are live, she smiles. So please, nobody swear. A pulse of polite laughter passes. The director raises her eyebrows.

Cormac tries not to search the group of performers, sitting together on a surplus church pew to the side of the room, for Caroline conspicuously. From the corner of his eye he sees the arc of hair at the top of a head and figures this might be her; he wonders about looking at her openly. He wonders if she will remember him and if she knows who he is already. He thought earlier of proposing to photograph her but realised how irredeemably creepy that would seem.

So, says the interviewer, to begin with let's talk about the use of space.

The director sighs heavily and unfolds her arms. She speaks to the ceiling in angry deadpan as if she has already explained herself. These spaces, right, these institutions, she grinds, were carceral institutions, OK? People were put in against their will and it wasn't a choice, and they couldn't escape. Bringing in dancers, she says, raises the question of how the body responds to that and what is the impact of that, like, on the body.

They want, she continues, the city council wants to sell the original site of the Sean McDermott Street laundry and turn it into a hotel. At this sounds rise from the crowd. It's unbelievable, the director agrees, it's absolutely unbelievable to hear, and yet there you go.

So you think, the interviewer has tilted her microphone towards herself, they should be preserved?

Commemoration is one thing, see, the director explains. Commemoration closes things off. That's not what we want to do. We want to keep it all open, and raw.

Cormac drifts.

He finds himself thinking of the stairs, of the tower at school, and of the hissing sconces and the samplers on the landings thick with radiator heat, of *Make me a channel of your penis*, of the owl and the fox rotting on their mossy logs. Why this place again?

Oh yes and the mild Mass-morning weather, the dry shiver of trees, the smell of mushrooms, on the day that Thomas died. And a yeasty stout-glass on a windowsill; a bulge of bulb-light; a saucer of cigarette butts.

Cormac's imagination shifts such things front-and-centre, quietly, in response to triggers so immensely subtle he is rarely able to isolate them. Each of these scenes, or rather the extinct instant of his apprehending them, is gone and over, and yet they feel so much realer than this moment of boredom. And that, he thinks grandly, is the reason for making art. It is to pin impressions down.

Pin and can or put in a glass cabinet: there was a story about the castle at school, a legend that foxes would gather to bark under the chamber window when the master of the hunt lay dying. Come dance with Reynardine.

He tunes in again to what the director is saying.

We can't do this again, is what she is saying. And we shouldn't even have to do it at all.

Do — now, what? Even the interviewer is lost.

Sometimes, the director says, it is like we are dragging this country kicking and screaming into the light.

In spite of this, the interview has to end eventually. The director has given so much of herself, she retires at once. Relief fans through the room with air from an opened door, and people begin to mix. Caroline is talking to a thin boy with a moustache, a small hat as tight as a condom on his head, by the pew. When Cormac approaches, she turns her face in sympathetic recognition, but, for all this, he knows it is politeness. He has not been recognised.

Heya, he tries.

Thank you. Caroline flutters her eyes shut. She had been expecting him to congratulate her.

He says, awkwardly, Yeah, great. I'm Cormac.

I'm Caroline, she replies. And this is Reggie.

Her instant introduction of, and deferral to, the moustached boy is wholly playful – she smiles, and Cormac shakes the boy's hand, not believing for one moment that the kid has been christened Reggie or anything like Reggie. He remembers Nina and Ned. These cute spontaneous triangulations.

I'm a fan, says the boy.

You are? Are you sure?

This is Cormac Mulvey, the boy tells Caroline, the photographer who started with *Lux*.

I know your work, I think, Caroline says. And you were at the show last week, weren't you?

I stayed out of your way this time.

I didn't see you. She blinks. Innocent.

Hey, we have a few snugs booked, says the boy. In the place, you know, that does Korean food?

Cormac's phone has begun fitting in the pocket of his jeans. It is Patrick. He regards it with dismay.

Are you around? his brother demands.

I'm at the, Cormac pauses, I'm at the theatre.

Weren't you there last week?

Yes.

Hold on – are you at that naked show?

At this, Cormac can only laugh, moving into a recess

and retiring from the force of the crowd. His eyes fall on a group by the door, waiting with their coats for one of their number: all have wide spectacles, remedial haircuts, ankles indecent. They look like a punchline without irony and this recognition makes him feel softly resigned, and old, and forgiving.

It's over, he tells Patrick. It's all wrapping up.

I'm in town, I'll meet you.

There are snugs. We're going to a bar. Cormac gives Patrick directions. As he hangs up he feels something slip away from him. Control.

He finds Patrick in the pub with a pint already.

What's going on? Cormac asks.

I need to charge this, Patrick shouts over the din, holding up his chipped smartphone. He is wearing a work suit, tie tugged off and disposed of, and has probably been drinking since the late afternoon. His face is red, his dark hair pasted in a swipe to the right by sweat. He begins to ask the barman for help, miming and brokering access to a set of sockets behind the bar. Even though he is drunk he remains alert, cheering at something the barman says as he is shaking out the charger cord and plugging in the phone.

So I won't stay long, Patrick claims, I just need juice.

It's a Wednesday, Cormac says.

I can't take it any more. I can't face it. And obviously, like, I can't drive. No, I don't mean that kind of juice. He barks with laugher at, and with, the barman.

Will I ring Ursula?

She told me to stay with you. She told me not to come back. Not in front, you know, of the kids.

Yes, I get that, Cormac says. He turns to a tap on the

wrist and sees, with surprise, that Caroline is standing next to him.

Can I get you a drink? she asks. To apologise for putting you on the spot in the name of art.

I'm always ready to suffer for art, he says, but really I should buy you one instead, to celebrate your – play.

He realises he is not exactly sure what to call the show.

I'm getting this, crows Patrick when Cormac holds out his card. It is an excuse to order another for himself.

This is my brother, Cormac tells Caroline.

Wow, you look nothing alike, she says.

After midnight, she also says, What's going on with your brother?

I'm trying to get him to leave, Cormac shouts over the music. This is true of the last half-hour but not substantially true of the evening generally.

They have left the bar and the actors, the director, the dancers, the academics, behind; Caroline, punkishly drunk and encouraged by Patrick, suggested they go to The Globe but remembered on arrival that the basement disco still operates and now they are in the basement disco, watching Patrick and Reggie dancing furiously in the surge of people. Cormac and Caroline have the prow of the bar to themselves, the floury bloom of steam from the dishwasher, the glow of a door to the smoking area.

The place is not overrun; it is Thursday now. Cormac knows how remiss he has been in letting Patrick lead them here. It feels like all is so tremendously lost and still the girl, Caroline, only speaks to him constantly, inclining her head to explain and explain and explain. She has been speaking all night.

He can hear most of it but not all of it, close to the porch of his ear, petitioning.

When I took my MA in dance, she explains – and she has, she further explains, to talk about this constantly, to arts institutions, funding bodies, family, festival committees, dates – I homed in on and became enamoured of ritual studies.

When she says *enamoured* or writes *enamoured*, she thinks, she explains, of the words *enamel* or *enamelling*, and thence of two different, instant, things: in the first, an antique enamelled bangle her grandmother had kept in a dish by the kitchen sink – flowers, birds leaking slightly of dye – and in the second, the poem 'Sailing to Byzantium', which she studied for the leaving certificate.

More specifically, of *hammered gold and gold enamelling*, of the three–two–four beat rhythm and the weird, redundant repetition of *gold*, a hammer becoming enamelling, a force becoming decoration, letter *em* receding and becoming letter *ell*: of hammered gold and gold enamelling.

She taps this progression out into the air between them with an index finger.

At school she was the liturgical dancer at every Mass until a priest put a stop to schoolgirls in leggings rolling and arching to 'Panis Angelicus' or 'Down by the Salley Gardens' or 'True Colours' in an Actual Church.

I read a thing, she continues. A thing about embodied empathy, she says, about watching and feeling, about the brain experiencing pain, movement, equanimity, from observing somebody else's bodily gestures.

And then another thing about the proximity, with regards to brain activity, of compulsive tendencies and the framework, the cartography, of *ritual*. Drawing a circle and lining it with salt. Lighting candles in this order but only this. Sealing out chaos with elegant and repetitive action: going mad, having rituals break against, like, the rational, having habit devour itself.

All of that kind of thing. I am interested. I bring this to bear on choreography. It's what I do. But religious – like, faith? Oh no, I'm not religious at all. It's not the same. Here, let me explain it again.

What's it like? Cormac shouts. This piece you're doing next, after the play?

Different in two places, she replies: on residency, where I started it, and at home. On residency, with the bare trees in their candour, it is stripped birch and bicycles, spoked and simple and continuous, a Catherine wheel rather than a Celtic spiral. She traces a circle in the air. In Dublin, when the studio she teaches in is free for use, the moves are contained within a mirrored wall, bright with spotlights, and a window behind.

The studio is in Stoneybatter, she explains, and broken into constantly. Once, an intruder dismantled a barre and smashed the window with it. She describes how they stuck the barre through the pane so that it shot into the street and remained in a fan of glass shards until daybreak.

Oh dear, Cormac says.

She says, Wait until you see me dance properly.

Oh I can't wait. Aren't you going to dance now?

No, Caroline says plainly. And then she asks, What's going on with your brother?

I think his marriage is in trouble.

She looks towards the dance floor in puzzlement. Her expression is similar to the quizzical impulse with which she read the nameplate on the coffin before demanding,

What? Strands of her copper hair are now pushed behind her ears, her body elfin and agile, her complexion a thin constellation of freckles on the cheekbones and nose.

I should take him home, Cormac declares.

I'll help you, says Caroline.

Patrick has been shimmying with women – some goth-looking students and a woman in her thirties, skittering on dagger heels – but he answers Cormac by lassoing Reggie around the shoulders and shoving the young man before him.

Tell them what you told me, Reggie, he shouts, clapping Reggie between the shoulder blades. The boy stoops shyly and laughs and leans into them, and says something.

Caroline cries, Oh for god's sake, no!

What is it? Cormac asks.

Reggie has M-D-M-A, Patrick says, spelling it out in a drone. Reggie has the nineties in his manbag.

You've got to be joking.

I don't mind. Reggie shrugs. I got it for free. Well, for a job I did. You can have some if you want. We can all have some. He smiles like a hopeful child.

It's a Wednesday, Caroline points out.

Cormac says, Actually it's Thursday now.

Man. Patrick leans on the bar. Patrick is perspiring. Tall and discrete and different from them all, Patrick has always been emphatically handsome; Patrick has always been powerful. Cormac looks at him now with pity and unease. Man, Patrick is saying to him. This is the last night out of my life. You know it is. You know what's going to happen tomorrow.

I don't, argues Cormac. No way. We're going home. We're going back to the flat right now. If you don't come now I'll lock the door and you'll have nowhere to go.

Oh fuck off, Patrick says. All right.

The four ascend the stairs and push through the gurning bar, the small crowd, to the pavement manned by bouncers and a girl with her hand out working, stiffly, from smoker to smoker, saying over and over without energy, Any change for a hostel, sir? Any change for a hostel, sir? Taxis slant, flaring headlights. The ingress with benches and a print of the Proclamation of Independence at the bottom of Camden Street has netted wanderers: a congelation of bickering drunks.

I thought you might like to stick with me, Cormac blurts out at once. I know it's not ideal. I didn't expect to have − him.

Well, I'll make sure, Caroline says carefully, that you get him home OK.

I actually live a stone's throw from here.

Really? Her face opens adorably with interest. That's amazing. That must cost a fortune. Unless it's a squat.

I promise it's not a squat.

Reggie lives in a squat.

Reggie my man! Patrick shouts. Come!

A wind speeds unbroken down the tunnel of Dame Street, whipping chip bags and cigarette butts. When Cormac shows them the door to the flat, Caroline says again, Oh wow, what kind of rent do you pay on a place like this?

He's minding it for a friend, Patrick brays.

I rent it from a friend. Cormac pushes the door. OK, he says. There are neighbours, so *bígí ciúin*, OK?

Patrick messes all the way up the stairs, lurching, but in the apartment he disappears to throw up in the toilet and sends himself squarely to bed. He curls up in his clothes and lets out a heavy sigh. Cormac pulls off his brother's shoes, feeling a pang of sadness at the feet, and when he returns to the other room, Reggie, who has not disappeared, is shaking out a bag of pills.

What shape are they meant to be? Caroline asks. She leans over, bent above the coffee table, and says, Oh right, they're lotuses. She laughs.

Half or whole? Reggie asks.

Half to start, concedes Cormac cautiously. A half-hour later, he says, This isn't working at all.

Have more. You just looked like a lightweight. Reggie spoofs kindly. I mean a little delicate.

They take the rest.

They really aren't working, Caroline agrees with sudden vehemence.

Take more.

It'll hit me out of nowhere then, won't it?

I feel sort of drunk, Cormac says. It's nice.

Put on some music, Reggie suggests.

Cormac toys with his phone and whispers, Don't wake Patrick, though. My brother, of course I love him. But – You know he has a wife, and kids?

He works in finance, Caroline says gravely. I don't even have a visual for that kind of life.

There are nights Patrick stays out, he gathers, but does not stay with Cormac. There are nights he cannot account for. Cormac doesn't say this out loud or even think it for more than a moment.

My brother is a journalist, Reggie announces. In London. This information glitters with a mediocre promise that shortly dissipates.

Reggie is sitting on the sunken couch with Cormac; Caroline, carved apart and perching upright on the arm-chair in a shower of lamplight, turns her profile to the window.

This window is interesting, she says.

Oh bollocks, Reggie says. He rises to dash for the bath-room, pulls the door shut, and retches.

I will bring him some water, decides Caroline. She fills a glass and knocks softly on the door.

Cheers, darling, Reggie croaks. They continue to listen to him heave. A splash and a moan of pleasure indicate relief.

That doesn't bode well for us, Cormac says.

It was stupid of us to do it all, says Caroline.

If they're cut with Epsom salts or something, Cormac grins, we're both going to die.

Don't frighten me. She shakes her head, knocking it side to side as if clearing her ears. Oh my, there it is. OK. That's not so bad, is it?

Do you want some more?

No! Don't push our luck, Cormac. She smiles at him. Do you want to check on your brother?

Forget about my brother for a minute. Cormac moves closer to her. Tell me more about embodied empathy.

I could talk, she says, all night about embodied empathy.

He has seen a clip of her dancing on YouTube: it was, he describes to her now, some point in a show called *Bridget Cleary*.

Yes, last year! she cries. Oh this window! She raises her hands, which are shaking. Explain to me, she says. Describe to me. What am I doing in the video?

I'll just find it. On my phone. Or wait, no, this is Reggie's phone.

He shifts, fizzing, to the arm of her chair. He holds it up for both of them to watch. In the video something has ended and there is no movement at all. Caroline sits, folded onto her calves, on a stage. Two white arms turn out and terminate in palms against knees. She stares down as if she is concentrating, but after a moment of stillness it's clear she is not concentrating; she is staring absently beyond, her body slack and decanted, not rigid but bereft, not tense but static. Caroline on the stage, that is. Caroline in the window watches.

That's the conclusion, Caroline in the window explains to him. Her voice has taken on the granular quality of the seashore. Everything in the pose, on the screen, is a null quantity. The other dancers stand about her, arched and mannered in a thicket of arms, panting visibly against pink-ish stage lights. Oh yes, Caroline says, Caroline in real life: I remember that well. She is moved. Did you ever hear of that mystery play, *Everyman*? *Everyman I will go with thee, and be thy guide, always and forever to be by thy side.* Anyway I was thinking of that. I was playing Bridget Cleary. She speaks softly to the windowpane. Her husband and family killed her, she says, because they believed she was a fairy changeling.

She breathes deeply. She closes her eyes.

It was, she says, in eighteen-ninety-five.

He tells her, That's interesting. And then, a beat later, Oh shit, I'm going to puke.

Reggie is now sitting in the bath. He tilts his head back beatifically. Wonderful, he tells Cormac. Feels wonderful now. That's right, man, throw it all up. So much better afterwards. He squeezes his eyes shut. Just chill.

Have we overdosed?

Yeah, maybe but, like, the body has mechanisms. It copes. Just wait it out.

Cormac grips the sink as he brushes his teeth, dizzy and finding the tiles and mirror pulsing slightly, falling into a state of demonstrable structural logic – squares, emanating squares, an auric ambience of squares – before shifting stiffly into new constellations of chaos, nonsense and nausea. He walks shakily back into the front room. His heart is pounding.

I know you want to have sex, Caroline announces, her voice now phantasmal but also everywhere at once, like the voice of God, like the voice of an art installation, but, she says, my body has switched itself off.

No, Cormac says. We can do whatever you want to do. Switched off?

Cormac's own body is twitching. Warm explosions of sensation travel through his arms and legs to meet spandrels of pleasure at each socket, ball and joint, to fill him with elastic space and genuine goodwill.

He sits down by the windowsill.

Look at this window! Caroline wails.

What do you mean switched off? Cormac asks, but he is also distracted. The lightbulb, bare and noble, reverts to its most explicit state: round, simple, fed by wires, nothing majestic to it but firm limits and elemental connections – a world of bulbs, and wires, and structures, and the streets around them webbed with frost outside.

Are you all right? she asks.

Yes, yes. He shuts his eyes. The sensations are electric, bursting and earthing, yet even as this unfolds he feels all the gaudy ordinariness of it, of everything: the meaninglessness, freeing meaninglessness, of an undemanding, given, spinning, indifferent world.

This is really quite good stuff, he whispers. I have to admit. No mythology.

From my neck down is dead, Caroline explains calmly. My brain is trying to stop it taking over. It's defensive. I have too much self-control. I have a superego. I could talk and talk. Don't let me. I haven't done this for ages.

Your voice is lovely, Cormac tells her. And it is. Like coins shingling, like guttate with a gust of personality behind it, like a veil of chimes. All of which is nonsense: all of which, he thinks fondly and sadly, is the garnish or the varnish, nothing true and nothing rare. Just drugs. She is right – he does want to have sex, especially with all these little explosions of chemicals – but knows they can't and always knew because of Patrick and Reggie. Also it would be wrong, ethically speaking, and despite certain sucker wisdom, ecstasy does not obviate rape – that's such garbage, Cormac thinks – he thinks clearly, slow enough to perform disgust and witness himself performing disgust even though this is taking place *inside his head* – it's quite the opposite really – cock curling into the stomach, a scrotal shrink. Wading in the bleak sea of the self, numb from the waist.

He sees this with a sad patrician clarity. The brain on drugs. Such ruthless but consoling clarity.

It's actually absurd really actually. It's really actually absurd. Something is abiding adenoidally in his head: it's *really* quite actually absurdly *really* quite actually absurd. Caroline is sitting on the windowsill too. She is telling him her life story, but her voice is blunted to a burr, which is good, he thinks, because her whispers, her hisses and shivers, are nice to listen to.

He can tell how much she likes to talk.

Reggie returns and lies on the couch. His body jerks and

tenses, releasing, and his breath becomes ragged. Cormac feels himself go cold; feels sweat slip down his back and legs. His shoulders spasm and his knees bend under him.

Water, Reggie? Caroline walks slowly across the room, her hands folded before her and her body as still and sad as a mourner following a coffin in a church; she fills another glass and brings it to Reggie. It's not clear where the first glass went. This glass is Fermanagh.

I'll have a sleep.

Drink this and sleep. Caroline sits on the couch and cradles Reggie's head in her lap. Wait for this to pass, she says. How stupid we are. My brain has switched my entire body off. It wants to protect it. How boring. How stupid we are. She is speaking leadenly now, as low and achingly empty as death. She looks like a tombstone or a goddess. Monumentally inert and pale and dead-eyed, cradling the sleeping boy.

We're only high, Cormac says. It will pass.

We will pay for this later though.

And they do. It's horrible.


Cormac comes to, tumbling in a tilting well and shaking, trembling all over. The words for what's happening will not form on his lips, nor any words: he knows only an animal focus on keeping control, on sorting darting cantilevers of dark wood at speed, on grabbing with urgency at context, mnemonics.

Something like a fit judders upwards from the perineal chakra and, then, he is suddenly hunkered on the floor of his bedroom and Patrick, lying in bed, is holding an arm out towards him laconically. Cormac is gripping the outstretched arm.

Are you OK? Patrick asks, also laconically.

Flashback. I think it was some kind of flashback.

You want to lie down?

Yes.

When he stands the blood rushes to his head and causes a swoon, and he again grips Patrick's arm.

Eat something, Patrick suggests.

Yeah. I can't keep anything down.

Cormac lies on the bed, above the duvet. The room is smoky and grey in the dawn. The world is viciously literal.

How was your trip? Patrick asks.

It was nice to begin with. His gaze sears the ceiling, eyes unwilling to rest or close and risk finding again the well of reddish brown. He thinks he was tumbling in it for a long time and can't remember reaching the bedroom at all. Now, in this vigilant and hysterical light, thin squares of childhood begin to descend, see-sawing or flaking serenely, snow. This used to happen sometimes, in the past, when he still did drugs. As now, blandly equanimous scenes and objects listed themselves, turned up like playing cards, non-violent and nondescript.

A tin money-box and a duvet set patterned with *Thunderbirds*. Soft rubber seat of a swing set facing black rocks to the sea, a sky of annihilation, smell of bladderwrack. A textbook curling at the edges. The twins who always came to school smelling dimly of shit; their house with no furniture; their father sitting on the floor watching television. Smell of a rubber basketball. Smell of a cast coming off a broken arm, like a locker room, like the annexe of a nightclub in Berlin. The tower – ravens – and the ice-house, *oubliette* (forget). Smell of the heavy-duty bin bags out of which Joy would make their Halloween costumes:

vampire capes for flapping, with a face of her own make-up.

The smell of polyethylene switched allegiances in adulthood and became the smell of sweat in cheap clothing, became a note playing into the bouquet of oral sex.

To endure this cascade of lifelessly encyclopaedic associations is torture, but Cormac knows he must endure. His brain on drugs lays out its contents in this way, joylessly limited, threatening to recall something painful at any moment. There are the howls, the losses and the dreadful death of Thomas in an accident at twenty-one; there are also the smaller, far more wretchedly suggestive memories – kernels popping in a saucepan, bedclothes piled for the laundry, a grainy shot of their mother smiling, so vulnerable, on a bench; a teething ring, a comic torn, a corridor – suffused with grief because they are defined only by their being past. They will never occur again, never be freshly met: the world itself is old now, stark and inhospitable.

Cormac sweats and forbears it. The brain on drugs always runs out of steam eventually.

Steam. Bath of beer-water: laundry. Beer of bathwater. Bath of breath. Caroline appears in the doorway and crosses the room in her strange processional way, with her hands folded over her stomach repentantly. Are you all right? she asks.

Not bad. Come join me if you want.

She glances at Patrick, who has begun to snore.

I'm really cold, she says.

Come here. Cormac stands up, tosses his side of the duvet back, and, slipping off his jeans, climbs in. For one wary and whey-faced moment she wavers. Then she gets in next to him. He puts his arms around her shoulders and chest.

This is nicer, she whispers. Her teeth are chattering as he burrows into her hair. What happened, she asks suddenly, to your brother? You were talking about him. Not Patrick – another one.

Thomas, Cormac says.

Yes. You were talking about him. He is – dead?

He died a long time ago, when I was sixteen. He fell off a balcony. He was at a party and he fell off the balcony when he was high.

I'm sorry.

I was probably going on about it.

Not too much, no. You weren't upset or anything.

I was sixteen. Cormac yawns and sighs. As soon as I can get up I need to eat something, anything. I feel like a Victorian invalid.

He fell? He didn't jump?

Well. I mean, we assume he fell.

Could he have jumped?

On purpose? I suppose. He was out of it.

Like we were last night? She turns to look at him. She wears a wobbly, ironic smile.

A lot worse I think, Cormac says.

Your poor parents.

They were broken. He feels his teeth close tightly together in irritation.

Are there any more of you?

No. Patrick and I are the only ones. Our father died a few years ago, but our mother is fine.

She must be strong.

She's made of iron, he agrees. He thinks of her with her paperbacks and her bone medicine. He thinks of the crust of light around her, the reading lamp, and feels freefalling guilt or shame or desperation and wants to keep her from dying forever. The impossibility of it, the dread, almost makes him cry out.

He thinks, Such a bad son I have been.

He asks, Is Reggie alive then?

He's drinking tea and everything. He's fine!

Is that his real name, by the way?

As far as I'm aware. Caroline has stopped shivering now; between them grows a gluey heat. He angles his waist away from her tactfully, because semi-erect.

Talk to me, she breathes. Talk about anything.

The solemn slivers of childhood are fading out, cold alarm and old moments drifting into the multiverse. The first time this happened he sat through each of them, his joints swollen in lotus position: he sat through every sequential, scorching deposit, awed sometimes by just how much texture could be preserved; he stared all this down until a peace came to him, sleepy peace; he walked around a roof garden in Barcelona, scratching at an insect bite on his ankle. Each scratch was like an elongated orgasm, vivid, with ripple effect.

Now the hard-on is pulling more blood from his head. Cormac clings to her, dizzily, for a spell.

I don't have the energy, he breathes at last.

I'd like to hear you talk, she says. I feel exposed by all of the stupid talking I did last night.

You don't need to. I forget most of it.

Me too. But god, I'm such an egotist.

We all are sometimes. He is falling asleep. He holds on, frightened of the plummet out of time and the torment of the red room. It doesn't come.

★

The rest of the day is chopped into plateaus.

After a time, he has to see Caroline and Reggie out to ugly alloy daylight, limply miserable in their coats, and eat slowly two slices of throat-catching toast. The city is rising and moving into its muscle memory. Patrick is not in much better condition and says, Don't ask, don't say anything, I'll explain, just come with me while I do this. *This* being a meeting with some kind of stakeholder. He's an academic, it's off-site, Patrick says; you'll like it. No, stop that, I can't fucking eat yet, just come on.

As they walk together to the taxi rank at Foster Place, Patrick talks and talks, low, his voice a throb, compulsively. Cormac only catches some of it over the sound of traffic and the commuter crowd. Patrick retells a story from years ago. Cormac has heard it before. Patrick went, for work, to Zurich – he was newly married, or nearly married, then – and the Zurich office took them for a huge meal in a beer hall; afterwards, some of the men drove them out further, to a squat cottage with dark windows, and here they watched a dark girl who must have been sixteen dancing naked around a pole. Her body was incredible, blooming with puppy fat, so that Patrick, almost married or newly married, grew desperate, and went back to the hotel, and phoned Ursula, and listened to her voice laughing over other things until he felt peaceable, able to go out by himself to a pornographic cinema, an experience he found – as he explains pointedly – squalid.

They are troubling him now, these memories, he implies. Implies or says. He is speaking rapidly.

Cormac continues to feel ill.

Patrick actually says: It was, you know, *squalid*.

They find a cab.

Sitting in the cab to the docklands – the driver is an unsmiling elderly man with a tracheal tube, his breathing like the last scuttling bubbles at the bottom of a straw – Cormac watches a grey heron rise with uncanny, Jurassic drama from the tidal flats. The cab is silent. It's kind of trippy. The heron that is.

Our father told me, Cormac says, that a heron taking off is a sign of luck.

Never heard that, replies the driver, in a wheeze so soundly other it makes Cormac feel a quality of discomfort he is able to investigate. The feeling is fear, but a thin, in-tuitive fear: a childish fear, a surge of objection smothered by civil strategies. It is not sympathy yet. It is a horror of what could become of his own life. He can see this dispassionately because he is still high.

Cormac tries to accept the terror. It does not integrate and, instead, he is startled by Patrick flapping at the door handle when they draw up at the riverside.

What relief.

Patrick, on the pavement now, wears yesterday's suit beneath a dousing of aftershave. He was fully himself for a moment earlier as he splashed it over his face singing hoarsely: I went down-to-the-river-to-pray, studying about that good-old-way.

Account, account, he says now, chanting the number, one foot in the grinding stream of trams and bikes and pencil skirts.

Cormac continues to feel ill.

He has been to this building before. It is glass-fronted and gaudily modern. In the lobby there are television screens and an area of white leather couches that look expensive but are wasted and threadbare at the edges – if you are observant – like the couches in a franchise dentist's surgery. The world remains hysterical, so Cormac notices everything: the mood of the room as well as the all-encompassing but subterranean gist of the room as the room produces a mood. Still high. Oh my.

To Patrick's visible surprise, the Principal Investigator from the co-funded project is already waiting in the lobby, a cup of coffee in his hand and a messenger bag across his chest. He is a young man with a monkish face, bland and inquisitive, and he is speaking to the security guard.

They'd be out from under you in a flash, the guard is advising the PI in a demotically Dublin snarl.

Patrick, having no idea of, or interest in, the context of this remark, merely interrupts, saying, Professor Deveraux?

Oh, it's Eamon, smiles the man, putting out his hand.

I let him into the machine, the security guard says. He looks at Cormac. Patrick does not explain Cormac to the guard.

The what?

Eamon holds up the coffee cup.

The guard says: The canteen.

Oh right. Yes, that's fine. Shall we?

The lift is spiced by the smell of coffee.

Did you have far to come? asks Patrick immediately, burring into small talk with sadistic flair. This is another Mr Mulvey; he will be observing. He's a lecturer in photography and fine art at DIT. If you are interested in any kind of visual element, actually, you might want to talk to Mr Mulvey. This one.

Cormac marvels at his brother's personal prowess. You would not think he was still, kind of, drunk; you would not think Cormac is only here at utter, giddy random, coming down from a low-end Wagnerian high. The enterprise begins to seem less incongruous and more like fun.

Cormac begins to crave coffee.

Oh no, says the man, who seems to be unnerved above all by formalities. I came from Drumcondra.

I'm afraid my colleague Mr Kehoe is not here today. You've been mailing him?

He mentioned it, yes. It should be fine.

But I'm all yours this morning. We'll confer. Patrick smiles. Patrick is almost flirting. Cormac thinks, not for the first time, of the ease Patrick has with women and the ease he would have with men if he ever tried. He remembers, thinks, of school: Cormac thinks unbidden of school. He thinks of supervised study on winter evenings, image of the study hall overseen by a pipe-faced Christ. It comes involuntarily but thickly detailed, intimately olfactory, and haptic as a bath mat: he pushes it down, crushes it, extinguishes it. The brain on motherfucking *fucking* drugs.

Cormac begins to feel vaguely horny.

Patrick's floor is empty but for a pigeon-chested techie leaning over a computer at the back. From this height, crowds of people coursing on the boardwalks can be seen. Morning air is hot and undisturbed, smelling of ink and toner, suggesting a slumbering force of industry. Wordsworth! Cormac thinks. That mighty heart is lying still. At school, he wrote an essay about that poem – about whether it was lying *yet* or lying *arrested*, lying stilly, tensely, threateningly: he had deeply cared. Goddamn study hall again.

Cormac continues to feel horny.

In a wing off the study hall with the pipe-faced Christ and behind crusted curtains, teenaged Senan sucks Cormac off and, of course, they never actually did anything in the study hall or anywhere near it, but wouldn't it be nice, he thinks, if they did. If they could. Nice to think.

I'm good! Eamon sloshes his cup. It rings near Cormac's ear. I'm good! Patrick has offered him more coffee.

Cormac shuts his eyes and shakes his head. Oh is this real, he thinks. The sentence has no question mark in his head. It is like a subliterate speech-bubble. Oh is this real, is this real. Oh.

All right. Patrick gathers a clutch of folders. Lifts the phone receiver. Pinned to his monitor there is a photograph of Ursula, on a picturesque wall somewhere Moorish-looking, smiling. It is a simple, pretty picture. She wears sunglasses.

Cab is coming, Patrick advises.

They descend again. Men in suits and a small number of nip-tucked women greet Patrick – who responds with a drowsy nod or wave, in the mode of an exhausted monarch – and double-take Cormac. He begins to feel a kinship with the portly sports-jacketed PI.

Cormac feels warmth.

Another cab, gulls like mortar fire, and the brash O'Connell monument a carousel of broad-shouldered stone angels. They drive inland. The driver this time is African and volunteers no opinions on anything. Rosary beads with a knot at one end swing luridly from the rear-view mirror. Cormac thinks of rosaries and funerals, which are the only occasions in his life he's taken part in rosaries, but sees the inference coming and elbows it expertly out of the way this time: funeral, Thomas, father, hearthrug, coffin, stems.

No.

They travel towards Ussher's Island, on the quays. Buildings begin to be boarded up, leaning sorrowfully over the barest portion of the river, but sudden junctions spilling out from Fishamble Street keep the atmosphere frantic and fleshy and alive. At the usual junction waits the usual juggler, the man who tumbles pins tediously in the air when the traffic is stalled, then looks for change. Patrick says with a spurt of fondness, Oh look, that cunt is still there.

There is a policeman on the area steps to the house they draw up before. It is full, splendid Georgiana: slender steps, wrought railings, lugubrious lintel. Thick doorknocker shaped like one of the Anna Livia keystones on O'Connell Bridge. It is also dirty and the lower windows blinded by plywood. Coloured rubbish snagged by the railings is heaped below, like a flowerbed.

Patrick demands, What's happened here?

Well, the protests, Eamon says.

Patrick pushes his face between the headrests of the taxi to remind the driver of the account code. Have you got that? he asks. The driver recites it back. That's it, Patrick says. Good man.

Eamon and Cormac are already on the kerb. Cormac tries to memorise the account code. Dublin on a bright day bashes about like a bully in a swimming pool.

Protests? Patrick is asking. He shuts the cab door behind him. It takes off and this street is busy and sunny, tourists opening maps over steel-topped tables on a café terrace opposite.

Cormac feels hungry. He nods: Protest.

Cormac thinks of, remembers, Lazarian. Tenements and ten-to-a-bed and boarded doors and housing crises and zoning holes and the interminable torments of land-lordism.

Eamon explains: The rent strike protestors were forcibly evicted from here two weeks ago.

Oh yes, echoes Patrick uncertainly.

The landlords brought in a private security firm. Eamon glances up at the guard and says, quietly, It was quite shocking. Balaclavas.

Some of my students were involved, Cormac recalls.

Can we go in? Patrick asks.

We can, I think. Eamon turns and addresses this to the guard with a nervous smile. Hello there.

What's your business? chants the guard, like he has not been listening.

As Eamon fumbles with some papers and Cormac tries not to give total way to mania, Patrick says, Yeah, no, we're from Deloitte?

Deloitte? The guard squints and seems amused.

We've got a permit, garda, Eamon assures. It's here somewhere.

Cormac squints. Permit. Oh to enter the building. Building is secured. Building is in private ownership. There is a movement – his students are moving through it – to expose slumlords and hoarding. He thinks: OK, cool. Solution-based.

Yeah Deloitte, Patrick drawls. He folds his arms and stares at the guard. Were you here, he asked suddenly, for the protest?

No, that wasn't our squad, but I'm not at liberty to discuss it anyway. The guard is from the west.

Cormac begins to feel fragmentary.

Don't worry, says Patrick. No one is going to ask you to.

He keeps his eyes trained on the man, who is wearing a padded vest. Eamon has produced the permit, waving it with a grimace, and is now shoving papers back into the bag.

Will the place come down on top of us, if we go in? Cormac asks.

It's all reinforced, reports the guard.

Cormac finally feels free enough to laugh and everybody looks at him. The study hall swabs before his mind and zeroes in once more on curtains and the pipe-faced Christ.

Cormac begins to feel incorrigible.

It is a forbidding doorway, panels set aside beneath a capstone that is locket-shaped and split, violently, by a structural crack. The plywood has been sprayed with graffiti and littered with boot prints. Cormac expects to smell piss within, but there is only the dully interdental odour of grout. There is also still carpet on the stairs, blue and bloating loose from the steps, inconsistently pinned in place by steel rods.

What was it before? Cormac asks.

Hang on. Eamon reads from a sheet, holding it close to his face. Residence, place of business, residence, doctor's surgery. Empty as of 2006. No evidence of squatting, oddly.

Is that odd?

It is a little, yes. But the buildings either side have stayed in use, so I suppose it would have been difficult to squat and not, you know, get reported and so on. Eamon clears his throat. Right then, Mister Deloitte. Do you want the tour?

I do, retorts Patrick. I'm intrigued.

Mister Moneybags. Eamon grins and searches Patrick's face for acknowledgement, admonishment, or anything at all.

Cormac begins to like Eamon.

As they enter the darkness of the building, tunnel-thick and disorientating after the street, Patrick says with abrupt intensity, My wife would get stuck into something like this. She looks at this sort of thing, this sort of wreck, and sees potential. She has a great imagination.

Eamon is climbing the stairs.

Be careful, calls the guard from the door. 'Tis easy to trip and fall. After a pause his voice carries with enthusiasm: Are ye insured? Are ye sure?

All keep their eyes on the bocketty rods as they climb the staircase. Eamon leads them into a reception room on the first floor. There is a collapsed couch under blankets, a fireplace gouged clean, and long windows throwing light onto cornices, onto a frieze of plaster violins overhead.

So these are the work of the eighteenth-century stuccodore Michael Stapleton, Eamon says. Who did—

Belvedere, Cormac supplies. And Leinster House.

So it's beautiful.

It is. Incredible. Well-preserved.

Not always. Eamon points to a brown stain with browner streaks radiating from it in one corner of the ceiling. A boiler, he suggests, or a bath, when it was bedsits.

Bedsits.

Gas, isn't it?

Christ, Patrick says. And now it's what – condemned?

Not quite. Eamon clears his throat again and sits into one of the window bays. It is registered to one P. Kearney and Associates, he reads. It's been theirs, and empty, for over ten years.

Why?

We can't say for sure, but probably it's one of several investments they bought for cheap during the crash.

They're waiting for the value to rise.

And it will. But at least these are based in the midlands. The next place I'll take you belongs to a fund in California. That means we'd label it differently, in the scheme: this place, however long it's empty and even though it is prime space and not being used, at least keeps its value in Ireland. That is, unless Messers P. Kearney and Associates have their funds offshore.

Of course they do.

They probably do. That is something we would investigate, through public accounts, and figure into the scheme.

What's the end goal?

A searchable online resource. Eamon raises his eyes to the ceiling, thinking, looking like a painted saint.

When he begins to reel off the other goals, he makes Cormac think of the director answering questions, after the laundry show, with her head tilted back. It is a pose that leaves the speaker, in that instant, pleasantly alone.

Searchable resource, Eamon repeats, policy submission, independent report. A full sense of what is empty, how long it has been empty, what kind of value it holds, who owns it, if or how or when or *if ever* – he laughs dryly now, looking back at them – they might be compelled to stop sitting on it.

In the next room, through a screen of folding doors, the walls are scraped and grey, the ceiling neutral, and a slogan has been painted on a board of plywood propped against the wall: Shame! This Could Be a Home.

A very expensive home, Patrick remarks.

Or twenty bedsits again, Eamon says.

There is a sink in this room, hanging from a wall. A thumping flutter in the hallway makes them jump.

Pigeons, Eamon explains.

Well, they have to live somewhere. Patrick opines this weirdly. Pigeons are resilient, he adds.

He falls silent, looking again at the plasterwork, at the musical instruments issuing like dreams from a cream of emulsion and trefoils. Cormac longs to touch these. The place is so singular, a whiteness distilled from the dirt and chaos of the world outside. Cormac realises he has passed it many times, passed by in the street, thinking nothing and knowing nothing.

Cormac begins to feel lonely.

Also dyspeptic: his stomach boils.

Would you like, Patrick asks Eamon, a cigarette?

Oh, I don't think you can smoke in here.

Really?

Well you won't want to burn it down, Cormac tells him. Cormac is dizzy and leans on a wall. It feels chill and constant, so thickly permanent that even the gall of a motorbike engine outside does not affect it. It is cold dust, bone dust.

I won't. Patrick opens the packet. It's damp as fuck.

Will we go to the next one? asks Eamon.

Lead on. Patrick nods with vigour, as if suddenly understanding something. I'm intrigued now, he insists. He says, You have my full attention now.

In this moment, Cormac realises he must cross the street urgently to the terraced café and use its toilet because he is about to void pretty much

everything.


So after that, he tells Alice, I went home, because I thought I was going to die. But, he assures her, it was never as bad after that.

What was? Oh right. She says, Cormac, don't be disgusting.

It's dark now. Alice lives in another old house, one of many craft cottages wrapped around a cobbled square in D7. On summer nights the new residents join the elderly corporation tenants and bring their kitchen chairs to the doorsteps, drinking beer and calling awkward encouragement to one another. They do this because they know they are taking over the area. There's a EuroSpar clattering with panhandlers but also a beekeeping supply shop.

She asks now, And what about Patrick? Where is he?

He drove home this evening.

She is quiet a moment before saying, Patrick is out of control.

He went home.

How do you know? He could be out boozing again.

If he was I'd have gotten the can-I-stay-with-you-man call by now. Look, Cormac says, I know he's making trouble. But you know, he was always kind of like that. Before he got married.

I think you should pay more attention.

Yeah maybe. Cormac is rubbing his eyes. They blur and snag strabismally.

Alice ladles pasta from a pot with a slotted spoon. They are in her kitchen; he sits at the laid table. She has a printout of the hastily edited interview with Lazarian from last week on a coffee table in her living room – a space dipped from the kitchen, with lights dipped over it too – for them to look at soon. The kid, she says, is upstairs. She has set a plate aside and covers it, expertly and almost unconsciously, with a film of foggy polythene. Cormac watched her hands do this, manacled almost by her many rings, as if disembodied, in a trance.

He has been home and showered again, changed out of clothes that were re-drenched in sweat, and feels hungover but averse to sleep in case the tilting well resurfaces from whatever hellpit and comes for him. He's figured it out by now, the well of his hallucination, what it was, with its red walls and floor: it's the Le Fanu room off Parnell Square, the council chamber of musket dust.

Thank you, he sighs when she serves him and sits opposite.

You look unwell.

I know.

You can stay here tonight if you like.

I'd like to. I will, he decides. They have a spare room, a white bed heaped with sheets and a box of tissues by the bed with the top tissue tufted always evocatively up. Or they had. No longer *they*: no longer Garrett and Alice. He asks, But is Garrett not in there?

No. He stays with me when he stays here.

Cormac stirs red shining penne with a fork. There are sprigs of something and nubbins of diced pepper. The kitchen is calm and evenly lit in a way he finds gratifying because so many places, so many rooms, are lit horrifically, including the kitchen of Nina's houseshare, where the landlord has fixed tactless spotlights that get too hot to work with: he's broken two of them already. Above the kitchen doorway Alice's spider plants sag suspended in crochet nests. There is a wooden chopping board and a plate of intact artichokes. Cormac does not know how or why a person would even begin to eat an artichoke. She has a gallery placard, framed, from one of Cormac's earliest exhibitions on the wall beside the dresser, amidst photographs of Ambie: it has been there for years and it's not the only art in the kitchen – certainly not the only art in the house – but its placement there declares something like love. A love for him.

It reads, the placard reads, *Father of My Children*. This was the name of a sequence of drawings and prints Cormac made when he was twenty-three. It was about his mother – it had a narrative, however gnomically – and no piece of it remains in his possession but there, by the dresser, hangs *Father of My Children*, without context: words to anchor, frankly, everything.

Are you divorced yet? Cormac asks.

No. She seems amused. It still takes time here, she tells him. When my father left my mother in the seventies he had to set up house with his mistress for years before they could make a petition. And even then they went to London.

Alice's father was a journalist. She grew up around cocktail parties and knowledge of political private lives, underground cruising spots and condom dispensers. The machine in Trinity with graffiti: *this chewing gum tastes like rubber*. This year, she and Garrett had a party in summertime when Ambie was away, riding horses or – god knows, the grand tour? – and they hosted people from the Institute with friends. Even Alice's hennaed sister was there, talking about sheep farming and leaving the city to sheep farm and getting weepy with wine before the trickle-home began. They had Cormac and for some reason Nina.

Nina watched with weird stone-faced avidity as Garrett, out of nowhere, announced divorce from Alice. Alice at that very minute was sitting, vaudeville-sardonic, on his knee.

It's true, she repeated with a smile.

The room came to a halt, people picking food from the table and talking – it was cruel and not funny, not funny at all, the way they did this with such denuded mischief – as the announcement fell entirely flat and one of the kerchiefed art theory teachers cried out – plaintively – What? What are you talking about?

It is over and done and we see no need to be bitter about it.

You're divorced already? someone asked.

No – no, going to be.

The *it* in *it is over* had been them, or this: had been their marriage, open and ad hoc as it was, and the very dead-eyed merriment this marriage seemed to consist in made the announcement all the more irrational.

But you are an institution, somebody else wailed, trying to be ironic against the backdrop of baffled silence with pockets of mutinous sibilance.

Children, Garrett crooned, you must grow up. You must understand that Mummy and Daddy have needs. It's not that we don't love you.

Garrett, fuck you, Cormac found himself saying without thinking. Albeit quietly. Garrett, that's not funny, he qualified. That's sad. I'm sorry for both of you.

Cormac is slow to anger, but this wasn't anger, only fear. I mean, he said, it's not a joke.

Fuck me?

I am sorry. I'm only shocked.

Yes, we are all shocked, one of the art teachers volunteered.

Nina, among the youngest in the room, was looking at Garrett and then at Cormac, still stony-faced.

All right, said Garrett. Alice slid from his knee and began to stack plates at the sink. Everyone in the room felt they were reliving some domestic massacre from childhood, a Sunday afternoon never to be recovered from, some quality of glassy light and despoiled joint and dining-room table. Silence like a pendulum at rest. A hateful wind that whines through the rest of your life.

All right. Garrett was kinder. What do you want to ask? Now he opened his arms to them all.

Someone said, You two have always been so relaxed about fidelity and shit. This person – a man – said it so candidly, drunkenly. I don't see why divorce.

It has nothing to do with that, explained Alice. It's just the right time. We always said. When it was the right time.

Cormac saw that she was pale, even for Alice, a naturally pale woman who kept her hair black to accentuate the effect.

He himself felt betrayed. That they would announce it like this without first taking him aside, that they would include him in the admixture of peers. It was perverse. Even the weepy sister was stoically topping up her glass as if this was not news to her. He looked at Alice. She avoided his eyes. He wanted to punch Garrett suddenly. He felt inanely certain Garrett was to blame. Nina's strange awkward stillness, looking from adult to adult with, now, a mild inquisitiveness, echoed his own emotional tumult and gave it muted shape.

Now he eats pasta with Alice, at the cold end of this significant year, and feels no more enlightened than he was on that summer evening.

You are still going through with it then, he says.

Yes.

Is it painful to talk about? I mean, can we talk about it? Can I ask?

Of course. But when she says this, Cormac realises there is nothing, in fact, he wants to ask. It's not curiosity he feels, just grief.

I think everyone imagines you owe them an explanation. He laughs, softly. I don't, like, want to be that way.

We've been a fixture, she acknowledges. It makes people question their own lives and decisions, I think.

Oh I know. Cormac begins to eat more enthusiastically. Thank you, he says, for this. You might be saving my life. He says, It's just that nobody gets it, now – the divorce – nobody gets why you would do it *now*.

Do you?

No.

It just feels natural. Like leaving a job behind.

That can't be true, Ali.

What do you think it is then? she demands.

I don't know. But leaving can't be easy.

Not easy, only natural. Because it is time.

Are you still? He hesitates. He wonders why the question feels indelicate. Do you still? Are you – still sleeping together?

Not for a long time, in that sense, no.

There have been others.

Well always, occasionally.

Cormac knows about this but also of its discretion. Some of her partners, some of Garrett's, must have been people he knows, but he's never been sure of any nor felt safe looking into it. To probe would risk awareness of a network of overlaps and common experience that would

128

have, he thinks, a desacralising effect. Because, of course, he's been her lover too.

He only hopes – he really hopes – Garrett never slept with Alva, for example. That would annoy him. It is unlikely, though, because Alva was puritanical. Even at college and among dancing troupes with unlimited access to fine physiques. In London, her cousin who danced with *Riverdance* crashed at their flat for a touring fortnight: the girl had wizened ringlets, a Matryoshka make-up case like the murkily metaphorical one in *Rear Window*, and a year or so – as she guesstimated – left on the clock before the regime of work would leave her legally too worn out to do anything but retire. Every night she and the other dancers skulled into Soho to party it out on cocaine. They did this, he figured, in New York and Sydney and Gothenburg, in Glasgow and Lille. Every city in Europe and a number of regional towns. He remembers the make-up case now.

Knee socks bleaching in the bath. The cousin told him that, when the dancers came off stage, they dunked their bodies in a barrel of ice. Straight away. It was the kind of offhand but insanely exact insight you never forget.

Alva, unimpressed, gave the girls nicknames: Chlamydia, Elvira, Border Fox. Cormac thinks of them still, upright in a barrel of ice, like longneck beers.

Alva would never have gone to bed with Garrett, no.

Cormac thinks also of Garrett sourly kneading his cock the one and only time they had a threesome, in – where else? – Berlin, when they were younger: Garrett turning over with distaste as if accepting punishment. Cormac fucking him with vengeful intent. Alice stroking her husband's hair, soothing but remote.

Jesus, where the hell was Ambie then?

Garrett would at least try to chase Alva, he reckons, to get back at Cormac. Not to get back for possession of Alva, nor even for the prosaic triumph of being on top, but rather for possession of the first, most certain, love of Alice. Which Cormac, undoubtedly, has.

I always thought you liked me better than Garrett anyway, he tells her now.

You think, she says, too highly of yourself.

After the meal they sit with coffee in the front room, Lazarian's printout and some test images on the table, and talk, instead of working, about JP.

Let me tell you about the last time I spoke to him properly, says Alice. I think it was probably about five years ago.

I wasn't back?

You weren't back. You were in London.

She says, I met him in the bar at the Shelbourne because he had work for me, he had a commission for me. And he was on fire. I thought he might swing from a chandelier or something like that.

Do you mean he was high?

Oh no. Alice shakes her head, emphatic. He was manic. He was bipolar.

I didn't know that, how do you know?

I thought everyone did. It was clear to me that day. He kept talking and hitting on ideas, or thinking he had, then jumping up and punching the air – like this – and calling out and waving to everyone in the place. And it was crazy because he was so very handsome, so beautifully dressed, you know? So dandyish.

She says, He was a lovely man.

After this, she continues, he kept asking me to come

130

back with him, to the house he was living in with his wife, for dinner – he kept saying we had ideas to discuss. I don't know why but I went. They had the house in Sandycove, an expensive house. Maria was there with the children and she had made food – it was a normal weekday, it was just chicken and chips, something so ordinary – but JP began to get worked up, excited I mean, and say: No, no! We feel like *Japanese*. We have to go into town for Japanese. He took every plate from the table and slid the food into the bin. He was saying, Come on, come on! Like it was all a big treat. The children were rigid and Maria, I remember, was staring at me. She didn't speak. I remember when she was on the books of every place in town. She was still beautiful.

It was as if, says Alice, he was on coke.

Maybe he was.

I really do think he was ill.

What happened afterwards?

Oh, I just left. She tosses her arms in the air, but she looks troubled; her gaze is distant and troubled. I didn't do anything. I can't remember now if I did anything. I left. I don't think that I spoke to him again, although I'm sure I saw him several times. Out and about. There are tears shining so subtly on her cheeks he doesn't see them to begin with and, when he notices, he is surprised.

Oh, Ali, he says.

I feel so old, you know, she laughs. She laughs smartly and thoroughly, as if shaking rain out of something or shaking sense into someone. We need to do this, she says of the interview. The backs of her hands dab at her eyes. Let's work, let's not get sad, she says.

★

Later: Cormac swings into the spare room, but there is somebody there already. The boy Ambie, lying belly-flopped on the bed. The kid wears a school shirt tucked at delinquent angles in-and-out of trousers. Cormac notices this because the kid is lying on his front.

Ambie, Cormac says.

Sorry, hi. Rolling over.

What's the story?

I do my homework in here. There is no homework in the room, but Ambie has a book: he holds it up. It's *Frankenstein. Frankenstein*, he says.

Your mother has put me up here. The room smells of sebum and antiperspirant and something sandy, something biscuity.

OK, sings the kid. He is not in a hurry. He sits up and swings stockinged feet to the floor. He scratches his head and yawns blankly.

Alice was back in Berlin mere weeks when she phoned Cormac. He was working for JP; he was idle an afternoon and went into the mountains to pick mushrooms mid-week. They were young. They had chunky, blunt, mobile phones. I will have to get married now, she said.

Of course you won't, he told her. You just want to.

I want to.

Congratulations.

It's Garrett's, she said.

Yes of course, of course it's Garrett's, he said.

At home that night, he and Alva listened to music. They rented the top floor of a tenement near Portobello. The fireplace had been staved in and bricked but there remained a long wooden mantelpiece on which they lined up books and rocks and candlesticks. The window opened on a long

132

yard of abandoned banquet furniture, trestle tables and rusted fold-out chairs, with an apple tree flowering fancifully in one corner. In that bedsit, the tapwater, piped loudly from Vartry and blasting out of the single tap, was particularly delicious, and because someone had said *It comes from Vartry* he always thought of the word, drinking the water: Vartry. In the evenings the smell of restaurant kitchens warming up filled the neighbourhood with aspirant ease.

Alva lay on the narrow bed and put her feet against the wall, elevating her hips. She saw only colours and mild prophecies and told him, slowly, the story of her day. She was soon to go to London – they would both go, together, to study and work – and their life at that moment was sweet and easy in a way he could not, just then, appreciate. It was the pseudo-adult world of twenty-one. He lay by her and tripped gently, hardly at all. He thought: Alice is pregnant. It meant nothing, it could mean nothing. She would marry Garrett now.

He remembers, barely, their lying there talking and sighing in tune. Their making love, probably; his dash to the chipper perhaps when it got dark and they grew hungry again. Even highs were effervescent then, or else this was Alva's influence, her soul a warmly ornamental pool. Perhaps it was Alice's promise – it is Garrett's, Garrett's child – that gave this memory a flavour of relief.

And here is the child: Ambie, abjectly fifteen.

Thanks, Cormac says. The boy finishes yawning and shrugs.

All yours. He leaves. His parents are divorcing. You forget about Ambie.

Cormac strips and sleeps. His muscles, stiff with poison and paranoia, relax gradually and painfully.

133

He wakes dehydrated in the early a.m. and rolls over in darkness, unsure of where he is, so many rooms – rooms he'd thought forgotten – appearing but melting out immediately until he settles on the right one and relaxes again. Someone is moving around downstairs and he knows this someone is Garrett, that Garrett is playing with the music system in the front room.

Wakes: there plays an instrumental piece. Garrett is playing ambient music, a thin computer shrill helixing flinchingly around wooden drumming and steering bass. It's good music but it booms provocatively to the roof.

Wakes in the spare room where the sheets are cool, the carpet is thick so the door resists and takes some time to shut. There are no curtains on the windows and a toenail moon tilts over mews, over some tributary, a body of water he doesn't know. There are lots of these under the city, rivers and pools, ley lines.

Wakes and hears the whisper of a woman's voice; he hears, he thinks, the considerate clip of the front door, a bike chain ringing fairylike over the night.

He lies vigilantly, anxious apostle, for a long time. He only knows that he has slept when he tears out of a dream – red room, naturally – and it is, greyly, day; he can rise at speed to leave before anyone else gets up. The house is close enough to Grangegorman to walk.

It is a grey day with a bitter breeze and pigeons in a powdery cloud on the road. As he passes through them they scatter and mutter and sift. The air smells of the Euro-Spar ovens finishing parbaked baguettes, a smell by now so known to Cormac it is folksily consoling.

At DIT, he lets himself into the women's ward.

Nina has written a long email in response to photographs he sent her last Sunday night. Not nudes: work. Tentative shots or explorations. He has asked for her input. The email is waiting in his inbox so he can read it and make pure use of the morning, healthy use, alone in the studio: dispersive sub-white light on partitions and tools, instruments, downed on site as if a workshop of shoemaking elves has just been spirited away.

Cormac makes a milky coffee at the kitchen and sits in his chair, which creaks, before the monitor, to read.

Your work, she writes, of course I admire.

Oh dear. Bland openings bode hammerings.

She builds a frame of praise, like a child with pipe cleaners. So I take this seriously, she writes.

Let us begin, she says, with art and death.

He laughs. The sound doesn't echo in the space, strangely, not even with its vaulted roof. Instead, something entraps it with an irritated snap. She has written, in fact: Art and Death. Let us begin with Art and Death. It's tongue-in-cheek, but he sees there are paragraphs to come and she means to take her time.

Common wisdom would hold, she writes, that the motivation for making art is the same as the motivation for making babies, but refined: that is, a need for permanence or some kind of trace in the face of our own mortality. Be assured this is a typically masculinist idea, and it's wrong.

Art, she continues bluntly, is a form of tending, of care, and no matter what you think yourself, my image of your art is one of *tenderness and care*, of tending and caring and observing.

Exhibit A: an urn, from *Father of my Children*, or the close-up shot of an ornamental urn in glazed green with

135

a crack, a photograph making of this crack or craquelure on the surface of the image an *accidental cunt* (of course! La source!) but only accidentally: really, the theme of the painting is the pity of the small domestic crack, not even a 'crack' in the façade of family life, but only a thing giving way, and of course the quality of light, the lighting, is the shade of sun through one of those gauzy curtains you see in sad houses.

Exhibit B: lichen-like infection, webbed and piss-yellow, on a board of wood. Also from *Father*. Pity the passage of time and imperfection! The lichen eats the wood carefully, with care.

Exhibit C: a photo, not by you, of your older brother playing Nintendo, so movingly nineties – the gauze again, the T-shirt, the idiotic expression, long hair – which happens to be a perfect matte, like a painting, instead of like a photograph. This work is care. Even though this work is made in the shadow of your other brother's death. Isn't it?

And that's it then, because after that you become *a photographer*, and you take pictures that gratify people because, among other things, they have people in them. All those raves. I've hardly ever seen you dance. You don't dance, you just record: once you realised you could be rewarded, you took more and more of this kind of photograph. You have mocked up nostalgia, a pre-internet-ish world of poetic partying, basically a visual for those spoken-word intervals about yokes on the bus to Electric Picnic. These works have a Dub-a-lin accent.

So it interests me to see these steps towards what you want to call 'asylum'.

In a way, she writes, this is of a piece with your work since the rave series, which is to say you have found a quirky little world of surfaces – an ex-institution, a mental hospital, something so saturated in sadness and Catholic repression one needn't do anything really, just photograph it: it's practically sociology. You who doesn't like it when women in Ireland make art lamenting past repression in ways that are marketable because, understandably, a whole load of chancers are chasing the *national treasure* label and you are above that. But those pictures you have sent me – a Virgin in a window (Cormac, please) and surfaces one, two, three – are not what I expected, or rather the surfaces are not what I expected, granted I was expecting something as easy as a Virgin, everyone expects that.

Here's what you've done that's brilliant though [thank god, he thinks].

You've photographed surfaces for the clean white movement of light and the lines of flight, the curvature, obviously there is something almost basilica-esque or renaissance to the harmony, you've done this with such care, you have returned to the human in you, you will let the world imprint itself upon you, instead of owning it with your camera and only ever immortalising a leisured class you have not been inducted to and never will be because the very fact of your needing to honour them declares your dependence on them.

All right, so full disclosure, she concludes: I'm fairly drunk right now.

Cormac is reflexively, unthinkingly thrilled by her attention but largely disappointed by her analysis. She's hardly said anything about the images he sent – light on white rendering, the dearest of airholes, little mouths like barnacles on a rock – and what she has said at all seems part of some thundering grudge.

He writes: Baby, I am embarrassed for both of us. You don't get me at all.

He rethinks. Does she deserve a generous gesture of play? No.

thanks for this lots to think about, he replies.

No punctuation nor capitals. He sends and sits in furious satisfaction for a moment, pulse quick.

Then opens the sent box and reads it again: he intended hasty, but it could also scan as wounded. She might release a cascade of apologies.

Too late to send anything else now, though. Come what may. She probably won't write back anyway.

He sits and thinks about her for a minute.

In August, three months ago now, they'd been to see the Harry Gruyaert photograph at IMMA because it was on display. The day was so fine the grounds were covered in bodies filling a dreamy battlefield, felled by the sun and bathing in pairs just like the people in the Gruyaert photograph: the photograph of gleaming limbs and faces in profile, lifted gratefully to the light, on a lakeside rock in Kerry.

The spacing and pacing of the image was perfect, almost twee: a man in the centre splitting the rock with its splintering lichen from the blue of the water in a way which also anchored a triangle of man, rock and outcrop of rushy grass above a woman reading on a towel. Even though, he explained to Nina as sweat crept down their necks in the white gallery space, the clouds are *perfect*, this kind of scumbled cumulus thing, the best thing about it is the dingy Polaroid feel.

It looks old, she agreed. She read the description. It was taken in nineteen-eighty-eight. I wasn't born until ninety-one.

Cormac let that one go. He said, It looks older than it is.

The photo of Patrick playing Nintendo, from *Father of my Children*, had that effect. It was an accident. It looked orangey, elderly; it looked like a photograph from the seventies aged by sun in a dusty album. It placed Patrick, sometime in the mid-nineties, in what felt at the time like mythology. The childhood of other people.

It's idyllic, but I'm disappointed that this is the picture that they own, Cormac said to Nina, referring to the Gruyaert. There are much more interesting ones. They only bought this one because, of course, it's got an Irish theme. His street photography is amazing – it's flat and tacky and static, all the cheap colours on the clothing, graffiti and texture – it's kind of primitive, like this, but there is chaos – the point is the shapes and the action, you know? It's not street photography as piety. It's not *human stories*.

Yes. Do you like the television shots?

I used to. They're frightening. I was mad for them at college. TVs in my childhood were these morbid machines that hissed and sucked and looked like coffins, you know. All this flatscreen discreet shit is just toothless and I'm not bothered with it.

She laughed. She said, This photograph makes me want to jump into the sea.

They wandered into the sun and sat under a tree. Its roots knuckled up from the ground and were littered with tree debris. He began knotting daisies around a twig and Nina passed him her bottle of body-warm water.

Garrett had one of the courtyard studios here last year, she remarked.

Only for three months. It was because they had a random opening and Garrett knows everyone.

Did you see the thing he made?

No.

It's a field recording.

He needed a studio to make a field recording, Cormac said. Seems contradictory.

To mix it, she said. Anyway. I will send it if you like. It's buzz saws and birds, but some of it was made at the burial ground up there. She pointed towards the Kilmainham gate, the avenue of gravel and trees. Do you know there are hundreds of people in there, it's a huge pit? There are pits everywhere. All cities are built on burial pits.

Sound doesn't interest me, Cormac told her, a whole lot. I don't know. Maybe I don't hear it like other people.

What got you into photos then?

I answer this differently all the time. I think it was early Ryan McGinley ones. They always looked like they were taken at somebody's house party, some grungy kind of house party; they always looked fun. Everyone skinny and lit too harshly. They were really sexy. You know?

No, but I'll look out for them, she said.

As if, he continued, this were an Irish gaff party, some-where with a dirty bathroom and mattresses on the floor, except everyone is happy and funky and naked. Which nobody ever was, at least then, at gaff parties.

He said: Not happy, funky, nor naked. Ever.

Let's go to this party tonight, Nina suggested, and see. She named the host: You know, she said, that one? Did you get invited to that one? It's tonight. She lay in the grass and shielded her face from the sun with her hand.

Yeah, Cormac lied. I didn't think I'd bother. But OK, let's go.

And they did.

That was, he thinks now, sitting in the high-ceilinged studio, the same evening, wasn't it?

Balmy and smelling of fried fat. Nina wearing a dress now shuffling along the brick tessellations of Dame Lane in heels, carrying a bottle of wine in twisted paper. Saying, If I fall and drop this bottle we will be in trouble.

It must have been the same night. In August.

Perhaps I should take it, he offered. The wine.

Perhaps you should.

She slipped an arm into his playfully. I want to get a cab, she said. I was wrong to wear these shoes and it's getting late.

The party was at a house on the Southside, ugly but wide-set, with big rooms opening onto each other and walls rag-rolled in the past then left that way. The effect was one of uncanny safety and perhaps infantilism: these were the rooms of sitcom families and, packed out with artists and producers, looked like something viewed in childhood from the top of the stairs.

People at the party assumed Cormac and Nina were a couple, addressing questions to both of them. Nina joined a woman with a baby on her hip at the kitchen sideboard, where lemons and limes were being sliced, and the women spoke with heads bowed as if sharing advice. Nobody got funky or naked, but they did seem happy, in a way.

The back yard, opening onto slopes of bold light, had a patio and a deck. At the end of the yard were long old stately trees. Upstairs, the bathroom was decorated with sponge effect. This was like something his mother would

cut from a catalogue and its big-hearted simplicity seduced him so that he started enjoying conversations about
income, a departure from what would have been gossip at
another kind of party – a party with cocaine – and almost
forgetting himself until someone gave him a joint. He still
disliked the cheesy screen of weed hanging over everything
but partook because there was no point in abstaining.

Sleepily stoned, he and Nina left at midnight, walking
long tree-fragrant streets by gated haciendas until they
found a main road and could hail another cab to her place.
She had the living room of a thirties terrace that made
him think of the house of his studenthood. An original
bay window of thin glass was crowned with painted panes
and devices: a star, a crown, a garland, a cross. There was a
deal table in the bay, which Nina used to sketch and read,
and a bed with two duvets, a pile of pillows, blankets;
on the back wall, where the mantelpiece remained, there
stood a huge looming chifforobe and the Klimt Judith.
Every intense girl he'd ever slept with had at least one
Klimt.

Candle wax splashed over the mantelpiece. Her yoga
mat and balance ball.

It was cold, now, in the dark shared house, and she
plugged in the space heater. Lit the red lamp with tassels.
They stripped and, shivering, clung to one another beneath the sheets, laughing softly and grinding his erection
against her pelvis, his chest against her breasts. She rested
her head on his shoulder and stayed there a moment, tense
in an instant of contentment.

Oh I love this, she said suddenly.

Maybe, she said, we should make it real.

He let silence settle like dust. He didn't want to stay

silent, but no words would come. Nothing he could say would approach what she wanted to hear.

They slept.

In the cold light of the studio at Grangegorman now, he thinks: It's that, it's about that. She's pissed.

Passing over the estuary on the train, Cormac realises that he hasn't seen the estuary in some time: its veiny marshland is still stark and dream-green against blue where freshwater meets seawater meatily.

It's Saturday night and the train is empty because everyone, if travelling, is going the opposite way. He sees the white wand of the lighthouse first and then the lights, in parallel pans, on the surface of the harbour. It is now, in this single lull, that his phone strikes with a message from a number yet unknown. Just to say hi.

I don't have this contact . . .?

It's Caroline!

Oh yeah, he thinks. He almost says: Oh yeah. The carriage shunts against the carriage ahead as the brakes apply.

Oh hi. Cormac accepts the contact. So nice to hear from you, he writes. He last saw her on Thursday morning, standing in a street that was viciously vivid through the sandy screen of the high. Her little rose-mouth, he remembers.

Fluttering dots of composition, like a flag in a wind. Typing, typing, typing, until finally a smile.

Through the turnstiles he walks down wet steps. It is all familiar and familiar as familiar: the gatepost and the boxing club and the greasy channel of street, the monumental frontispiece of the old bank, the cars exiting the car park. He finds himself thinking of childhood involuntarily.

Memory of a tyre swing drifting over grass, of a rubble of mushrooms in the grass. The bank has become a funeral parlour. He indulges himself and walks to the window, where a printout lists the recently dead: there are surnames he recognises – town names, names of schoolmates – and the name Adebowale, which is new.

The house – his mother's house – is always cold. Cormac looks at the thermostat on a wall of the hall, which emits a whiskery click and insists it is working fine, before putting his scarf back on. In the kitchen, a nine o'clock news segment on the radio warns of black ice and freezing fog. It has been extraordinary all day: leak-water light and sleet that is lacklustre, flurrying almost, not sticking like snow. Upstairs, in the cold heaven of sealed bedrooms, it will be raw.

When they were children the fresh-cleaned chimney would let bird sounds – scrape of crows, thuggish gulls – clatter down the flue unfiltered, loudly, and this was wonderment: no sieve between the sky and the living room, the house and the street. They left their letters to Santa Clause on the rug to be magicked up. Thomas threw a T-shirt of Patrick's into the fire; Patrick threw underpants that belonged to Cormac into the fire too. Cormac spat quietly, watching it hang and drop onto Patrick's food when he wasn't watching. Patrick told Cormac, There is a dead body stuffed in the chimney, you know.

Cormac dreamt about this, with frequency: skull gurning, bats erupting from a tower – Norman Thoor with vampires – and *oubliette*/forget. Sometimes he dreamt, with shameful privacy, of footprints on the stairs.

He remembers it now, in the afterglow of Sadbh, with less passion. Less interest. He is embarrassed almost by its total ordinariness.

Cormac makes coffee and waits at the table, now, reading the newspapers. His mother buys every broadsheet to read methodically on Saturdays, wearing her spectacles on a beaded chain, cutting coupons and articles on childhood nutrition she keeps for Ursula. He is reading still when Ursula arrives, hissing: Cold in here as it is outside. She says, I like that scarf. She moves as busily as ever, unpacking a bag of bread and cheese and tomatoes onto the countertop.

How long do we have? she asks thoughtlessly, or phatically. For certainly she knows what time it is down to the pip.

About a half-hour.

The roads are bad, we should leave now. I won't take off my coat. Ursula stamps her feet. Cold in here as it is outside, she repeats. I can just . . . she looks at him doubtfully, just go to get her on my own, leave you here?

No, I'll come for the drive.

That's good because I need to talk to you.

Yes.

But not in front of Joy.

No.

Are you ready?

I guess. Should I leave, he asks, the heating on?

It's on? Lord. Yes, leave it on.

Cormac met Ursula long ago. He was a teenager, Thomas was dead, Cormac and Senan had travelled into Dublin for a gig. They bought cans and swung these by the wire wicket boldly, pissed on rum-and-Coke already; bailed into the Trinity Pavilion on a purple night in June, exam time, mildly agog at the people – all those people, confident and sexy and older than them – carpeting the cricket pitch; met Patrick inside, who shoved them onto a patio with a picnic table, students smoking and looking coolly at them from the picnic table, and said, Jesus, you gee-eyed prick. But also Patrick, in his third year of accountancy, laughed at them.

Senan, who never smoked on account of his voice, took a strained-looking drag on a casual fag and had his legs buckle under him as the blood rushed to his head. They sat, gangly and acting out, on the edge of the table.

This is Ursula, Patrick told them, introducing the doe-eyed, deer-limbed girl in a purple jacket.

Hiya, they mumbled.

Ursula scuffed Senan about the head, scuffed his blond hair. You are the cuter one, she declared. Her lipstick was purple too. She looked, to Cormac in that moment, less like a woman and more like a music video come to life. Patrick only ever went out with beautiful girls, but Ursula defeated any of the small-town prodigies of adolescence – the virginity lost in an ornamental garden behind the cattle-dealer's ranch, the debs date who slapped him in the face – just as singly as she outshone all the girls around her now.

She was not even wicked but intensely good and interested. After messing with Senan, she looked at Cormac and sang, I know all about you!

The woman firing up her car now, in fingerless gloves and a scarf with pom-poms incongruous, inviting investment in a childlikeness she has outgrown, preserves early Ursula's urgency but less and less of her optimism. This, he thinks, is not her fault. She is brisk but resilient. Cormac feels sorry for her because he would not wish to be married to Patrick either.

So did Patrick take drugs on Wednesday night? She asks this almost as soon as they take off.

No. Cormac is used to her abruptness. No, that was only me. Imagine going home and telling your wife that, he thinks. Telling your wife on me. Patrick can be so pathetic sometimes.

Why, though? I mean, why? Ursula asks.

In all fairness, that's kind of my business, Cormac says. I can do what I like. And no, as I said, Patrick did not take drugs.

Because that would be the final frontier.

She has turned into Main Street. So much of Main Street, he sees, is boarded up. The dry-cleaners, the gift shop that sold photo frames and christening plates, the commercial hotel. The old AIB and the old Bank of Ireland buildings and the old pub that got the makeover during the boom, looking and smelling and finally turning like cream liquor. Behind the pub and the British Forces Assassination bridge, a culvert of land-water sprays over rocks and ferns and shopping trolleys. And yet there is a spirit to the place. It passes over him occultly, exquisitely familiar.

Drugs, Ursula says, would officially cross the line into insanity and, quite honestly, social workers.

Lucky it didn't actually happen then, isn't it.

Don't be a dickhead, she says.

You've got to stop attacking me. I'm on your side.

At this, Ursula laughs harshly, too loudly and too disruptively, making him think with rude alarm of Alice.

Oh Cormac, she concludes.

Where is he now?

He's at home, and he doesn't drink when he's minding the kids. I do know that. I think I should leave the kids with him all the time (another laugh: thunderclap). He does it at work.

His job is stressful.

Yes, thank you, I know that, so is mine.

A little slower here, maybe? They have left the town and entered a tunnel of trees, an unlit back road over which silos loom intermittently.

Fuck off, Cormac Mulvey, Ursula says, you unbelievable little fuck.

Cormac cannot stop himself laughing, leaning on the dashboard and looking at her. He echoes, Little fuck!

Little fucker. Whatever. Never even learned to drive a car.

You bully me. There is no need to bully me.

Fields settle around them like a great shaken-out sheet. It's no longer sleeting or even raining: the sky is clearing, simple stars, pitiless plummet in temperature. They see the twinkle of hamlets and the beady bulbs of runways at the airport across the expanse. Two planes pace silently inland. It's awesome out here – it is open, shameless, without sound. Growing up, Cormac never appreciated it. He thinks about living out here and meeting recurring surnames. The family that owns the land and quarry, every single daughter blonde, like in a fairy tale.

Really though, the ice, he says.

For a moment it seems as if Ursula will persevere above the speed limit through spite. This chaotic evil in her temperament is glimpsed these days but rarely realised. She applies the brake and they pass an old bungalow with an arcade of broom trees at the gate. Cormac knows this coach road, knows it better than he realised. These trees. The townlands with their boggy vowels and digraphs: Clogheder, Ballyboughal, Courtlough.

Somewhere nearby is the school, the castle, and the

bell-jar with the owl and fox. The cattle grid and the vin-egar swimming pool, the shower room, tang of boy-sweat and lingering steam. Memories of the early nineties, when Ireland was still nowhere: when women had perms and few civil rights and no apparent interest in gaining more and half the fathers of the town were serving in The Leb.

Although not theirs. Cormac's father worked for Córas Iompair Éireann, first as a bus conductor and, finally, in the offices. This gave them slight distinction and their mother ran with that and sent all three of her sons to the Francis-cans instead of the technical school. He remembers this era with more symbolic acuity than the flabbier noughties, era of idiotic American incursions into Iraq and also into pop-ular culture and the exchange of grunge – a genre which always felt so morosely appropriate – for pop metal. But he was in college by then, listening to Throbbing Gristle and John Cooper Clarke and Gregorian chant.

He freewheeled down the whole of Collins Avenue on acid and didn't die. He started taking photos for JP. He migrated from Alice to Alva and then left entirely for Paris, Barcelona, Berlin, and London at last. Sequences of novelty interspersed with mendicant jags of regret and whole moments given over to the acts of ordering food, plug-wiring, train-missing, vomiting, money-counting, laundry-doing, lovemaking, in variously pastel or rain-cloaked metropolises; his memories of these years were, until recently, current.

I joke, but I'm losing patience, Ursula says.

Tell me honestly, she commands, what you think.

I think it's a phase, answers Cormac uncertainly.

A midlife crisis.

Yeah.

And what if we don't survive it?

Ursula, I am not in your marriage. I can't say.

I know. He sees her chin flick up, her mouth harden, in silhouette.

Is there, she asks quietly then, anyone else?

No.

How do you know?

He would have told me.

And you'd tell me?

I would make him tell you. If he wouldn't tell you, I would do it, openly. Like, I would tell him I was telling you. I would.

You'd draw the line?

Yes.

Over me?

No.

She glances at him when he says this, taking her eyes — tired — off the road. The road is swept into existence by headlights.

No, he repeats less confidently. Because of Maude and Jake.

Ursula continues to look at him. Her expression empties. She hits a pothole with the wheels and axle of the car and reverts to the road with shock, jumping in her seat. For a long time after this she is quiet. In this time, they pass down a widening strait to meet at last the crossroads that was Tanner's Water once but which now crunches a care home and a motor dealership, spraying both with sodium light. After the dim vault of the coach roads this light is distressing to behold.

Ursula changes gear and charges forth, taking the incline

to the golf club silently. Gravel pings and the lights behind them simmer down.

They see a stray woman with a phone held aloft for coverage, wearing a ball gown and a jacket, in the avenue: she shoots up like a flare in the headlamps, then shadows out on the rim of the road.

Cormac wonders if he has failed or consoled Ursula. The fact that he cannot tell leaves him concerned and, in the silence, ashamed.

Ursula kills the engine, now, in a parking bay. They face a high hedge and, behind them, the clubhouse is richly lit. Cormac sees the stray in the ball gown inching, high-heeled, back towards the doors, her arms banded around her tightly and face bent to the screen. He asks Ursula if she'd like him to go get Joy and she answers, Oh we will both have to go. She's gone AWOL on this. Ursula holds up her own phone.

All the complaining she did.

All the complaining she did, she echoes sweetly, and now she probably won't want to leave.

Even without Maude and Jake, Cormac thinks, he would tell her.

He feels terrible for saying otherwise.

He wants to correct it, but she has stepped out of the car. On the threshold he pauses, but decides: he would tell her, certainly.

I'd tell you, he tells her now, getting out. The sound of the dance floor carries from the clubhouse giddily. Air is distilled, snow-smelling. It smells of ice and open space. I would tell you, he repeats, if my brother was cheating on you.

OK. Ursula's voice lifts, flickers with fear.

There's no one. But I want you to know. I'd tell you, even without the kids; I'd tell you because I respect you, and you are my sister-in-law.

Patrick is your brother, she reminds him.

It doesn't matter. I would tell. I'm sorry if you ever thought I wouldn't. I should have been clear.

I haven't dwelt on it much, she says, for she is now stepping back from this conversation and disavowing it. Retreating into ambient irony.

Just so you know.

All right. She raises a gloved hand with the fob and clicks. The car bips its two-note assurance of security. Lock-pins in soldierly assent. The car seems to take this task so seriously it is comical.

When they find Joy inside, she turns and totters to the bride, a second or third cousin-niece.

Oh they've come for me! she cries over the music breathlessly. Oul killjoys have come for me.

The bride is distracted and drunk but gathers the stuff of a skirt in one hand, her arms showing large tattoos. Jesus, thank you all so much for coming! she shouts at them – at Cormac, Ursula, Joy.

Outside, gravel spinning about her block heels, Joy gathers a shawl around her green dress.

Well, I just don't know about people any more, she says. But I wish them the very best of luck.

Jesus, the music was too loud, she continues in the car.

And you'd think she'd cover those tattoos. Isn't it easy to get one of them – lacy, batwing things?

Two kids she has with the other and one of them with that autism, apparently.

I wish, all the same: wish them the best of luck.

Chuck of chin and she looks out across the runways, on the fathomless unlit space that is fields and ditches and wastewater and bramble and thatch under cover of darkness. Leaves them, the newly-weds, like everything, to God.

Cormac will stay with you tonight, Ursula tells Joy too loudly. Help you with some things in the house tomorrow. Ursula weaponises this volume because she cannot, ever, tell her mother-in-law to shut up. Joy has become like a child grown out of cuteness but some years from cop and coyness and, knowing this, Cormac feels tenderly towards her.

Well, he won't get very far, Joy snaps, when you take this car. Sure he never learned to drive.

But then she softens, saying, We'll go for a walk in the morning then. That's two Sundays in a row you're out here. We won't see you for a while now, probably.

Good to get out, she concludes absently.

Over breakfast Joy says: Your one who had the post office, years ago, is after dying. Mrs Lynch.

I don't know who you mean, Cormac tells her calmly. He spreads Flora Light on white toast. The cork placemats are decorated with a Flemish *Vanitas* of tumbling grapes and polished apples, pumpernickel in a copper dish. The teapot wears its cosy scorched with ring-marks from the hob.

And do you know who's out? Of prison.

Let me guess. He guesses her second cousin, the one who drove away from a drunken collision in ninety-six but then mounted a pavement and took out the parish pump.

She dismisses this with a wave. Sure he's out years. I mean McPherson, who went in for—

Donie Foley, Cormac remembers. Wow.

With a ripple it is given back to him. He was twelve, and Thomas was still alive. The house was asleep. It was a Sunday morning in summertime: the day was bright and scented and tensely feminine. Because he was up early, he ate breast gouged from a cold roast chicken in the fridge. The screen of firs in the garden cast the kitchen in shadow, but outside it was spring.

I can just see myself, he thinks now. There is a vertigo to going back and letting scenes compose themselves again, the rag and bone, the swallowing wallow of emotional recall.

He took the bike and cycled out of the narrow street towards the town. The day was so nice he wanted to break it in bits or destroy something. Years later, in cities, he would marvel at Sunday mornings and their gorgeous industry: café terraces clattering, twisted bedsheets, headaches with the weight of sexual complication. Weekends in childhood were interminable. Either tautly solemn as the services of Easter Week or dull with rain and spinlines, with grinding Formula One races on TV.

At twelve he would have begun at the Franciscans. He would have been masturbating morosely three to five times a night. He would have entertained that dream of slitting throats.

On this morning, there was a route Cormac could take on the bike – a brother's cast-off – to the top of the town and the long green lane of bungalows at Flemington. This would siphon him into Gormanston, a tunnel of trees and clamouring birds, and past the cattle grid at the school. He could take this road as far as a barnyard with a pig-smell just before the turn for Ring Commons, Jordanstown, where the quarry with its drone of engines was open: workmen captivated by reversing trucks, standing in a spell like saints, raising their arms eventually to beckon forth. They never noticed a boy on a bike weaving the perimeter. But he didn't feel like taking this route today.

He circled the block instead. All was melancholy. The familiarity made him melancholy. The blue sky and the creamy smell of settled air, sweet with the closeness of fields uninterrupted by traffic yet, were laid on like the forced fun of an unwanted holiday. He was drifting by the silos of the factory that had been condemned, about to pass the football green, when the flicker of a squad-car light caught the side of his eye and Cormac turned at once to stand on the pedals and piston thickly in its direction.

There was a small crowd on the football green. Through the bodies he saw gardaí, tape, and a deposit like greyish snow, which he realised on approach was a dead person with a duvet – an uncovered duvet, polyester fritted visibly – thrown over it.

What is it, what is it? he asked, so desperate to know his voice came in a whine.

Some lad got his head smashed in, a man explained. He was a lean man in a tracksuit and Cormac recognised him from football practice, which was undertaken in serries defined by age and league under floodlights and between little coloured cones of plastic. This man, satisfied with his simple authority, turned back to the scene with folded arms. Most people were quiet. The police stood basking somewhat in their attention. Then and afterwards they reminded Cormac of harmless, hand-fed animals. They were waiting, somebody said, for a tent.

One garda at last detached himself from the hood of

the car and walked towards them, saying blandly, Here now, nothing to see here.

The absurdity of it made Cormac laugh. His laugh was so stupidly loud, strained with a stressful glee, that everyone – some dumpy women, some children with bikes, the man in the tracksuit – turned to him. Of course there is something to see! he cried at them, hysterical. Seconds passed as the strangeness of the situation caused him to feel cleaved from the moment as if he were standing alone, outside something.

At last, the tracksuit man put a hand on his shoulder and said kindly, Shut up the fuck.

Move on or we'll call your parents, warned the garda.

Who is it? one of the women asked the garda plainly. She asked in a tone of resolve as if, vehement, she was done with being messed around.

We don't know yet.

We do, said another man. It's Donie Foley.

Cormac was pained to realise he had no idea who Donie Foley was. The name suggested someone ancient and uninteresting; an old man purple with age and alcohol ambling blank-eyed over the football green after the pubs closed. In fact, as he would learn later, Donie Foley was a loner in his thirties who lived with his mother and fell asleep smoking cigarettes. This became part of the myth since he'd come to the attention of police for starting two separate fires in his mother's house, fires that spread aggressively because, they said, of a superfluity of VHS tape: videos, their ribbons loose, in untidy and proximate stacks.

Foley had now been attacked and his head kicked hard; under the exposed duvet, without envelope – this detail callous, afterwards – his eye sockets were black with haemorrhage.

I made that part up, Cormac thinks. I embellished.

He is not remembering the death of Donie Foley by ir-ruption of violence but remembering the retelling of this death to Alva, writing it with her, thinking about visuals.

Cormac sees this now: more ripples, more restoration.

This was the year she tried, through contacts, to break into film. She had ideas of moving from choreography and producing plays to collaborate with a retired film director and a cliquish link got them out to the director's house for a weekend. It was in Wicklow and far, far away from both Joy's dining room and Donie Foley's VHS. It was also far from their flat with the mantelpiece of books in Portobello, the place they set out from in a car the film director sent, driving into the white veil of the mountains and ascending the weird Olympian world of vales and valleys floating above South Dublin.

It was winter. He reconstructs it now – amazing to forget such things, even for a little while. It was his script, or his treatment, they were going to use. They had such stupid ambition. They must have been – twenty-three? They arrived late. The place was very old and very huge. They were given supper by a middle-aged couple who turned out to be staff and shown to a beautiful room, like travellers in a gothic novel.

The film director did not receive them at all. In the morning Alva let Cormac sleep in, or tricked him into sleeping in: he woke up alone in the high bed they had vaulted into after midnight, setting gin glasses down on the ebony dressers either side. It took him a moment or two to believe he was not dreaming, lying dry-mouthed underneath the canopy of satin ruched and drawn up in the centre like a rosebud. She was up already, gone.

He felt she had tricked him. It was playful; it was also rather cruel. In the kitchen the staff were absent and the radio was playing, incongruously and alarmingly, death notices. He made coffee and sat at the long table and waited.

When he'd mentioned to JP what they were doing, the other man told him the story of a Hollywood actress who came to rent the house the director owned for a year in the eighties. She kept it out of the press and brought a retinue of adopted children. They must have done something perceived to be impolite because, explained JP, they woke to find dead rabbits nailed to the door of the house. This happened two or three times before the actress fled. It was still bandit country back then, JP said.

In telling this story, JP didn't laugh, but put it to Cormac instead with the terse urgency of an induction. He was useful for that kind of thing, having rattled around this world since he was a child. Cormac sat in the glow of death notices at the table, alone, and imagined hammered rabbits, the actress throwing an American tantrum. He smiled to himself angrily.

Where was Alva? It was eerie, or wounding. Perhaps she left him in bed because she wanted to speak to the director alone; perhaps he was an embarrassment. Well. He banged back up the stairs to dress, washing quickly in the bathroom attached to the red room, and emerged with determination.

There were corridors, a sinking carpet and oak doors closed firmly all along the corridors. Cormac stopped outside each one, inclining an ear carefully, to listen out for movement at the other side. It was like listening to a seashell: blood or breeze, the settling of air, the settling of the house itself, a pulse, nothing. He came to a staircase and a parquet hallway he recalled from the previous night. Off this – he pushed the door to, intrepidly – there was a reception room crowded with dust-sheeted furniture, white and waiting photogenically, like the Arctic.

He found his coat, left by the back door, advanced into the morning mist and followed instinct down a gravel path beneath an arch of grey stone.

She was not being a bitch, he reminded himself. These jets of irritation threatened to become destructive soon. He was reading things, he knew, into her actions unfairly: she had more power, he believed. He stopped dead on the path when a gunshot cracked and echoed in the valley, which was damp and blurred but rose into birch trees picked out finely as brushstrokes, the hills bridging into each other melodically. In a moment, he realised what it was. He would need to face forward and keep his back to the house, to the garden, and slope safely to where Alva and the film director were launching skeet from a spring-loaded sling and aiming at them with a shotgun.

There came again the whir of release, the shot, the explosion like a breaking plate and the tinkle of debris spraying over the ha-ha. No birds, he marked, reacted to the shot – they must have moved on, up the valley, already.

Cormac raised his arm in a dour motion, back and forth, to signal his approach. He felt foolish as they turned to watch him. Alva held the gun but cracked it open and lowered the shaft, plucking a moment later at the shells. The film director, an elderly man in a greatcoat, sat in a garden chair and smiled and called ironically, And here he is!

Carry on, Cormac said. You are good.

Oh I'm not, Alva replied. Then she took down another streaking skeet; the shot carried again, profound and loud. The director wore headphones. Cormac only covered his ears. The next shot was not successful, however, and the little disc fell all the way to the slimy grass beyond the ha-ha. Cormac hated himself for thinking instantly of the waste.

Never mind, he said. And there it was: revenge.

The director turned to him with an outsized, campy movement that was clearly meant to be censorious: She's been excellent!

She has hidden talents, Cormac smiled.

Alva ignored them both and failed to hit another skeet. This time she cracked the gun again and said, My shoulder's killing me.

You try, the director suggested. He himself remained in the garden chair, sublimated by greatcoat, a lean and avid head emerging like the head of a heron. Of course the old man preferred Alva because Alva, with her hair crackling dryly in the damp, was a woman stalking boyishly about. She'd been at school with the director's daughter. There was probably some association there: daughterhood, a fox-eyed appetite for life, even if it seemed the actual daughter had grown up to be a mess. She met them in a bar once, morosely made up, and explained she was archiving every voice message from an ex-boyfriend to build a web resource for anyone who met him now.

Here, Alva said. She held the gun out. Do you need me to explain?

No, I've been shooting. He took it. Her arms were trembling. Was that significant? But: the gun. The discharge would hit her small ribcage violently.

Cormac released a skeet and missed it, then again. The pain was shocking. After two more shots into the trees – a bird broke then, a late bird, terrified – he could hardly pull the trigger for the numbness in his arm.

He'd been shooting as a teenager at the clay pigeon range in Ballyboughal. Older cousins with beer guts and bootleg jeans who could smash clay plaques with a hired gun all day. It was this world he wanted to draw out, revivify, with the film treatment. At the time, this was how people like JP and Alice and Alva saw him, he felt – as a toughened messenger from the lesser social world. Thinking of the project now brought warmth and relieved the shame of failing openly in the valley.

Cormac failed twice more. And that's how it's done, gentlemen, he said leadenly. The director laughed, but Alva said, Open the gun, and when it was safe took it from him and looked right at him wickedly. In this moment, the director was sealed out: they were two people who had spent the whole night fucking, most of it, and existed still in some mutual heat.

You killed it, she told him sarcastically at last, going slightly too far, and he squeezed her upper, opposite, arm, the one he knew would not be bruised.

They returned indoors. In a hot parlour loaded with books – the coffee table covered, the bookshelves, the mantelpiece – the director took tea with them before a small, merry fire. Cormac stripped to his T-shirt to cope with the heat but did so openly, deciding in the instant to inhabit a roughness and expand, instead of avoid, his sense of not belonging in this world.

Alva sat in an armchair with one of the director's cats, which perched on her knees without easing itself across her lap. The animal remained erect, like a sculpture, and stared rigidly at its master, intermittently pricking the tights on Alva's knees so that she twitched in pain and stared into the distance with a look of puzzlement. Cormac wondered also why she didn't just discard the cat. He felt an active, but relaxing, pity for her.

So did you see this – dead man? This black-eyed man? the director asked.

Cormac had been writing, pressing heavily, on a notebook. He sat back and raised his face with mild surprise. No, he said, I didn't see it, they had a duvet over it.

The director held up a large hand, weathered and webbed thickly at the interstices of fingers, wearing a wedding ring. He swept it over his face.

Cormac nodded. Like a shroud. It was kind of haphazard, I guess.

What actually happened? Alva, prepped for it, asked.

It was just three other men from the pub who followed him home and jumped on him. I don't think there was any reason but, of course, for the purposes of the script, we give them one – they think he is, I mean, a paedophile.

Alva had scripted a short production about Artemisia Gentileschi as part of her graduate portfolio, and the actress she cast – a thin whim unfitted, physically, for the role – was also the person she wanted to play the tomboy small-town girl from Cormac's film treatment, should they go into production. Belinda would surely want the part. Belinda was Alva's friend; a shivering, rabbit-eyed girl who took – he thought – a lot of tranquillisers, who daubed paint across sundresses for her own graduate show. She made more sense as the girl-iteration of Cormac than as Artemisia Gentileschi.

Something about this girl, the director said. Who is, I believe, twenty-five.

She'll play herself later, said Alva quickly, too. She'll play herself at thirty. So we'll need to do her over in both directions – but Belinda, I mean, it's easy. She's childlike.

Felix, stop that, the director said. Come here. As the cat padded underneath the table, he explained, My wife named her. They had seen nothing of the wife since they'd arrived and this was the first time he had mentioned her. The carriage clock on the mantelpiece, which looked like a seventies wedding present, had instead a foil banner underneath the timepiece reading only *Locarno, '91*. If we don't see it, the director turned to Cormac again, where does it come in then – the black eyes?

I'd like to open on it. Like a strike. Like the end of *The Shining*.

Like what?

The face of Jack Nicholson in *The Shining*. Dead. In the snow-maze.

The director frowned a moment as if, unbelievably, he had forgotten, but then said, Yes! Well, I stayed with Kubrick in Hertfordshire, did you know? When nobody was asked. Did you know he was a recluse? Or so he wanted people to think.

Everyone knew this: Cormac, in his T-shirt, decided to say, Yes. The face, he said, is a shock at the end of that film.

Ah but, the director said, that is because of him – Nicholson. It's because the whole film hinges on his facial expressions. Or a goodly part of it anyway. Now. The director seemed to enjoy schoolteacher challenging. Tell me: do you use this man's face, this – pervert, this oddball, whatever – and make him heavy-lidded, you know: the director raised his hands and placed fingertips over his own, closed, eyelids. Do you do this? Do you earn the dead face?

Yes, Cormac was firm.

Splendid, the director said.

The film was never made, of course. They left for London shortly afterwards and Cormac enrolled at the RCA. Alva's troupe pooled money to rent a studio. She did not travel back with him for Patrick's wedding – she was starring in something – ensuring, he realised afterwards, that his sense of Alva's separation from his family, from the worlds they respectively represented, remained intact. One night they ran into Belinda at a party in Hampstead given by a wealthy actress who insisted on being Irish profession-ally. Belinda was then playing second gentlewoman and swinging from the arms of married men. Many of these memories are dented for Cormac now because they all got so fucked up when they socialised.

Donie's eyes are coffined in a file somewhere: *fade out*.

Belinda's body was chiselled at by self-starvation, as if to release a birdlike soul, but last year he caught one epi-sode of an RTE documentary in which she led cameras down the corridors of drab institutions, eyes carved steeply with kohl, and explained anorexia and spoke about board-ing school.

Alva is married. Cormac is at liberty.

What do you do, he asks his mother pointedly now, when you get out of prison anyway?

I suppose you just get back to things, she says.

A week of work passes imperceptibly, mundanely, like a train.

December begins and there are coloured Christmas lights in the city: it happens overnight, as the air remains bitter, twisting with flurries of graupel and sleet. The boulevards of light are valleys in the darkness from four o'clock each afternoon.

On Thursday, an invitation arrives at the School of Visual Arts and Technologies. As Cormac lands first thing, the administrator calls from her scabbing hatch: Post for you!

He raises a hand and passes at speed and says, I'll come right back. He forgets to come back and so Alice drops by with her ginger tea at eleven o'clock.

Post for you, she says.

He takes it. It's an invitation to Nina's launch; a co-launch, a collaborative show, in Temple Bar. I was in that show, years ago, Cormac says with injured energy. Remember?

Yes. Alice takes the card from him. And here you are now, she says. Haggard and establishment.

Everyone keeps telling me I am old these days, he complains. He complains in play and half-serious.

It's because you go out with gymslip girls.

I go out with no one. I am a lone coyote.

You are the *puer aeternus*, Alice says.

He props Nina's card against a glazed pot of cacti. Alice leaves; they are busy, everyone is busy, because it is the week of the graduate show and sliding to the Christmas break.

On Friday afternoon, the afternoon of the graduate show, students descend on the gallery early to supervise mounting and to talk in close, dramatic clusters and to cry at one another, Oh my god, hi! Each wallop of the fire door blows cold in like bellows. Inside, bodies keep it hot.

And then there are their pictures, their final, graded, works. A large canvas in matte shows teenagers sitting on a low suburban wall, against a screen of guttering privet, in the headlights of a car just seen within the grid of the right foreground. Some of their eyes, turned forward in irony, reflect the flash, and this has been allowed to remain, suggesting a defectiveness belied by the richly textured quality of the privet and their ankles – thin and white above a spongy clump of trainers – and the golden, gorgeous path of headlight.

This photograph has won the prize and its author is a serious, shaved-headed boy in a Harrington jacket and skinny jeans. In his earlobes he wears silver ingots. Standing, now, apart from the group, he scrutinises this and his other pictures. He is going, he says, to finish his final term next year and move to Berlin. The boy has spent hours in the workshop at the Institute, making austere mood-boards and developing prints. One day he showed up with the copy of *Lux* from years before, the Sutton rave; Oh wow, Cormac laughed, where did you find that?

Yeah, I stalked you, the boy shot humorously, roughly, looking away. I really liked them, he said.

I can see your influence, Alice tells Cormac now. Most of her own students this year are Challenging Gender Norms.

Say it quietly, Cormac smiles.

His second favourite is a strange display brokered at a supervisory meeting right before mid-term. The student had pink hair and held up, in his office on that day, a square of stretched canvas with a single photograph. This print showed two hooked trout against the white of a hull or a harbour wall, their eyes as pricks settling deadly in the centre of shining discs. The photograph sounded of surf and smelled leathery, like ocean spray. The trout were blade-like, metallic.

I want to hang them like this, the pink-haired student explained, in the graduate show.

With thumbtacks, you mean?

High up. She shaped it with her hands, laying the print on her lap. Near the top. This size.

They'll be hard to see, Cormac said.

Not from the mezzanine.

Ah. Cormac smiled. You've been to check out the space?

The student looked surprised. Of course, she said.

Cormac glanced down at the folder open before him. Her grade point average was average. This impulse to independence seemed pure, however, and commendable.

167

OK, he told her. Why? When the student shrugged, Cormac shook his head. No, no, he said. Won't do. It's quid pro quo. He reflected for a second. Clarice.

The student stared at him.

*Silence of the Lambs?*

Oh! The student blushed and lowered her gaze. She folded her arms and pinched her elbows with chipped fingernails.

I want them high up, she said to the floor, so that they look like they drifted up there, like paper. Well, I mean they *are* paper.

You want them small and high.

They are not meant to be, like, big, deep portraits. She was shaping it again: her hands held something invisible, oblong. Cherished. I want them to be little, little wisps.

They'll be hard to see at that size, even from the mezzanine.

But we don't get graded *on* the show, she said obstinately. We get graded on the project itself.

True. Cormac snapped the folder shut merrily. Very well. As you wish. High and slight. You'll have to come down the night before, and come a bit early, he advised.

I will. She was grinning. She still looked like a child, unremarkable. Can I go now? she asked.

You are free to leave.

She giggled. His girl-students usually giggled hollowly to signal the close or acknowledgement of something. They seemed to do it without thinking.

Through the pane of glass in the classroom door he could see one of her friends waiting for her, emerging from an alcove with a grin, but then the pane was filled with Alice, who pushed it to and asked, That it? It was the night of the laundry show three weeks ago, he realises; Alice had arrived to invite him.

Now, when the student with the fish-photos — slimy decks and paste-white hulls of hookers in strong sunlight — arrives, the gallery assistants spend a long time steadying the ladder and following her instructions. As they work, they tell her it cannot be seen from the floor and, as the student nods blandly, chewing on a thumbnail, conclude with angry shrugs.

What's that about? asks Alice.

I don't know, to be honest. She never explains anything.

She won't get her grade if she doesn't explain.

The weakest projects have the longest explanations, he thinks in defence, although he refrains from saying this out loud where a student might overhear. He thinks of Caroline suddenly too, and feels bad about that. But it's true: A4 pages mounted by every image droning on about Questions and Interventions. Students calling their own work courageous. He has come to respect the strange fish-pictures, the way they shine with grease and saltwater and winter sun.

I think they're perfect, he tells Alice.

She says, All right, let's get something to eat while we can. And then, Oh no, too late, he's here.

The Dean has arrived. He spreads his arms and his spade-wide farmer-hands. All abuzz, he sings. Is it all abuzz? Students, as unfamiliar to him as the Dean is to them, cast crimped glances of disdain; return to their work and their buzz.

Oh you'll have to come eat with us now, says Alice.

But can we leave them? the Dean asks, looking around. Can we leave the students to it, do you think?

There are postgrads here, Alice says.

There are two postgrads – a girl with a bored expression pressing her back against the only empty wall and a boy who has spent the day heavy-handedly browsing photo-books downstairs. At one point he raked a freestanding spinner and caused it to totter, almost topple, before Alice caught hold of it.

Yeah, no, they have our phone numbers, Cormac says.

In the Square there is a smell like calamari mixed with candyfloss. It is still and the evening is approaching in noctilucent powder-blue. Cormac thinks with a jolt of his paint tin in childhood, turning over the cap to see it dusted in a thrilling shade: newspapers spread over the floor of the dining room. A flash of Parma violet against a fawn floor. How important, once, was the floor.

We should eat, says Alice, in the Film Institute.

In the Film Institute, at a table before the inactive fireplace, sit three women in full-mouth conversation, bending together, and one of these women is Caroline. Her eyes flit towards him in recognition before returning to her plate. Girl One has a long ponytail and is holding forth; Girl Two, who is sallow, reads from something on a phone. Caroline's hair is tied as tight as a squeak at the top of her head.

Alice, who has not noticed her, is saying to the Dean, What's the uptake for the master's like this year?

Remains to be seen, replies the Dean distractedly. Now. He looks about for a menu. Now.

Hey there, Cormac says to Caroline with a smile. He stands at the end of their table.

Girls One and Two cease speaking and turn sharply to him.

Hello. Caroline is curling a slow bale of spaghetti around the tines of a fork and against the incline of a dessert spoon.

It's all abuzz, Cormac jerks a thumb, over there: it's our first graduate show tonight, you know, for the Institute? They have a winter and summer. Two shows.

Ah, says Caroline.

Girls One and Two stare at him glassily. Alice, from their table, is beckoning in bright despair.

Otherwise I would come to the talk tonight, about the play – that's tonight, isn't it? I got your message about it. And you're taking part?

Caroline raises her eyebrows. He has not answered her messages in a week. She sent the link in a WhatsApp too.

You're missing out, says the blonde girl suddenly. It's going to be brilliant. I am Lisa, by the way. We dance with Caroline.

Cormac. He shakes her hand.

We know who you are, Lisa says.

The tall girl lifts her face and chants her name, something complex and over-Irish. Caroline says nothing, but her lips twitch in amusement as she watches this. She continues to turn the fork against the spoon. The action is droll and her expression droll, and she tilts her head, and in this moment she becomes the one with the power again. It happens in an instant, like a spell.

Feeling obscurely humiliated, Cormac takes his seat next to Alice.

They eat, with the Dean, and talk about the department; all three perform coded gestures of diplomacy and

171

intimacy. Alice keeps an eye on the time, saying several times, OK, I'm keeping an eye on the time.

Cormac sees the three dancers rise and leave, paying separately, standing each by the register and waving debit cards with impatience. A girl comes to crunch the plates they have left together, gather up glasses, wipe the table clean.

OK, I'm afraid we need to get back, says Alice.

The gallery is empty now, sympathetically lit, since all of the students have left to dress and meet their parents.

Dismissing the postgrads, Cormac and Alice finish off the hangings; at the podium, the Dean pokes the microphone and clears his throat with a clatter. Guests begin to arrive with the first skid of moon. When the place is full, it glows gregariously onto Meeting House Square.

Cormac, calls Alice. He is in conversation but turns around. The student with the ingots in his ears holds his prize certificate and looks glumly from her right. Next to him is an elegant middle-aged woman, hairless, her egg-delicate head lit by a face of colourful make-up.

This is my mam, the student says.

You must be delighted with him, smiles Alice.

Oh, he's always been a dark horse, the woman laughs, turning to her son in teasing appeal.

Yeah, mutters the boy, blushing. Ha. Dark is right.

The face that looks into Cormac's now is lean and ill, showing hungry contours, hungry hollows, eyes open and soapy underneath mascara crumbling from the lashes. Looking at her takes him, with a jerk that is also instant and cruelly fluent, aback. The woman, he realises, has the same pallor and spirit – more spirit, really, squeezing the student's arm and letting copper discs swing from her ears

– as his mother after Thomas died: lit from within by some tenacious filament, the kind of thing extinguished in an instant, something frightening.

When Joy was lifted onto a stretcher in catalepsy, her head tipped, lolled helplessly to the side, and it was the first and only time he'd ever seen her unconscious. He felt abandoned, and he knew the feeling, it was physical and primitive. He felt hate for her, and squirming guilt, and social shame, for the fortnight she spent in hospital. It was as bad as the death itself.

What a thing to remember.

Let it pass and remain in the moment instead.

We are hoping you'll come back from Berlin and enrol in the master's, Alice is telling the boy. She raises a hand to pat Cormac's shoulder theatrically. This one is never done praising his work – nodding at the mother now – and he's something special. We want to hold onto him.

I never doubted it, the mother says, looking at the boy again with flirty intimation. Shall we go? she asks.

I'll drop you a mail, the student tells Cormac, who nods. Finding his voice again, Cormac coughs.

Congratulations again, he says.

Cheers, man. The student has found himself. He puts an arm around his mother and cocks his head at her. Like sweethearts, they leave and cross the Square, the boy breaking off to perform one liberated skip: to jump eccentrically into the air.


Cormac sends a message to Caroline. It asks, Hey, do you want to hang sometime? She lets the read receipt glow freshly for two days before answering, OK.

No more drugs! he says.

Yeah obvs, she says.

Nina is not welding on Monday afternoon but sitting on the mezzanine stairs, dangling her feet in scuffed runners and tapping on her phone.

As Cormac arrives, a woman with a scarf tied in her hair passes him and nods in acknowledgment. One of the cats – plush but flat-faced, a dainty runt – dabbles after her. The cat glances back at him. Nina lifts her face. Hiya, she calls, surprised. I'm sorry, I was drunk, she says.

When? He knows what she means.

The email! I was harsh.

Oh. You were not wrong, though.

I was not wrong. She slips the phone into the pocket of her coat. She doesn't move from the top of the mezzanine stairs. It stands on steel stilts; it's still some six feet from the vaulted roof of the shed.

I want. Cormac stands at the foot of the stair. I was thinking, he says. We could revisit this.

Nina doesn't stand, but swings her runners in. She sits forward on her heels.

I mean like. His throat is dry. I mean *cosa nostra*.

She pauses for a cruel, dilatory time. She says: Oh?

Us. This. He raises a hand uselessly, fussily. You know. This thing.

You and me.

Exactly.

She looks blank. I can't right now, she says, this minute, because I have a delivery coming really soon.

Oh, of course, I don't mean—

But. Yes. Of course.

Brill. Fantastic. Mind yourself. Cormac pivots on a heel and hastens out, sucking breath. The woman with the scarf, together with Ned, raises a rusted structure shaped like a tower in the yard. The small cat watches keenly, cutely, from the rockery.

His next destination is a café by the basin, a spot that looks happily haggard when the tide is this low. In summer, kids from the flats come down to dive and swim in the basin, but now it's only swans harassed by gulls and Christmas coffees in Starbucks. The gasworks bought entirely by Google rise behind in accordion; the reddish streets of terraces belong to Google too. Patrick, when he meets him here for lunch or drinks, tells him Google anecdotes, like: Google bought units in all of the residential blocks around here to rehouse the council tenants they are, like, obliged to house in their own residential blocks.

What do you think of that? Patrick demands today, peeling up the topmost of a sandwich to scrape relish off the cheese. It's late afternoon, getting orange outside.

Not surprising, I suppose, Cormac replies.

His brother watches him. Now the private blocks that were sold to, like, finance people, normal people, have two and three times the number of council tenants, he continues. They go mad. Some people paid three hundred or four for those apartments. But if Google pulls out, the jobs will go.

Those are not local jobs.

Exactly! Patrick points into the air with emphasis. This girl I work with, he laughs, tells me, listen to this – Tinder in Dublin is apparently wall-to-wall lonely techies from, like, Iowa, bussed in.

The modern dream.

But she also says I can't say *drink the Kool-Aid* any more. It's offensive to, you know, survivors of Jonestown. This is deadpan and Cormac tries to crush his grin. To prevent Patrick from triumphing.

Offensive, Patrick repeats leadenly, to survivors of Jonestown.

They are eating sandwiches and chips in the afternoon slack. Lunch hour is over and the piazza busy with slender mothers in furry coats pushing Bugaboos. Fairy lights twinkle even on the silos of the defunct flour mill.

That was some night we had there the other week, Patrick says then. What was it, a fortnight? Time flies.

You passed out.

How were the yokes?

Terrible.

Well, he chuckles, there you go.

I notice you told Ursula.

I had to blame you. When you stoop to marry, dear boy, you will understand. Something to say. He holds up a hand before Cormac can speak. Something to say, he repeats. I am not being unfaithful.

I know.

It's nothing about that.

I know. It's not funny though.

Hmm? Patrick is eating now, limply and messily.

Ursula thinks I'm a bad influence.

Ah pet. Patrick puts on a wheedling, old-woman voice. Ah pet, shure Cormac is harmless as a floy. He's mine, leave him alone, he's mine!

Ha.

*He's mine:* this is what their mother would say about Cormac as a child. Leave him alone, leave off, he's mine.

176

Patrick spins a knife, a pulse of light across the blade. The café is flossily lit and the tables are rugged lumber, as in a canteen. The waiter looks like one of Cormac's students but he can't decide if he knows the kid or if the kid is merely a type.

He checks his phone and sees, blessedly, nothing from Nina.

The kid comes over to take plates. He grins and says, Howiya, sir.

I thought that was you. How're you getting on?

Not bad, not bad. The boy stands back and begins to speak, at unbidden and arrestingly pointless length, about the place – the shifts are long but you get a weekend night off every weekend; most of the staff are Polish but they have a real laugh; the best part is watching a lot of preparation and layout of food because he thinks sometimes about food photography; yeah, that's actually a thing, he answers Patrick, yeah, it's actually, like, a really growing industry.

When he leaves, Cormac shines with obscure pride. The kid was just so nice.

That was sweet, Patrick says falteringly. The digression has broken his stride. He finishes his glass of wine. Here, he says. I want you to read something.

From Eamon, is it.

Who?

The academic.

Who?

That academic lad from the other day. Cormac's vowels broaden in exasperation.

Deveraux! Oh fuck yeah, sorry. What?

I presumed now I am a co-producer or whatever, artistic

consultant, that I'd be contracted or something now. By Deloitte.

No, Patrick says slowly, frowning. It's something I wrote myself. It's a manuscript.

Cormac doesn't know what to say to this. He tries, eventually: Oh?

Yeah. I mean, obviously I've never done anything like this, obviously I don't *write*, so I've only shown it to Kehoe –

(Kehoe?)

And, like, you. If you want to have a look at it.

Well of course. What's it – about?

It's a memoir.

Cormac stares abjectly. Patrick nods at him slowly, as if helping him to process this, and then says, I know, I know, you wouldn't think I'd have the time. But I do a bit here and there. I find the time.

Have you – does Ursula know?

It was her idea to be honest but, like, she hasn't read it yet. Patrick looks, only now, uncomfortable. I'd like it to be really right before I show her, he confides.

Right.

So. Maybe let me know what you think?

Sure. But. Where is it?

Oh sorry. Yeah, no, it's in an email I sent to you just there. Patrick laughs.

Great. Brilliant. OK. Cormac opens his inbox on the phone superfluously. There it is, he agrees. That's a PDF. OK.

I just write things as I see them, Patrick adds as they stand. It's not fancy. I don't embellish, you know? It's just as I see it. As they pause, he holds Cormac by the top of the arm a moment. All them books in the suitcase, he bends to say. Lots of memories. See what you think. Just see. OK?

He crosses to the register to pay. Patrick always pays for everything. It's late in the afternoon now and the place is, Cormac realises, empty but for them, banquettes by the long windows glowing in leather yellow from candles lit in the centrepieces. He finds the peace of this interval between lunch and dinner beautiful, as if it is working on some bittersweet memory of beholding a room filled with yellow candles and winter light, as if the lumber and burgundy menus popping tug at something he's seen before and known before, if only for one shining moment of aesthetic delight. It might be a roadside pub or the ballroom of a christening in childhood.

The melancholy makes him sedate until they step into the cold again.

Nina, he remembers.

Why did he sweep into Nina like that? He'd left work and the impulse only carried him arrogantly.

He was in work. He was going over the graduate show. It had gone well, the students all drunkenly surging towards him and Alice in the Square as the shutters went down, shrieking, Sir, aw sir! Hugging him, rushes of peppery perfume and Lynx deodorant spray, before breaking off jubilantly and swinging around one another, charging into Temple Bar. The quick shame he felt at finding them annoying most of the time. He'd walked home happily and thought of Nina, wanting to talk to her about it, about the feeling of gratification Alice understood too well to really *receive* Cormac's iteration of this feeling and make a small room out of it, hospitably.

He got back to the flat and messaged Caroline. He felt fired and suffered the lack of anyone else to talk to or make out with. He sat in the snowy light of the front windows and listened to carnival clutter from the street, the banker leaning with his shoulders hunched against the chill on one of the trees, the guy on the newspaper reading a piece of his newspaper. Excitement ebbed, chemically, to moroseness until Cormac went to bed. Dwelt on the Nina email. Felt alarmed at the antagonistic impulse within. She was angry with him.

A day passed and then, a glittering sensation of something breaking or dissolving inside. I mean, he cared for her, Nina. They were fun together.

Why not try? He'd made arrangements to see Caroline at the end of the week and saw no reason to unmake these. It was a gamble, walking on into Nina's studio after work. The feeling now was confusion. Anxiety or excitement? Physiologically, more or less the same thing.

It might be all right, he thinks now. I'll let it cool and wait a while. All the same, the idea of seeing Nina's name at the high surf of WhatsApp contacts felt like cold fire suddenly.

Life a casino. Shots into the ether, and the dark.

You know I'm done now, Patrick says. I'm meeting the lads.

Jesus, do you ever work at all.

This is work, he protests. It never stops.

That Friday night, the DART station is wild. Wind slams the caged walkway above the tracks with a strength gathered over the bay. Cormac can see mountains and a thinning thatch of lights on the mountainside. Planes pace inland. He closes his coat to duck with everyone else from the DART – commuters in waterproofed or camel coats, all turning away from the gulf of the sea – into the gale. The green reek of the coast makes him think of home.

Caroline is waiting in her little car. It's wild, she agrees, as he claps the passenger door shut.

He kisses her, cheekily, on the lips, and she responds. They are going to stay in her parents' house because her parents are away. Her parents are academics and evidently rich.

As she takes off, under curled Victorian lamps lining the ramp to the road and a block of villas white as soap, she protests, What makes you think they're rich? Not all academics are rich.

We're in Monkstown, Caroline.

Is that rich?

I can't believe you would even ask me that.

It's a very old house, she insists.

That makes them even more rich. Look, I am not criticising you, kiddo, for the sins of your fathers.

She laughs. Fuck off, she says.

I am merely making an observation.

Growing up in your pothole, I guess, she returns. Eating broken glass.

Exactly.

One expects bitterness. She is driving uphill with amateurish acceleration, the car as brittle and subject to the mineral texture of the road as a thin-soled shoe.

They pass a church and a crowd of people breaking like water around a hearse, and turn into a street of large white houses. Caroline manoeuvres the car between others at the kerb. Doing this, she twists to see behind, scarf and cardigan bunching about her. She doesn't wear make-up and her skin is so dewily young, her eyes wide and moist by the lamps of the street.

Cormac always feels some embarrassment when being driven by a younger woman because he has never, in his ambulant and ascetic life, learned to drive. He is happy to get out of the car and hop from one foot to the other in anticipation of warmth. Wind roars through the street, if less brutally than the station. The house is square and sedately ornate, with a deep garden in front, and topiary shrubs in pots that have toppled onto the step.

Oh crap, says Caroline, picking these up by their necks. Welcome to the palace then, she says.

A large shoe-rack inside the door indicates and celebrates a family of trampers or flaneurs: rubber boots stubbled with sand, softened walking shoes, Birkenstocks beaten into idiosyncrasy but dried out and neglected due to the time of year. Caroline removes her boots, wobbling on one leg as she grinds down the zipper of its other. A staircase ascends to a landing and another case of stairs. Cormac is surprised by the walls of old-fashioned flock, but not by a shelf of spidery ferns and a framed poster of faded notation which, on closer look, is actually trees in thin pencil lines. Cormac cannot help himself – he never can – and points to it, saying: Origin of the species. That's the illustration, isn't it?

Yes! Caroline is impressed.

Cormac thinks with pique that it has been some time since a girl who was not his student seemed impressed by him. He thinks of Nina's email, which was unwarranted, no matter what way you look at it. He doesn't want to think of her: no.

Inside, the house is imposing and crowded with large pieces of furniture. Herbs grow in little pots on the kitchen sill and three walls of the living room are bookshelves toe to top. Ceilings are high and cornices are moulded. Caroline lights big billowing table lamps to illuminate urns and flower heads and curlicues.

Right. She turns to him. She looks at his boots.

I'll take these off, he says.

You'll be cosier. She walks into the kitchen. He follows, in socks, and catches up with her, putting his hands around her waist. Her mouth is muffled by a kiss, the curve of her back beneath his hands, and at once a salty urgency overcomes him: something that wants to wipe out the house and its inferences, the world, the wind, and to discharge itself before the evening can begin.

He hardens immediately and she draws back, laughing with amazement or dismay, as he whispers, I like you, I like you, I like you so much.

They go upstairs to a large room where the wind butts loudly against the panes of a window bay. As she removes her clothes, she shivers and says, I'm cold. He crushes her underneath a duvet and several blankets, sucking a nipple until she breathes, Easy, and dragging fingers through her hair; he digs with his tongue into the hollows of her mouth, unable to prevent himself again, then draws his face over her belly to push it between her legs.

He kicks awkwardly out of his underwear and strains to hold off as much as he can, slowed by the pause for a condom – as contrived and dry as a pause for the Angelus – but driving into her heat after this and crying out.

He wants to fuck her on his lap, sitting up, burying his face in her breasts and clinging to her thighs until he can tolerate it no further and comes, rasping with relief and regret at his own haste since the whole endeavour has taken less than ten minutes.

Jesus, he whispers with spirit. He collapses next to her. He moves to pleasure her with his fingers, but she whispers, Later, we'll do it again. He is terribly thirsty now. He tries to catch his breath.

Your pussy is ridiculous, he says.

Thank you.

And your ass.

You're not bad yourself.

I was going crazy.

And are you better now?

I am.

The sound of the wind is wonderful. It feels as though they are safe from the world and from anything complicated. It feels as though they have the whole event, the evening and the night, ahead of them.

Caroline re-dresses in her layers and says, Let's eat.

On the night they got high – the first night – a moment occurred: for Cormac, this moment now crowns from the mess of moments preceding and following it, presenting itself as a picture before his mind. This is the instant in which Caroline had been sitting in the window with her back straight and her face turned to the streetlight and her hand, fragile, half-raised, paused or exhausted in a gesture suggestive of administration or benediction, like the languid gesture of a holy figure in a stained-glass window.

This hieratic pose and blazing moment stayed with him. He feels he will always have it and wishes he'd taken a photograph. It makes him think of drawing or painting, conservative forms he has not used since art school.

In that moment, Caroline's quality of remoteness was expressed with the prehensile emphasis of an archetype and, Cormac realises as he watches her tossing her hair in a mirror now, this remoteness is equally raw and visible at the close of *Bridget Cleary*, that show about a witch or something he watched on the internet.

She leads him, now, downstairs.

On the hob she begins to reheat a pot of soup she has made with vegetables and barley. He admires the simplicity of her style and the way it is served in blue bowls with a loaf of bread. Butter puddled in a dish. As they eat wind whistles kookily through gaps in a pair of French doors. Beyond the doors the garden is dark but for occasional moving fronds of green or tree branches; beyond this, and a wall, are the elegant white-lit windows of villas. In a nook above the sink he sees a battered collection of cookery books, dust jackets ratty and hanging, in places, off. Even the spoons have fantails of interlace. There is a tipsy, jolly, bohemian vibe to the place. When Caroline mentions that her father has gone mad for krauting now and makes his own sloe gin – they could have some later – Cormac is not surprised.

It's in the pantry, she adds. He wants to laugh and repeat *pantry*, but feels that joke is getting old.

I thought we might watch a film, Caroline suggests.

That would be lovely. That would be perfect, he says.

We should do something other than fuck. She gives him a sardonic smile. We should get to know each other.

Of course. Cormac feels chastened. An image of himself as sybaritic and slightly pathetic floods his system with resentful vigilance; Nina is always kind of fine with it. Nina

185

flashes painfully, then, before his mind. Which is twice in one evening.

I'm sorry, I didn't realise you were – offended, he says.

Well, you should have more patience, she returns dauntlessly. She dips over her soup and seems, he thinks, to suppress a smile.

Of course, he repeats. I really like you, he tells her.

I like you too. She is smiling fully now.

Are you annoyed?

He asks now that she is no longer annoyed.

Not at all. I'm just – maybe I am a bit wary, she says, tilting her head to the side as if entertaining the thought. Because a lot of men come after me, you know, with the dancing and so on.

Cormac is a little confused.

I have a nice body, Caroline explains.

You do.

But I'm not an object.

I in no way want you to think—

I know, I know. She reaches across and rubs, briefly and non-committally, the back of his hand. Let me tell you about my last boyfriend, she says.

When she advances into monologues, he realises, she is never actually asking for permission. It is more of a tic or a cultural indicator of impending volubility, like *hark* or *hwaet!* He is becoming aware of a need to glean for economy and practise a selective attentive stamina to receive her stories intact. This, her first speech of the evening, also makes him conscious of how quiet she has been so far: how quiet before, and during, the sex. How singular her silence when he saw her in the Film Institute and she was

186

angry. The volubility, it seems, signals contentment. The silence is unhappiness.

He feels some shame. He stirs his soup and focuses on her, following the story as it unfolds. Trying, sincerely. The story she tells this time is of an ex, a rogue with a long-term partner stashed away. An older man who danced what she calls *addictive* attendance on Caroline. She discovered the deception via Facebook when on a somatic movement retreat. In a fit of vicious spite – her words – she told the other woman, thus, as she saw it, passing on the pain like a charge of electricity from one node to another; this, the sadness she was sure she had engendered, doubled back in karmic catapult to cause a sprain that cost her a marginal role in a well-paid and well-placed production.

All was interconnected.

On a somatic movement retreat, she explains, you are supposed to be deep in your body, not the mind.

I failed completely, she explains. I felt rage.

Maybe your body was angry too, Cormac says.

I should have worked it out, then, Caroline says listlessly. I should have moved through it and worked it out.

I shouldn't, she says, have done what I did.

What was so much worse was that the whole thing left her gutted by shame, since she felt in her heart she had known all along – about the other woman, that is – but had been taken so passionately with the pedestal this man had put her on: her legs and belly, bone structure, profile, red hair like fire and gold; the books of poetry and post-cards he'd given her, the secrets he'd confessed, the way he'd double over in a kind of agony across from her in bars and coffee shops and at this very table once, so much in love was he, so tortured and prostrate.

She models this passion: she puts her head in her heads. Just like this, she says. The words are muffled by the pads of either hand. She lifts her face. Now her arms are up-turned on the table and her hands are clawed.

He was an ordinary man, you see, she says. He was living in quiet desperation. My life looked very different to that.

My life, she continues, to a man like that: it looks wild. He thinks with me there'll be sex and craziness and no consequences.

She says, This is not the first time a man like that has come after me. Then punished me for it afterwards.

She continues with the tale. When she found out about the partner and the semi-D and the cocaine habit, the port-cullis of love came crashing down. This man, her boyfriend, called her a Crazy Slut, a maniac, and now, as she knows from Facebook, he and the other woman are still together.

It sounds like he was nothing but a scumbag, Cormac tells her firmly when the narrative has closed.

The bowls of vestigial vegetables are cold.

There's nothing you can do with a person like that, he says emphatically.

He feels highly disturbed because her articulacy on the subject is terrifying. Caroline looks at him with pity now, paler somehow and tired from the telling. The loaf of bread is a stiffening stub between them. He finds her vehemence and sadness depressing and feels it is early in their acquaintanceship for such dark intimacies. He doesn't want the tone to turn.

Well, it doesn't look like that when you're taken in, she says at last. It doesn't seem so simple then. Like, just a scumbag: move on.

No. It doesn't, he agrees.

What I felt for him was real as well.

Of course, he says. Actually a lot of people would say you did the right thing, you know, telling the other woman.

I didn't. I did it out of spite, she repeats. It was over between us by then. I did it for no reason other than spite.

You were hurt.

Oh god, I was out of my mind. She begins to chuckle, to Cormac's immense relief. Oh god, she says. Out of my mind.

When was this, can I ask?

It was a year ago. It's over and done with now. For a long time. She pauses. She breathes deeply. For a long time, she says, I couldn't live with myself.

That's harsh.

I always thought, you see, that I was a good person.

You are.

You don't know yet. Now she is laughing. Oh, she says. Oh, I'll shut up about it. You get the gist.

I do.

Don't mess with me.

Do you hate him now?

I hate him so much, Caroline says with antic severity, I watch the death notices in the paper for his family name. They laugh together, but Cormac attends to an after-echo of alarm.

Caroline clears their bowls after this, and Cormac springs to his feet. When they have loaded them into the dishwasher, she slaps his backside playfully to signal some release. There is an art film she's never seen and she wants to watch it, it's called *The Double Life of Véronique*: has he seen it? He has, but not for a couple of years. In the living room there is no television but a projector with a screen that can be unfurled before the fireplace. They settle like cats into the wide wad of a couch with many cushions.

The photography of the film is perfect, a disenchanted flatness revivified by rich colours and welling complexions of creamy light. Véronique, Caroline remarks, has the kind of Lady Diana haircut that only works on the luminously beautiful. She says it with a mock solemnity, as if she took it from a poem: *the luminously beautiful.*

She pauses midway to make gin and tonics. It tastes flowery and foul to Cormac, like the perfume of some childhood authority figure, but he drinks it anyway. Caroline further says: *Amélie* really ripped this off, and then: a sex scene with eighty-denier tights. And she's been wearing them all day.

He laughs. She says, eyeballing him, They make the feet and crotch too hot, no woman on earth would submit to sex without at least a birdbath.

A birdbath?

A top-and-tail, if not a shower.

Maybe this is just set in a more spontaneous time.

No, it's that men don't understand hosiery. Her mood has expanded, sweetened, and enveloped both of them. Véronique, she further complains, has fallen in love for no reason.

It's romantic, Cormac says. He makes puppets.

Maybe it's like *The Birds*, she speculates. Tippi Hedren says to Alfred Hitchcock: Why would I climb the stairs to a room full of psycho birds? I need a reason. And Hitchcock says: The reason is I said so.

When the film is over they talk into the luxury of the

late Friday night. It is raining, more tranquilly than before, on the papery privet outside. They think aloud about drains roaring with overspill and flash floods streaking down streets. They discuss the British election, which took place yesterday: on her phone, Caroline opens Twitter and says, Hashtag Corbyn, will you?

I don't have Twitter.

Oh right; never mind.

He has no chance.

He does. It can't happen again.

There is an argument on the left for leaving Europe. What do you think of that?

It's an argument against neoliberalism, not Europe, she says. And it's wrong.

They discuss Brexit. They discuss the laundry show. They discuss the new appeal, that week, for information on a ten-year-old police case, a man who vanished on a stormy night walking home from an office party. I remember that night, Cormac tells her. The weather was terrible, as bad as tonight. I was home from London and everyone was out for Christmas because it was nearly Christmas. There was a taxi strike, you see. I remember the posters going up very fast. His face was everywhere, you saw it constantly.

You were in London?

Doing my master's. I lived with Alva.

Alva Flynn the choreographer? I heard.

The one and the same.

I love her. What is she like?

Oh, you know. She's – nice.

In West Hampstead, she broke her phone against a wall when he climbed the stairs to their flat and told her he was

191

unhappy. He remembers her scream-breathing but finally fixing herself. She is married now to a film producer and has a child, a trampoline probably – he imagines it silvered with dewdrops as the sun crowns over the gardens of suburbia – and he is always running into her husband on shoots when he works commercially.

What do you think happened? Caroline asks then. He halts in surprise at the question until she qualifies, To the guy who went missing, I mean. Do you think he killed himself, went into the river, and wasn't found?

I don't think so, Cormac replies. He's pleased or relieved they have dropped Alva. Because, he continues, they would have found him by now. Especially since he disappeared near the canal and there are locks. It doesn't flow straight into the bay.

He remembers the night, or perhaps he's remembering another night. Senan with a guitar case in a doorway, sheltering from rain, pointlessly – it would keep on, drains curling forth with a garbage froth and pealing down pavements – and he wonders, Did I spend the night with Senan, as in spend-spend? I can't remember.

They searched it straight away, he tells Caroline now, they searched the canal. There was a state visit or something and the city was checked – they checked everything, the sewers too. Let me see. He thinks. Bill Clinton was visiting. They could check the sewers easily, the canal; they had Special Branch at work already.

Although, he concludes, I suppose there's still a chance it was suicide, yes.

She pauses a moment strangely. Rain rattles with an almost animate pragmatism in a gutter outside and occupies space. Caroline says, Sorry.

What?

Your brother. Suicide. I didn't think.

I'm not sensitive about that. You don't have to be on eggshells or anything about that. Cormac is irritated.

I'm curious, she says with oddly unfeeling frankness. I'm curious, I suppose, about the impact it had on you.

Well, it was horrendous, obviously. Cormac speaks sharply. Her circling back to the topic of Thomas shows, he thinks, her inexperience with life and pain – with certain strata of reality – and this is the only thing he considers negative so far in their interaction. That and the sex reprimand over soup. Also the story of the villainous ex. Actually, there have been a few things.

You don't want to talk about it?

He shakes his head. He nuzzles her neck, breathing her ginger-and-onion-skin scent, and wraps his arms around her. The first time, the morning after MDMA, she shivered in his grip until they grew clammy and comfortable together. Her cold feet and long toes and strong arms. She has, tonight, more vim: she struggles against him with puppyish petulance to instigate play-wrestling. It concludes with an entwined topple to the rug and her leaping up, asking if he would like more gin. She resettles herself with a refreshed glass, and him.

I don't think he killed himself, she says of the man who is missing still after ten years. Looking at the evidence, it's clear somebody else did something to him.

A week after Thomas's funeral, Patrick – then nineteen and in his first year at Trinity – broke the embargo on the back bedroom and made Cormac, while their parents were out, help him sweep it decently for contraband and porn.

They did this still in the giddy phase of adrenal denial and shock. Patrick told him: If I die, I want you to do the same for me.

Cormac blazed with blush and said, Yeah, me too.

Patrick himself was greenly pale and perturbed but holding it together, opening a pane of Thomas's window on a womanish impulse of purification.

The place still smelled of scalp and aftershave. The bed, as ever, was made, and cold, since Thomas had been living in student digs for two years at that point. This was the room he used on weekends and midterms and, for this reason, it was tidy, stripped, and bare: a shelf filled with paperbacks of complex foxing, posters of bands, dumb-bells and the hulking, forbidden computer – *stay the fuck away from that!* – with its dust-filmed screen and dust-gritted frame, its latent smell of plastic heat, its keyboard rattling like teeth.

Patrick switched this on but did not know the password. They won't know either, he reasoned. Mam and Dad.

He pressed the button until its whirring internals staggered, dampened and died with a hiss. He then found a tin of pre-rolled joints with a speed and ease Cormac suspected and felt faintly awed by, since Cormac had always been too frightened to come into this room or impinge upon Thomas in any way – to risk revisiting early rituals, humiliations and punishments.

Thomas, as a child, led Cormac into the kitchen one day and said simply, Touch that. The red-hot hob. Their mother steeped his hand in water for an hour. When he came to from the sobbing he had pissed himself, thoroughly. This came back on the table, with heat, with Sadbh.

Patrick said, in the room now, Try that drawer, and that one. On the wall, Thomas had painted a version of the artwork from *The Dark Side of the Moon*. Patrick lifted the mattress and slid his hand back and forth, catching on something and drawing out a modest stack of magazines.

Ah, he said.

Even he was distracted. They flicked a sample open on a vulva, waxed and pink and enrapturing, belonging to a tanned and smirking woman whose breasts were like things designed to squeeze or maul for stress relief: OK, OK, Patrick repeated at last. Keep looking, he said. They discovered nothing more. Patrick hid the magazines at the bottom of their shared wardrobe, in the room they also shared, and piled on dirt-flecked, mud-crusted, and studded gym holdalls – errata of his school career as a long-distance runner, which had won him much esteem.

It was very neat, the room, Cormac remarked carefully.

Yeah, he's hardly in there any more.

It struck Cormac that Patrick, like him, fully believed their brother was coming back. This brought him the consolation of solidarity and kept something unbearable, perhaps unlivable, at bay.

He was pleased to break the anxious intimacy they had shared in Thomas's room when Patrick left, when Cormac was free to sweep beneath his own mattress and retrieve the sooty centrefold he'd come by underneath a bush at school. This did not have vulvas on it but showed two men, shaved-headed and leanly muscular, linked at the groin like spokes on a dizzying wheel, an image he had not yet been able to look directly at, an image which caused exquisite terror to fountain through him with such vibratory violence his ears went blank with blood, the world shrank to his own beadily muffled pulse, his cock stiffened according to the same atavistic urge which informed rage and fantasies, lifelong fearful fantasies, of pure destruction, explosions, dismemberment.

Cormac crumpled this image and ignited it with a lighter and burned it, partly, in the bathroom sink, running the tap over grit and glue and balling it into a paste and squeezing this tight, opening every window, depositing the sticky ball in the outside bin before cleaning the sink and batting his arms about to diffuse the smoke and, finally, shattered and aroused by this tight escape, attempting an ameliorative bout of wanking while perched bare-assed on the edge of the bath.

He sat in aftermath, then, and felt a glare of solitude – clammily insular, bodily – envelope him until the birdsong and the twittering cistern, the afternoon going on boringly outside, returned.

With breakfast in the morning there are papers, delivered, like in a film or a television show. Breakfast is boiled eggs in Tesco Value cups, so basic it seems ironic or self-consciously kitsch. To this Caroline responds, What? Oh. Ha, ha.

Here is that thing you mentioned, she says.

In the arts spread: Lazarian, photographed close and with his mouth miraculously shut, autumn light behind. Also embedded in Alice's text is an image he did not take himself, of Beatyard – it was taken in summertime, showing the yard behind a green ridge of hanging plants and bicycles with baskets leaning up against the hoarding, as if nobody would steal an uncuffed bike with a blithe basket in Dublin 2.

Cormac has read the interview, of course, and sifts through the paper with little interest. It pleases him that she, Caroline, should come across his work by accident in this way, featured – which is unusual – in a broadsheet newspaper. It makes it look as if he's someone in a way that anyone can understand.

He was gas to speak to, he remarks. Very energetic.

Fuck, that was the day I saw you there!

It was. Such serendipity.

God, Dublin is so small!

It used to be smaller, Cormac says. I think it's more dis-connected, now, than when I was at college, say. Things like Beatyard. He thinks a moment, finding the words come confidently: Contrivances like Beatyard, he says, don't do anything.

Are you, Caroline asks from the hob, on about your broken glass again?

The eggs drill as they boil against the bottom of the pan. She slots toast into a cast-iron slinky. Cormac could be man-of-the-house, with eggs and newspapers: because it is only an act, it is not a threat. Upstairs, the bedroom remains muggy and eggy from sleep. He was reluctant to leave, but she bolted up, chivvied him down, put on coffee in the canister like a compact bomb.

No more rain. Vigorous chilly sun. Plants on the patio spilling about like hammy actresses. The world robustly stretched as a canvas.

He pulls her onto his lap and she asks, spiritedly or per-haps hysterically, So, what's your plan for the morning?

Nothing, he tells her. He tells her fulsomely. Nothing planned, nobody to see until later. I'm free. And you?

She says, I know something we might do.

★

197

They drive up the coast. There are tall blue-blooded trees, pines and cypresses, lining the residential streets beyond the embassy district. The houses are palatial and there is an abundance of them: there are gates and gravel driveways, Victorian teapot-towers spouting from the sides of piles, ponderous modern cubes built onto ground-floor wings inconspicuously. The streets are absolutely quiet, like the streets during a plague, even though it is Saturday. There is simply so much money frozen calmly in these walls and windows, cubes and mansard roofs, and he's been inside houses like this – at art school, when he briefly went out with the daughter of a property mogul, her teenage brother witless on Ritalin at Sunday lunch – but so long ago, before he was old enough to understand.

So autonomic it feels like premonition or second sight.

Fancy area, he says to Caroline.

She is next to him, driving. Official Ireland lives here, she explains. Not the ones you hear about. The ones you never see.

He thinks of Patrick: beautiful soul.

Thinks of Nina.

Does not want to think about it on this, a bright afternoon, driving to the Vico with Caroline, to swim.

In her parents' house he'd said, OK, swimming, cool, immediately, concealing fear.

We have a gang and we do it on the regular, Caroline explained. All year. I can get you trunks from my brother's room.

Sea-swimming in winter is a thing now, as he knows, a status thing – when the kids on the docklands retire their wetsuits until summer, South Dublin's bourgeois descend for their medicine aggressively. He's done it in summer but never December. He reckons he will be OK. He is young and strong and sexual partners tell him all the time that his body looks good, he reasons. They really do. Women and everything. Has to be true.

Driving, now, down avenues of calcification, Caroline wears her hair back in a band, her ankles bare. They leave the palaces behind and climb Killiney, passing haciendas in sight of the sea. There are many cars parked against hedgerows here. A man walks a spindly greyhound that takes an interest in Cormac as they get out of the car. Here, staggered palms hiss in the breeze. The palms are windburned, veering back or groping forward, and they stand everywhere, giving a kind of colonial melancholy to the place.

Have you been here before? Caroline asks.

Years ago. Want me to carry something?

He finds himself saying this too often: *Years ago*.

Only towels. She grins. You ready? It's cold.

They pass over a stile and slant down the dirt path between squeaking bulrushes. A middle-aged couple pass and angle around them, nodding pleasantly. There are people at the rocky bathing-place – a small crowd of people, undeterred by the fact that it's winter and icy and baldly bright. Cormac wears his jumper and jacket and gloves, the red scarf piled at his throat, and begins to feel dread at the prospect of removing these, but Caroline raises her arm to shout, Mila!

The sallow girl with the Irish name, from the Film Institute, sits despondently on a stone platform, wrapped in a towel. She is sheltered from the breeze but something of it ruffles her hair and whisks it up, exposing bone-white scalp. She is slow to smile, but salutes. In this instant, the

199

scene is a winter invert of the Gruyaert photograph: bathers move jerkily instead of lying around like cats.

You've met Cormac, Caroline says a little saucily as she drops the organic tote of towels at Mila's feet.

Of course. Nice to meet you again. The girl's feet are crazy long, monkey-long, slenderly grotesque. She has a snub-nose and wears her hair parted austerely in the centre.

Have you been in? he asks her, even though it's clear she has been in. Her lassitude, the bang of lassitude off her, is irritating.

Yeah, but I'll go back.

Hurry up, Cormac, Caroline instructs. You have to do it fast without thinking. If you think about it you will choke. She has come into sudden confidence, it seems, due to the cold and the cries rebounding off the rocks, or due to the presence of her friend, or due to some excitement radiating from the sea.

Yes, ma'am. Fuck me. He has opened the coat and scarf, lifted up the jumper. Fuck me. It's Baltic.

Mila tilts her head to the side as if this is a curious thing to say. The towel is tucked beneath her arms and above her meagre cleavage. She is winter-tanned evenly, like the girl at the laundry show, and, even with the monkey-feet, distractingly attractive.

Caroline is in her bathing suit – she calls it a *bathing suit*, cutely – her body as pale and angular as her energy is warm. She cavorts a little, barefoot, on the platform. The ground beneath them is uneven and seamed, but the cement shelter opposite is filled with families changing and especially with nasal mothers shrilling after children as fathers in wetsuits ignore everything.

Caroline says, Come on, and so they go.

The cold of the stone steps, with water ragged and spume-white all around, is a nagging cold. But the cold of the water, into which Cormac pushes himself chest-deep by descending the steps, is nullifying.

For some seconds there is no ego. Cold, cold, cold. There is only a klaxon of dissent that feels urgently cellular and a sense of suffocation. With vicious will he lets go of the handrail and shoots ruthlessly into a rootless suspension. The current is not unremarkable. A hotel glows like England up the coast. There is a yacht bobbing before Blackrock. It is a view of Dublin rarely seen, carved into garish greens and white cavels like the stone smile of some immense deity: a flooded buddha or a sphinx, so weird and vivid he is stunned by it as much as by the temperature, which remains fucking unbelievable.

Cormac cannot speak. His teeth chatter in shock. Bodies surface and call to one another. After a minute of treading in torment, the cold dims slightly and the scene steadies before him and he looks for Caroline.

Can't see her. Waves roll without surface breaks bearing swim-hats, grimaces. He makes a few strides in breast-stroke, proud of the strength in his arms and legs, which propel him as solidly as they did at school – shot of Senan at the edge of the turbid pool, snot and steamed goggles, head capped too tightly: stink of chlorine running to soap-scum, stagnant water, smegma, bleach.

Can't see her. He swims, alone, pushing into a wire of current that reliably resists. This will – the staying in it – makes him ecstatic with triumph and novelty. He wishes he could see her; he wants to press against her and entangle their legs, he wants to find his voice so he can laugh. He likes this, and he likes her – fully, now, in this ecstasy of

shudder and swell, this moment of objective wholesome-
ness. With each second the feeling grows more and more
ludic in its purity, a musical mushrooming of ambition and
desire finding perfect expression in a Platonic triangle of
health and affluence and security.

Why don't I do this all the time? he thinks. Why don't
I do nothing but this, all the time?

There she is. She is waving from the slipway, which is
slimy and ghoulish with seaweed, wrapped in a red towel.
He begins pulsing towards her and a group of unthinking
people, screeching at each other and congregating, ob-
structs him, annoys him.

On the slipway, a breeze snags on him and, just like
that, he wants nothing more than to be away from this.
But there is glee, back at the concrete wall. Mila in her
clothes now and the other girl, the girl named Lisa, towel-
ling off. She is Caroline's age but her face is so hysterically
expressive, rising up to him now, she looks older, more
volatile. Oh you! she exclaims.

That was great, Cormac says, even though his body is
shuddering and catching with cold and fright.

Isn't it great? We come down here all year. It opens the
amygdala. Lisa is scrubbing her shins now, one after the
other, with a towel. It loosens up your amygdala, where
you keep your trauma. It makes trauma, like, come out.
Standing, she frowns at him and gestures with her hands.
You know?

I think so.

It cures.

It feels amazing. But it's shocking in there, cold.

Caroline has given him a beach towel that smells of
detergent. He is tired suddenly, and overstimulated. He

202

feels all three women watching him and is happy with this, happy to be the object of their telepathic attention. Mila wears a raincoat with a pointed, elfin hood.

Now that we're done, Caroline instructs, we have to eat. And he cannot help but think for one laughingly insane moment that they're going to eat him.

It turns out a chipper in Dalkey is much like a chipper on the Northside except for the widescreen television showing Sky News with the concussed subtitles. Cormac points to this and says, That subtitle robot thing is one of the many banes of my life.

I know, it's like you can't stop looking at it, Caroline says.

When they were still at the Vico drying off, a good-looking man in a wetsuit approached them and offered swigs from a bottle of Powers. He did this to undermine Cormac in front of the women but, all the same, Cormac drank some, they all drank some, and now they are warm and satisfied. They are also ravenous. He feels a hunger unlike anything experienced for years.

They order fish and chips and decamp to a plastic table by the window, watching Main Street growing dark but nipped by festive lanterns on the façade of a heritage pub opposite. He is amazed by how much they eat – Mila, Lisa and Caroline – in between speaking to one another fervently in a girlish vernacular. This week, as he gathers from a conversation which dust-devils ably without his input, they have been seeking out a new venue for the rejigged *Bridget Cleary* and settled on a disused warehouse behind Capel Street. As they viewed it, Caroline explains, a *hands-on performance* hosted there was finishing up and for this reason the floor was sprinkled with flour.

I liked that place a lot, she says now. I'm happy with it. I'm happy to go with that in the spring.

Three cardboard cups of milkshake fade on the table. Cormac has ordered Coke and feels unsure why since he doesn't really like Coke; he considers it something mindless or obvious; something people who don't care about their body, or indeed about anything, drink. The reflex is weirdly classist and belligerent.

Who of us can say, after all, we know ourselves?

So long as the dais is removed, says Lisa firmly. She traces her fingers down the side of her cup, its beads of clear sweat. Do you agree?

Yes. The other two nod.

There's a dais and we don't need it, Caroline says. There is a beat before Cormac realises she is speaking to him.

Oh yes?

It's mechanical. It sinks into the ground. It opens up and then sinks back down, on, like, springs.

Right.

Mila says, So is that settled then?

Yes. Caroline smiles.

Lisa is frowning thoughtfully into her chips. Cormac also smiles and folds his arms and looks at them all with a doggishly accommodating nod. Caroline has introduced him as *Cormac* without a descriptor, no *date* or *friend*, and he knows by this she has told them all about him, but not what she's told them exactly.

Wasn't the flour great? Lisa asks. She looks gentler and paler now, less vivacious. I wonder about that, something like it, she says. For us. Something like flour or sawdust on the floor.

Sawdust would be good, suggests Caroline, and especially if it had that, you know, sawdust smell.

Lisa is nodding vigorously.

Actually, Mila offers, sipping, clay makes more sense.

Clay? They all look at her. Even Cormac, feigning engagement.

Earth. Soil. On plates. Like in the *Dubliners* story.

What's that? Lisa asks. The flare of irritation and inferiority in her look is so obvious it makes Cormac, watching all three with increasingly anthropological interest, feel sorry for her.

Mila, the dark one, comes, Caroline has explained on the drive from the Vico, from the Gaeltacht, not from South Dublin at all: her full name is *Maolíosa*, but she possesses, to his eyes, the languidly secure and separate aura he saw in members of the minor gentry during his times at the Royal College of Art. He wonders about telling Caroline that. She might not like him thinking about her friend.

It's a story from James Joyce's *Dubliners*, Mila begins to explain. It's called 'Clay'. This old woman who lives in a laundry, she's like a laundress or whatever, goes out to visit family in the suburbs, she's unmarried, she brings them a cake – a kind of cake – and they play these Halloween games. The children blindfold her and she puts her fingers on a plate of clay. That means death.

Laundry, he thinks.

So what – this is a Joyce thing? (Lisa.)

It's a superstition. Like the *piseóg*. Clay. When she puts her fingers into the clay, it means she is going to die. But nobody names it. They go quiet. It's brilliant.

For a long moment it looks as if Lisa is going to say

something critical, but the frown becomes thoughtfulness, interiority, and finally a nod.

Yes, yes, she says. I can see it. Clay. On different plates. There's a ring in the middle.

There's a ring in the clay, hidden in the clay, on one of the plates. And whoever finds it gets married next.

But they have to find it in the dirt.

Yes. But it's also, like, the burial place?

All three upspeak: together, it seems, the frequency of upspeak increases.

They begin then to talk, absorbedly, all at once. Cormac feels impatiently his exclusion. Their way of talking, these younger women – the affirmations and exclamations that parry between them, the humour safe, the extraordinary earnestness – means he can neither disengage nor fully take part: he doesn't share their metabolic swell of self-delighting, self-affrighting exuberance, but all of this, its zeitgeist, requires a kind of indefatigable attentiveness: it's like an algorithm, spurting and converting itself. Even Mila, whom he at least suspected of a sexy species of lethargy, is fully involved and whipping the volume up.

They are making more noise than anyone else in the chip shop.

Alice has explained this phenomenon in respect of their students. Nobody, she says, ever told them they were worthless growing up. Not the church, not the state, not – you know – the insidiousness of culture. Not their parents. Nobody.

That can't be true of all of them, Cormac protested. I'm sure some of them were told they were useless.

Not these ones, or not so many of them. Or rather,

you know, it's a cultural thing. They have to *seem* really enthusiastic. About the right things.

Right.

The same way we had to seem like we didn't give a fuck.

I think they have it harder.

They do. We should go easy on them.

He sits now and wilts, therefore, at the coalface of their self-esteem. They nod and take notes on their phones and when they agree on something, they sit back to stare into space, still nodding with certainty.

I've to go soon, announces Lisa at last. I'm going to run now actually. OK! I'll send an email to that woman, what was her name? We'll take the venue. Is that settled? Bye!

Yes, Caroline smiles: perfect. That is a weight off.

Lisa leaves. She leaves behind a woollen scarf, liver-coloured, with tassels melted together by dryer heat.

I'll mind that for her, Mila says.

Caroline tells Mila, Your clay idea is brilliant.

Are you sure?

Yes! I love it. It's so good. You know the story, right? (To Cormac.)

We did it at school.

The space in the story, Mila is tracing shapes on the surface of the table with long fingers, is like the space of the Cleary cottage – tight, you know, old-world: primitive, like the peasant play, or whatever, but transposed to the city, the old traditions and stuff, you see?

I do, Caroline nods. It's a relevant overlap.

Cormac fears another undulation into festive conversation. He wants to leave. He needs to leave anyway – he is accompanying Ursula and Maude and one of Maude's little friends to a carol service at Christchurch. He is taking Patrick's ticket for reasons that look faintly like a ruse. When he reminds Caroline of this obligation, she says, I will drive you, we are going into town, we're meeting people at the Lord Edward anyway.

We're all going to stay up, Mila tells him, and watch the British election count in Reggie's house.

God yes, that was this week. It goes on all night though, doesn't it?

There'll be snacks, she says.

They do this – they drive into town – when they have screwed up their chip wrappers. They drive along the coast road, passing presences, the Poolbeg chimneys, the Soviet estates of Ringsend, and many weak examples of Public Art. They can see the bay like a black gash and the manic candescence of the coastline, sliding with cars, broken by the pier at Poolbeg.

In the city Caroline parks badly but with bizarre confidence in a lane of cottages off Kevin Street. As they wind their way around people in a fanged wind, icy and intent, up Francis Street – almost reaching his apartment, as he notes mournfully and privately – she and Mila discuss the border feverishly. They know nothing about us in England, Caroline says. They've taken our history out of their curriculum. You hear unbelievable things.

Remember when the DUP came into Westminster to prop the Tories up? Mila asks.

Patrick conceived of a joke when this happened, a few years ago; he tried it out on people with underwhelming success. Cormac admired it and replays it now. That move, he says, was like Dorian Gray and Dorian Gray's

208

portrait being in the same place, the same parliament, at the same time.

Mila nods but Cormac fears she does not get it.

With the Conservative Party, he explains, as Dorian Gray – staying bluff and appealing, you know, because all the sins are being hidden in the attic of Northern Ireland. That's the sexy face of conservatism and the Democratic Unionists are a bunch of, like, bible-thumping creationists – the unsexy face of conservatism.

Very good, Caroline says.

Their father took them, Cormac and Patrick and Thomas, to Armagh for High Mass one weekend when they were children; no reason but exploratory point-making, telling them the doleful story of conflict and ensuring they understood that there was no difference, no difference at all, between Catholics and Protestants. Their father, he explains to the women, unsure as to why he is saying this but needing urgently to discharge tension by reinstating himself in the conversation, had joined the Christian Brothers as a teenager but left within six months. He never lost his moral woundedness.

He would, Cormac says, have made a better Jesuit. He was a thinker, my da.

All the way north, he recalls, he and his brothers wished for, and squealed at, the prospect of being blown up, sky-high, or lined up for interrogation by villainous Ulstermen before going nobly to the gallows for the cause of Ireland. He recalled this now – his first trip over the border, aged ten – as an erotic experience.

I would not make it into an ethnic thing, he says. Not like, an England-versus-Ireland thing.

Why is that? Caroline asks. They are coming in sight of

the cathedral, splendidly lit, a light show sliding snowflakes over a broad old wall.

Seems petty to stamp your feet and cry nationalism.

It's not nationalism, she protests.

I'm older than you, he tells her. I remember the violence.

Oh give over. Have a good time, she says, where the queue begins: *no pasarán!* Mila gives him, he thinks, a baleful glance before both women duck into traffic and towards the lean stook of the pub. The pub is a strange building that cants forward in that eighteenth-century style, like a skinnily vehement drunk.

Cormac pauses to text Ursula and then watches his sister-in-law stand out of the queue further down, waving a gloved paw and wearing a padded coat.

Joining them, he dips to the children first, and gives Maude a spin. The little friend is milk-blonde and delicately watchful. Ursula's own face is pinched and her eyes under-smudged with blue. She embraces him suddenly, pinning him to her before releasing him with a chapped kiss on the cheek.

All right, she says firmly, to herself. Who was that?

Some friends, he replies.

As their small group – he and Ursula, Maude and her friend – pass under a Gormenghastian arch, Ursula waves fretfully at another woman, a woman in a red elegant coat, who is settling more children on fold-out chairs. This is Sarah, a friend of Ursula's, he is told. Cormac shakes her hand, which is slim and minimally, nuancedly, beringed.

You're the brother-in-law! Sarah cries with a crashing smile. You're the artist!

I have been known. He bows. He flirts.

That's just amazing, she says.

He can tell by her accent and tailoring that Sarah belongs to that school of women his age who sincerely believe he is hobbled for want of a wife. Ursula is also one of these but her reasons are more precise.

Maude's mouth opens as she looks up at the garlanded nave of the cathedral, at the ribs and pillars of carved flowers from which eerie little faces peek. Lights have been criss-crossed in a cold space and the crowd is filling it with secular sibilance. It is beautiful. He feels glad to be here suddenly. He feels glad to be away from those exhausting young people.

Cormac bends to Maude and points things out, sensing the hot proximity of her cheek and her smell of soap, wool, until Ursula bonily bundles Maude to her other side and sets her up with the children – four between two women, Sarah he notes now honey-blonde and wind-flushed, not unattractive – with Cormac at the outer edge, exposed. Maude's squeak of protest is diffused.

Ursula says, lowly, I've been meaning to speak to you again.

Of course you have, Cormac replies.

Are you free tonight, for the rest of the night?

Uh – yes, I guess?

Will you come back to Donabate?

Sure.

Kehoe is there. Sarah will come back with us. She gestures to the other woman – Sarah, he realises, is Kehoe's wife.

Right. He remembers her. He remembers Sarah, aeons ago, when they were all at college – was she the one who—? No, probably not. Kehoe would not have married

211

that one. Kehoe had been a member of Young Fine Gael and even then never left home, rain or shine, without a golf umbrella.

We're going to do it, once and for all, Ursula explains. She means Patrick. She is gathering allies to accost and confront Patrick.

You could have warned me, Cormac whispers.

I knew if I did, she explains without shame, you would find a way to bitch out. She does not look at him but surveys the crowd. He didn't, she says, come home at all the other night.

Jesus.

Shush. Sarah can distract the kids, you see.

There was no need for the plot. He tries to make her laugh. He feels a flicker of redundant rage at *shush*.

It's not about you, Ursula says.

He didn't stay with me.

I know he didn't, she says.

Choristers in crimson cloaks have congregated at the back of the cathedral, arranged neatly and waiting. Maude cranes around to look and Cormac looks too, close enough to see them, all quite young and glacially made up with one man of height and handsomeness towering over the rest and another, a man to the tall one's left, cocking his head and nodding in Cormac's direction meaningfully.

It is Senan. Cormac waves.

Senan is, he thought, in the Netherlands. There was a post on Instagram: Beautiful Nijmegen! Photograph of a Teutonic beer hall. Europe spared by bombs and communism looks like a toytown. Senan was in Switzerland last month: photograph of a child-eating ogre on the plinth of a dry fountain.

Cronos, Senan posted. Antisemitic, someone sub-posted. A fight ensued, but Senan stayed out of it, commenting only later: Beautiful Bern!

Now Senan is here. The singers begin to sing 'God Rest Ye Merry Gentlemen', parading up the aisle. Cormac feels short of breath with surprise.

He hasn't seen Senan in person for months and yet his vision still telescopes in, urgent and unreconstructed, so that Cormac sees and knows again he loves him with a scratchy passion that returns reliably as a rash. It is not a nostalgic feeling and casts no shadow, existing always in a self-sustaining now.

How acute it is: immediate déjà vu.

Cormac stands obediently with the rest to join in for 'O Come All Ye Faithful'. As it progresses, he tries to contain a troubled welter of lust. He thinks despairingly of the night ahead with Ursula and Patrick, with Kehoe and Sarah, with children and righteousness and a world he has never belonged to or never felt he belonged to. The unfairness of this opens out like decadent technology: self-pity striated by desire, sensations that seem queerly at home in the cathedral.

Cormac feels sorry for himself.

In the interval Senan travels down to them, kissing Ursula on either cheek before secreting himself into a seat among them.

I got called in at the last minute, he explains. Someone is sick, and I was in town. I've done it so many times.

So no rehearsal? Cormac croaks. He clears his throat.

No need really, it's the simplest of stuff.

And you just what, have these to hand? Cormac flips

the lapel of Senan's robe. Tucks it back into place slowly and taking too long.

Senan says brightly, They give them to you.

Yes, I know they give them to you, kid. I'm messing.

How are you anyway?

Dandy, Cormac insists. Excellent.

Cormac watched Senan sing Latin Mass for Good Friday – statues under purple drapes, small girls in mantillas, a kind of libretto listing the many apocryphal adjacent torments endured by Christ – when Senan was studying at Maynooth. Afterwards they got so drunk with a bunch of friends no one could remember how they made it back to the student residence.

Senan's tenor voice had been thin but deeply sad. It was the dark jus shades of mahogany and the panelled council chamber Cormac photographed for *An Triail*. Senan uses it rarely now, this voice – he's gone through a folk phase and a *sean nós* phase and that phase of barefaced girls in pub backrooms singing *There was an old man came over the sea / Aye but I'll not have him*. His voice is less a container for personality than an adenoidal instrument that can be set aside. At school of course he was lambasted, often – a chorus of gouging sneers – for being the Mass soloist, pure and girlish and best of all in the small snatches of Latin:

> Veni Creator Spiritus
> mentes tuorum visita
> imple superna gratia
> quae tu creasti pectora

But he did not care for the sneers. Senan did not notice them, or care, so cheerful was his vanity. This made him stand out strangely at a bottom-rung boarding school with no arts provision run by seedily weather-beaten monks. There was no substantial music provision either: Senan and Cormac had to share a damply surplus lumber-room in the old tower, set aside for stackable chairs and morality manuals that had become limp as butter pats with disuse, with a honking piano and the giddy reek of glue from Cormac's portfolio sculptures.

The saggy couch where they began.

Senan came back from the Gaeltacht. He said: I'll show you some things I learned in the Gaeltacht.

Cormac was a day-boy who went home every evening, but Senan had a bed in one of the sad yellow remaining dorms. Cormac never invited Senan home; Cormac was asked to Offaly but never went. No one knew what they were doing and he doesn't think anyone ever figured it out. Patrick had finished school. Thomas was gone. Senan formed a prog-rock band in final year: they were called, Cormac explained to Nina once, Footprints in the Sands of Time. They were as bad as that name would suggest. We drifted apart a bit, to be honest, after that. He had a band now. He had other friends. What we called – the things we did. We used to call it *as Gaeilge*, as a joke: labhair as Gaeilge.

So he was your first love then, Nina said.

I don't know. It was nice to have him. After my brother died, when all of that was going on.

Maude likes your singing, Ursula tells Senan now. Maude has turned away and buried her face in her mother's coat for shame. As a young person Senan was blond and frail-looking and unwittingly twinkish but, heading for forty now, this abject youthfulness is aging unevenly.

You'll be at the flat, then? Cormac asks.

I'm not sure. I'll get back to you. Definitely next week, though. I might be in Offaly – you know, my sister is home again.

This will be the sister who married badly, the one who periodically seeks asylum from drunkenness and cruelty with her kids in the humble bungalow. How is she? Cormac asks.

Sad as ever, Senan says. It bothers me. For someone with such a fatiguingly oversized family, Senan is close to his siblings. Cormac has known him long enough to retain random information about some of their marriages and business loans and cancer scares, their timeshares and failures of nerve. Even if months can pass, and years have passed, without he and Senan seeing one another or being alone.

When Senan leaves, now, with hugs and apologies to re-join the choristers, Maude gives way to a fit of giggling. Cormac smiles on her but wonders with a flash if she understands what is happening, what is going to happen, with her father tonight.

The singing recommences and becomes wearing.

'In the Deep Midwinter' suddenly, however, makes Cormac want to weep. He thinks of his boyhood and the ponderous sadness of boyhood, of his brothers and his parents, of faces he cannot remember and places reduced to freak olfactory snatches of recollection and of death, of mortality; he thinks of bones as thin as pencil shavings in alcoves beneath the cathedral.

The organ harps, indecently opulent and solemn. So many people have left in the interval, the space is gapped. It's rude.

Thinks of Nina: cities are built on burial pits.

He is pleased when the performance finishes and lays a hand on Maude's little duck-down head. His niece glances up with an open but tired expression that makes her look in this instant like a little woman.

Are you coming home with us? she asks.

When they gang up on Patrick, he says at once, What the actual ever-living fuck?

And then, What is this, an intervention?

Yes, says Ursula.

What, did you know about this? He rounds on Kehoe. The other man is standing at the mantelpiece, watching uncomfortably.

Yes, he knows everything, Sarah says.

We're united, adds Cormac lamely.

Patrick begins to laugh. Sit down, sit down, he cries.

They see his fear and commit to it, lean into it. The exit poll has been announced and the Tories once again are storming the lead. Patrick asks, How can you ambush me at a moment like this?

It's almost Christmas: a tree twinkles pitiably.

And it is late, so late, when Cormac leaves.

Ursula says, Stay, but wanly. She is pale as a moth and lying with her head on a scatter cushion. He calls a cab.

Senan, on the couch off Essex Street, is asleep, having unbaled the spare duvet and pillows and sheets in a gesture of tired politeness – placed his shoes considerately side-by-side underneath the coffee table – and left a suitcase zipped tight by the side of a sleek unstickered guitar case. Even though the windows are closed, the sound of the paving stones is constant, meteorological, and the power button on the oven glows a sentient red.

Cormac pauses in the doorway and looks. The other man is curled, his back and the fabric of a T-shirt by street-light, and Cormac could toss some hair from his forehead or wake him up with the screw of a bottlecap or say, Hey, Senan, Senan, yoo-hoo. Sleeping on the couch indicates Senan's intention to be chaste, either out of loyalty to someone in his life or out – which is the more likely reason – of that shyness, that shamefacedness of character, he retains like *noblesse oblige*.

Cormac is so tired he has become dryly wired and he hasn't answered any texts from Caroline. Sense memories of the pranging cold, the silky water, have returned to him all evening. They are like the nervous spasms of sensation that would wake him at night as a child: ball-pools, hot sand, chairoplane. Grinding approach of the motorbike race.

He has been pausing in the doorway for a long time, both arms opened out and leaning on the frame in the pose of a man who is dominant, a man who isn't going to take it any more. But take what? He is tired.

This is the pose he is still holding when Senan wakes up sedately, turning and exhaling, falling still, freezing ani-mally in the semi-dark. Cormac?

Hey. Cormac releases the door and crosses to the arm-chair by the windowsill. This is where Caroline sat, he remembers, hieratically.

Did you, Senan asks in a whisper, get the results?

What? Oh, no: they're not final yet.

But it looks like Tories.

Yes, it looks like Johnson.

Senan sighs and turns again and for a moment it seems as if he will go back to sleep. Instead he says, I'm sorry I didn't let you know I was coming, it was last minute. You know how it is.

You could have messaged, Cormac agrees. He's so tired.

I know. I don't know, I forgot.

I think you like ambushing me sometimes. Cormac uses Patrick's word. He might use it more often because he can think of numerous recurrent scenarios in his life which warrant the word *ambush*; which are ambushes of some description, if one looks at them justly.

What? Senan laughs a little, in the gloom.

I'm messing. Cormac is tired, but repentant. He says, Senan, do you want to come into the bed?

Can I?

Of course. Only I'm wrecked, you know.

Of course. But thanks. Senan sits up. His eyes are small and half-asleep; by creepy streetlight he stares up and down the room, taking it in, and stretches a little. Cormac realises that he, Cormac, has to rise before Senan will. When he does, Senan follows him into the bedroom and tosses back the sheets.

Aw, they're clean, Senan says, nuzzling. Good man, yourself. He is asleep almost instantly, as usual, breathing with a distant catch and squeak. Cormac undresses and lies next to him, still tired and wired and dry. He needs water. He bounces up with vexation and returns to the kitchen to fill a glass. This one is Wexford.

The plaintive tone, the *Can I?* These are turn-offs.

He prefers Senan unapologetic. All evening, the prospect of sex lurked numbly behind the indignities and endurances: Kehoe against the mantelpiece as sinister as he had been at Trinity, Ursula in white-hot martyr mode shading painfully into disbelief. Patrick laughing at all of them but finally losing it and yelling and Cormac deciding, with a shock of ingenuity, to say: You look like Mam when she went mental. Do you remember that? *I'll not stay in this house! I'll not stay in this house!* Mental is the Dublin term: *insane, crazy* – these are elsewhere.

Joy had continued, raving at one time or another at her husband, And you, the father of my children, you do this to me. You do this to me.

What did he do? Nobody knew.

In bringing her into this, her unfortunate period – or one of them – Cormac knew he was throwing his mother on some callous pyre, on some chopping block: he knew this but did it anyway. Patrick stood at a loss because Cormac remained the only man he couldn't hit.

I'll go then, I'll go, Patrick began to bait. Lowing like the overgrown toddler at closing time, rearing up to everyone else in the pub.

You're not going, you're being put out, screamed Ursula. Their kids were right upstairs. Sarah came trembling down and put her head around the door. Have you lost your minds? she hissed at Kehoe.

Shout at me now with the children upstairs, Ursula shot.

Oh, hit me now with the child in my arms, Patrick sneered.

Cormac thought, I could put a knife in you. Clean through the ribs. Beneath the ribs. He shook but stood.

He said, Ursula, don't engage with him.

You, little fucking faggot, I don't know why you're here.

This was Patrick.

Little fucking sneak, sneaking around my wife. No family of your own.

Afterwards they would all think Cormac was the fount of calm, but actually he was only frightened, then mortified, then incrementally – opulently – indifferent. Detachment, a familiar mechanism, dissolved and settled in him like seltzer.

Yeah, all right, he said. Fair enough. But here you are shouting like an animal at the mother of your children. What are you going to do now? Murder us all?

Jesus, Patrick said with real surprise. I am only defending myself.

It was so pathetic he, Cormac, felt that everyone assembled died slightly on the spot of embarrassment and disillusionment. A dart or prick that punctured human hope and poisoned many years of better memories. They waited, creating a breach in which Patrick might absolve himself or at least rethink. He did not do this exactly, but he opened both his hands in a gesture of concession: he looked like Garrett in the Stoneybatter kitchen, also being a prick.

What has caused all this? Patrick asked.

You! Cormac said desperately.

He said this because for some baffling reason Ursula did not. She had set herself against the counter and lit one of Patrick's cigarettes. Her eyes were reptile and they travelled to everyone, looking at everyone – at Patrick, Cormac, Kehoe, at these three men – with the same bloodless lizard quality, calculations without emotion, discrete as a pin-eyed ikon.

She continued to smoke for some distended seconds like the fiercely unkempt love interest in a paperback noir, a role he had never seen her step into before, a role which was alien. She looked at them as if she had not brought them together for the purpose of serving her. There was not one stroke of loyalty in her look and he, Cormac, hated her in that moment, just a moment, or contracted the contagion of hate moving through the room.

*Hit me now with the child in my arms!* Attack and insult me here, in front of lesser men.

Cormac sits in the window of his apartment, sipping water now, alone.

The street beneath looks stunned by ice. White eaves and the rotunda of City Hall invoke pictures in a storybook, an out-of-time world in which animals stand on hind legs and juggle pies. The world is an uncanny place and in certain moments you don't know it at all. The last visit to Sadbh for example. The red dust in his centre – the heat, rising to be sliced out of him – subsided and he drank a pint glass of water and set off along the rim of a country road, past the spikes of the Virgin shrine he felt no motivation to photograph, on a cold day turning to turbid and turning, then, to rain: out-of-season rain, the dogmatic species of downpour that breaks heavy weather in August but seems overstated in December: it had saturated him by the time Bray came on in bike lanes. It seemed personal. He turned his face to the rain and tried to laugh with it, or at it, and the laugh was like kicking up gravel impotently.

By the time the nervy navy dawn begins, he is lying in bed next to Senan with his hands behind his head, thinking further about strange things. Thinking about the *piseóg*. Caro-lisa-mila, that dainty hydra with milkshakes, have mentioned this: it is a curse you plant in someone's life – anything rotten, blood or meat, anything decayed –

and hide it so they don't know where the rot is issuing from. Until they can find it, everything in their life will go wrong.

He knows a relationship rots similarly, mysteriously, but inevitably. He finds this bitter belief in himself as sudden toughness, as gristle between teeth, as a nut or a nail or some other hard thing. He pauses as he thinks and waits and detaches himself.

Sees the thought resolve itself.

Sees the thought as a thin, autonomous thing.

Do I have to believe this?

There's a flickering interregnum when he might think otherwise, but the night has been too depressing; Cormac feels hateful and overtired.

He turns towards Senan, slides to scoop the other man from behind, puts his face into the warm crook of neck and the smell of perspiration. Senan sinks into the embrace in his sleep and things get warm between them, a knee to a knee pit and a cock to a coccyx, a calloused heel to an anklebone, the lonely photorealist light of early morning bitingly cold.

I'm glad you're back, Cormac whispers.

Are you?

Yes.

Are you surely, surely glad I'm back?

I'm surely glad. Cormac reaches around to stroke the line of Senan's jaw, press his palm against Senan's abdomen and find the loose frill of a waistband, the scratchy slope of hair against the heel of his hand, the erection silky but damp at the tip. He, Cormac, is already moving rhythmically in a kind of mime. He thinks, I'm tired, I'm thirsty, I'm fucking miserable – but O.

This O opened years ago beneath the blue trees of a school demesne; a couch in a lumber room; a lumpen bunk-bed with its frame overpainted so that blisters formed and diminished with time; a wall of posters and a drip of curtain against which Senan as a boy is turning, turning to look over his shoulder, mouth an O of implication. So nice and precise it could be a photograph.

Caroline sends articles responding to, and reflecting on, the Tory landslide attached to messages. She sends the emoji with the monkey shielding its face and tells him they are all going to a town hall meeting on Tuesday night, and Cormac realises he has no idea what she is talking about.

When she asks what he's doing on Wednesday, he answers, Memorial, for an old friend.

She sends the monkey again.

She says, Shit sorry, didn't look at that properly. I'm sorry about your friend.

It's OK, it might be fun actually, he tells her.

Senan has come and gone from the apartment since arriving, and this time it is a leather shaving bag laid open everywhere. When he is there, he strums a guitar sadistically and leaves the hall light on all night. In daytime, as ever, they do not touch one another in any way. He says to Cormac: Do you want tickets to things? I can get you tickets to a bunch of things.

On Wednesday evening they eat omelette together, extractor fan gnashing over the hob, and Alice drops by at six o'clock.

Oh, Senan, she says – will you come with us to this thing for JP?

He didn't know JP, Cormac says.

I will, actually. Senan crosses his knife and fork. I did know him actually. Vaguely from around and that, back in the day. But I should change.

We need to go now, Cormac says.

I'll catch up! Senan slaps the door frame as he darts by. I'll follow you!

On the street Alice asks, And what is the nature of this visit from the Milkybar Kid?

Who knows? says Cormac. He listeth as he will.

He's the nicest thing about you. I'm always happy to see him.

She wants to know next about Patrick. When he tells her Patrick is exiled to Joy's, she claps her hands and shakes her head and says, Priceless.

The city is full of lights and the pavements dense. The atmosphere makes the place vivid to Cormac, the cushioning pulse of habit dimmed by the abrupt alterations of Christmastime – it takes him out of himself, so that he remembers the thrill of arriving here first to go to college. The terrace in Kilmainham, cones of sage spiralling to the ceiling in stinking mist, a wall of mandalas and the route of Venus sketched onto the underside of some wallpaper for contrast. Memories.

Turning from sex on a coat pile at a party to see a boy he knew masturbating – out of it – in the doorway; flushing into the street with a fleet of shrieking girls the night the living-room ceiling collapsed and snowed plaster – it looked like disaster – as the house alarm belted out across the cul-de-sac inconsolably.

My feeling is that JP would be furious, says Alice now, the Shelbourne was not available. Her voice brings him back.

Together they step into the Central Hotel. The lobby remains like something off a dated freight road in the deep country, the paintings of horseflesh and merchant skiffs as hick as they've ever been. It is one of the best places in town because it is so reassuringly uncool.

Do you think she'll be here, he asks, the wife?

Maria? Let's see. Maybe not.

There are a great many people crowding into the bar and all faces turn to the door when it swings. From a window under a velvet curtain, Garrett waves. Opposite him there sits an exceedingly handsome woman, in her thirties or forties but with a screen of dark hair, pinched knees in sheer tights pushed together as she sinks somewhat into a chair of flabby leatherette. When Garrett waves them down, the woman follows his gaze and raises a hand to copy uncertainly. As they approach, Garrett pulls two lazy stools close to the table.

Some crowd, he remarks by way of opening.

Are they all here for this? Alice bends to the task of unlooping her scarf as the other woman beams up at her with kindly regret.

I'm Claire, the woman says. Do you remember me, Alice?

Alice sits smartly down. A hand crawls over her face to rake back hair, the lips pushing into a polite smile. I do, she says. Claire.

I'm Cormac and I'm sorry to say I don't remember you. He sticks out a hand.

Here. Garrett bounces forward suddenly. He pulls out his phone.

Oh no! Claire laughs.

Here. Aha. Look. Garrett holds up the screen: there, a

young woman – Claire – lies insolently on a bare mattress, dressed in a yellow ball gown.

I took that, Cormac realises.

Autumn/Winter two thousand and four, Garrett reads from the screen. I remembered her straight away.

God, I've changed so much!

She has hardly changed at all, apart from the haircut: in the ball gown photograph it is pixie-short around a face as slight as a choirboy's.

I was good, wasn't I? Cormac says.

We all were. We were great. Cheers. Claire lifts her wine glass at Garrett's signal and they clink.

Alice asks atonally, Cormac, what would you like to drink?

I'm on Guinness, pipes Garrett.

I don't have enough hands. Next time.

I'm scared to turn around, Cormac grins at Claire when Alice has left, because I don't know who else I'll see. I was away for years, he explains.

Cormac lived in London briefly, Garret says. When he came back, Alice got him a job.

Oh but I see the old gang all the time! Claire exclaims.

I wasn't in the old gang. I didn't know there was a gang. I feel left out now. Did you all have a gang? Did you meet up in secret?

Claire laughs at this, for a surprisingly long time.

I suppose I mean the girl-gang, actually. We used to meet once a month in Reynard's, and of course then it was Avoca, because we all had kids; it's harder now, of course, but Belinda Roche and I both have daughters at Alexandra College. I talk to Rose Crawford a lot, although she's in America now.

She says *Alexandra College* because she thinks he won't know what it is. If she felt he would know she would just say *Alex*.

Rose's husband, she continues, was transferred. She wasn't sure about such a big move, but I said, Rose, go! Her husband is with Merrill Lynch.

After a beat she also adds, The bank.

These woman. Cormac is goofy. I didn't know any of them. They wouldn't look at me.

You were the photographer, Cormac, Claire scolds. I think you would have been looking at them! Though, of course, you were with Alice. You two were joined at the hip.

Alice was me, Garrett corrects.

Alva was me, Cormac says.

Alva! Claire turns from him and scans the room. Alva is here!

Oh. No way.

Alice is returning from the bar, cutting through the crowd impatiently, and when she sits she says at once, Alva is here. She has recovered, it seems, from the blow of Claire.

Last time Cormac saw Alva she was harried and waiting to begin a post-show Q&A, watching the clock and reading text messages, asking him ardently inconsequential questions: What are you working on now? Are you still teaching? And are you, like, *happy* with that?

He really doesn't want to speak to her here. He feels, these days, almost clownish when he approaches her or has to discuss her; there could be a laugh track trailing him. Even a mild look from her when they run into each other is dick-shrivelling. And, of course, this kind of thing is excruciatingly routine in Dublin.

Who's that? Alice asks suddenly.

A woman with dramatic make-up and lace gloves to her elbows, a glass of champagne, stands before the fireplace to address the room.

I want to thank you all for being here, she begins. Her voice holds that American inflection which in fact is just an accident of nerves. I want to thank you all for coming here, she says, so we can remember John Paul together. We'll be reminiscing and having, we hope, a laugh. We'll be celebrating. Some thank yous that I have to say tonight, specifically, are as follows.

I don't know who she is, Garrett says.

Me neither, says Claire.

She looks like an astrologer, Alice observes. It is so savage in its accuracy even Cormac is discomforted. Some people nearby might have overheard.

It's not the wife? he whispers.

Oh no, god no. She doesn't seem to be here. I don't think we're at the official thing.

There's another thing?

I just doubt this is bona fide. These are the groupies. It seems. Alice drains her glass and sets it down. There's Senan, she says.

Senan has slipped in the door and is crossing the room discreetly. Everyone looks at him anyway. I went into the wrong function room, he explains in a hiss as he crouches down. I think it was toastmasters or something.

You know, he turns to Cormac, Alva is here. Push up, he commands, into that seat.

Senan sits close. There is a jammy razor nick beneath his ear. His long hand closes over a knee. They are crushed together, now, in the chair. Cormac can smell his own cologne, which he has not put on tonight, meaning Senan has.

The astrologer continues, It's important that we have a chance to come together and support each other.

I still don't know who she is, Garrett says.

Well, she probably doesn't know who you are either. Cormac reaches for the pint of beer Alice has bought for him. He takes an opportunity to scan the room but doesn't see Alva yet. She might be with her husband who works in television.

He thinks: Faggot, no family of your own.

To his brother, silently, in the veiled realm of telepathy or aspiration, Cormac says, Our other brother died of acting the maggot. He fell. Just like JP.

This hasn't struck him before now: it's true.

To Patrick, silently, and impossibly, Cormac says, I was at school with Senan when Thomas died. I was in the blue woods of the demesne. I heard my name being called, and I was afraid. I thought we'd been found out for fooling around. I was sure that's what it was about. I couldn't understand.

The prefect in the small potato-smelling room; the fireguard; owl and fox in action pose; corridor lights staggering, going pop, pop, pop: little font for holy water dry. Shaped like a silver throat, a burdened Christ. When someone tells you *There has been an accident*, you know already that the subject is dead, because only death warrants abrupt courtly reversion to respect.

Senan packing himself up palely, looking at Cormac in fear as if he was to be blamed, when they heard Cormac's name being called. Both boys hurrying into the avenue, by the leaf-littered speed ramps, hollering, What? The willow tree was there of course – limp but furnituresque.

You are wanted, you are wanted.

This is what people said when you were in trouble: You are wanted. Never in a good way. No adult actually wanted a child. None ever had. At school, the ball alley looked like a prison yard.

JP's family want me to thank you all, finally, the astrologer says.

I was only at school, he thinks, I was so young. He is yelling this, somewhere, at Patrick. Cut me some slack and give me a break and stop watching me, all of you.

Stop calling me. *You are wanted.*

I'll get in a round.

Senan, darling, Alice objects. Allow me. She joins in with the last of the applause. Claire is leaning forward, feeling for her handbag while maintaining rabbit-bright eye contact with Garrett, who is speaking to her.

So amazing, she says. I'm sorry to say I have to go. I have a baby with an earache and a husband back from Boston less than twenty-four hours. How amazing it's been, she says, to see you all again.

She leaves the room like all well-bred and beautiful women leave the room: apologetically.

People have begun to mill about again. Senan slides into her seat.

So then, tell me, Garrett, he says tartly, how've you been?

Cormac frowns, beholding them both. Surely not? Hardly. No. Alice has returned with more drinks for Senan, Cormac and herself.

Pretty good, answers Garrett with vigour.

I saw your installation piece at Limerick. Senan names

a collaborator: I've worked with him, he tells Garrett, and so have you, I see.

Oh yeah. To anyone else this would be warm or at least helpful information. To anyone else this would be recognised as politely site-specific small talk. But Garrett looks keenly at Senan instead of replying, as if he's been criticised.

The astrologer woman approaches and leans buxomly over them like a hostess.

Hi, hi, thank you, she smiles. She is gregarious and tipsy. She doesn't want them to feel bad at all at the fact that nobody knows who they are. Thank you so much for coming, she insists, holding Cormac's hand lingeringly.

Alice is cranky and, when the woman moves on, clicks her tongue.

I seriously think we are at the wrong event, she says. Who the hell are these vampires? Good grief, look at the *fascinator* on that thing.

A woman wears a sprig of black wire, webbed out, at an angle on her head.

Performance poets, Alice says. I think they may in fact be performance poets. Or cabaret singers. Or that burlesque collective who do performance poetry.

Do you want to leave? Cormac asks.

I can't leave yet, Garrett interjects. I'm meeting someone. They have my bike. Everyone regards him with a shared, spontaneous surprise.

I didn't know you had friends, Garrett, Cormac says.

Just a few.

Senan asks, Do you want to speak to Alva?

Of course not, Cormac says. I don't even see where she is.

She's in the corridor. I passed her. I told her I'd go back out and chat.

Cormac looks at Senan but says, OK then.

Outside, Alva is standing — long in a flame-coloured skirt — against a wall of robust flock and at the edge of a circle of people. She turns her face at once and nods at Cormac and Senan, smiling tightly, but doesn't approach. Steers her attention back to the group's speaker. She is with friends.

Alva has a small chin, a weak chin, which narrows her face to a slant and makes the flesh of her bottom lip jut out. With age this feature has become prominent, but the way she holds herself now means it's less a flaw than an aristocratic quirk. She still wears her hair romantically long, like Ursula, which is unusual in women of their age, or used to be. It has the effect of looking girlishly artificial.

You look so well, Senan tells her as he leans in for a kiss and places his hand on the small of her flicky little dancer's back.

Hello, Cormac, she says. How are you? What is going on with you?

Still at DIT, he says breezily. All photography. Technical and theoretical. I was made permanent — he counts on his fingers — four months ago.

Congratulations.

It was inevitable really. From a legal perspective. A pause falls between them because Senan has begun speaking to somebody else. Like, they can only have you on rolling contracts for so long, Cormac qualifies. She looks back at him softly.

It is frightening to look into the eyes of a person you have known so intimately when the time, the intimacy, has passed. You don't see this person but you see yourself as exposed and diminished suddenly.

The real, representative image he retains of Alva, the primary one, is from London. It is framed by dry canopies, comingled trees crunching above him in a breeze, which are shot through with streetlight.

In this image, it is late, it is dark, but the birds sing by the fake daylight of streetlights enragedly. Five floors up, at the top of the art deco building they rent a flat in, in the window of the kitchen, which is bright and wide, he sees Alva washing dishes – he knows this is her, it always is.

He's coming home late from something with reluctance. He's just turned thirty. For his birthday they went, ironically, to the zoo. In the lion's cage there was a block of frozen blood the size of a filing cabinet. It was too hot all day long. Tonight, he hadn't wanted to come home. He had waited by the conical Eleanor Cross for the bus to NW2 and hungered, and angered, and watched people cross the street before him until he was practically panting with loneliness; he came home, he always had to come home, and there she was with her hair down lifting dishes from the sink and turning away, turning back, the great buttery bulk of the window bigger and more urgent than any other window in the street.

He stood under the trees, where the atmosphere was sooty and shaded and gracious, somewhat wild, he stood and looked up and felt a paralysing shame, a strangled rage: he wanted to leave, he wanted to leave, why did she have to be there? Always? It wasn't her fault, but he couldn't do it. He watched her placidly lifting dishes. This was years ago; so many years ago now.

He'd climbed upstairs at last, then, and wrecked it. It

was the work of minutes in the end. There was no lift in the building: five floors, mezuzahs by every door. Different dinner smells.

He remembers now how lonely he felt afterwards, and that he had no right to feel lonely, as he'd believed: how lonely for months afterwards in the city they'd arrived in together. Suddenly its edges and discrepancies were sorely visible.

What does he feel now? Shame. For hurting her.

Well, it was nice to see you, she says.

Alva, Cormac came to understand afterwards, was an elegant and resourceful woman whom everyone respected. He, Cormac, was a messer, falling frankly in their estimations in commencing a campaign of sleeping with a lot of people who told other people and soon he was written off since he didn't make enough money to compensate for this generalised indiscretion.

That's part of it. How he lives now.

There is talk around him, in the corridor, and it closes Cormac out.

He turns to the staircase, which is sweeping and busily carpeted, just in time to see Nina, small against the maul of wallpaper as she ascends.

Nina now. He registers it.

Oh hi, she says. Where's Garrett? I've been texting him.

Hi! He's – inside. Are you—? He stops.

He doesn't know what he is asking her. She wears a distracting bobble hat. Something comes to him.

Your show.

She looks at him. My what? she asks.

She is standing, under the bobble, oddly and provisionally at the top of the stairs.

Your opening. Your—

That was last week, Cormac, Nina says.

But I saw you—

The Monday. Yeah, like, I haven't heard from you since. Can you tell Garrett, she asks briskly, that I locked his bike outside? It's at the rack opposite Dunnes. Here is the key. Please give it to him.

Of course—

OK, she says. Goodbye!

In bed, Senan says: I don't know why you still have it in for Garrett. I mean the thing over Alice at college, sure, but you wouldn't have married her anyway. And that's what she wanted, you see. Senan says: People want you to take them seriously.

Have you ever fucked him? Cormac asks the ceiling.

Jesus, no. What, have you?

Caroline is surprised, in the morning, when Cormac calls.

She says, Hello? slowly, as if the number is unknown. She then says, Oh hello.

He dives right in to derail her. So have you heard of Cian Bohan?

The singer.

Yes! I have tickets to his gig tonight, in the Olympia. I don't know anything about him. I don't even know if he's good or totally shit. But my friend Senan is playing in the band and he has tickets for us if you'd like to come.

I mean, he says, I would like you to come. I mean, will you come with me?

Tonight?

I know it's short notice. I only found out.

Well hey. Cormac hears a dragging groan in the background, like furniture being moved. He hears her voice relax. I'm at the studio, she says. I don't finish until seven. But I could come to you after that – is that too late?

Not at all, that's perfect. Do you want to meet in Brogan's?

Sure. She sounds happier now. She sounds happy at all. I didn't know if I'd hear from you, she explains.

What do you mean?

You've been flaky. Like, answering messages.

There's been a small family blow-up. No, nothing mad – it's fine. But sorry, I've been distracted. I'll tell you tonight. The whole ring of the Nibelungen.

Looking forward to it, Caroline replies.

Because he has no classes in the afternoon, Cormac takes the tram into town to visit the gallery where Nina's work is being shown.

It's a small space, high-windowed and gently retro, like a boutique restaurant modelled on a milking parlour. Dozing in the winter sunlight sits a girl with neon loops in her ears. She wears heavy-rimmed spectacles. She flicks through a textbook. She is a student or an intern probably. When he opens the door, this girl sits up at once, looking sleepily stunned.

Hello, she says.

All good to look around? Cormac smiles.

Of course, of course! Let me get you a brochure. She disappears into the back, earrings clackering as she goes. One of Nina's mesh huts sits, small-seeming, in a corner of the room; after this, everything is visual. Canvases, big and spaced, between the exposed girders and the tranquil walls. The hut is now welded down to a sheet of metal which is dimpled, thin as an oven tray, mistily insular.

The paintings are not unlike work of Nina's he has seen before. A candy-coloured bough of tongues, a nose perhaps, dancing to primitive music in a border of wine-puke pink; black abstract figures, a human and a duck against a Klein-blue undulation; a strange and appealing mouselike creature with cute ears, insides parcelled into panels of primary colour and a black stain where its brain should be. He looks at the caption card. It reads Teddy Bear.

There is work by other people in the gallery. A bird feeder of untreated pine, on a podium, with pads of moss tacked to it and sprayed with glaze. A baby's mobile made from cut-up sheets of government correspondence, squares of paper stamped with harps, suspended by phantasmal catgut from a hoop of balsa wood.

Nina's paintings are blunt and happily anarchic, in Gauguin colours, and you could hang them in a house without people feeling uncomfortable. There's a glee to them that is, he feels, distinctly feminine.

The intern returns with a brochure that smells deliciously of ink just like schoolbooks in the nineteen-eighties smelled of ink: knockout cheap and erotic. Its gives him stupefying flashbacks of a classroom with long windows and a drill for pulling blinds whenever a funeral passed by, which was often enough for a drill.

The pictures are amazing, aren't they? the intern says.

Cormac asks, Did you paint them?

The girl giggles and waves her hands. Oh no, oh no! she cries. I just watch the door.

In the brochure, on Nina's page, there is an introduction:

In the age of mass media, artworks must compete for attention with garish and mutative, heterogenous but manipulative, forms of public affect and display. Critic Garrett Murray describes the work of Nina MacLeod as fighting against this onslaught of 'affecting' imagery we encounter continuously in the contemporary landscape and describes how, as a result, MacLeod's paintings in particular are *'assertive and exuberant, transgressive and opulent, but sincerely and unrepentantly naive. They celebrate childhood and spontaneity, plasticity and play, without ever being pious or innocent.'* The images are figures or fleshy forms, which have a plastic density, open to transform-ation. Matter and its potential – not information – is at the heart of this vision.

Fucking Garrett, Cormac thinks. They could have asked me.

He wonders. He wonders how, for instance, a person thinks into this way of seeing with enough interest and texture to produce four or five, or more, canvases exam-ining it without ever getting bored. Personally he likes the tongues and the teddy bear, but to be honest it's difficult to get fully into the rest of it.

He leaves the gallery and walks into the sear of winter sunlight on cobbles and bookstalls. The large bearded man who runs the canvas-covered bookstall on the square scrubs his hands together.

Baltic, my friend, he remarks.

Surely is. Cormac turns over photobooks of Dublin – tourist stuff, sentimental – and foxed university classics, the fist of shamrocks on an urgent eighties paperback: *Trinity*, by Leon Uris. This was a book his father had on the shelf,

239

at home, throughout Cormac's childhood, and the fist of shamrocks brings back more memories with a tender jolt. He remembers *Visions and Beliefs in the West of Ireland*, a woman clutching at her shawl as red hair unravelled melodramatically into the spine. Nina's paintings, he thinks, are like the abstract shapes on baggy clothes in the nineties. Maybe all millennials have some kind of epigenetic emboss from that time. The design must date back to something: Basquiat, subway graffiti, disco. It's uncynical.

Cormac picks up a book about Gestalt therapy. Life as shapes that integrate new shapes. He remembers the suitcase of books. He thinks of Patrick's manuscript, still loitering awkwardly in his inbox. He turns at this thought to the bookseller.

Have you heard of a book, he asks: *The Bicameral Mind*?

The bookseller has not.

It's an early theory of consciousness, Cormac explains. Explains unbidden, admittedly.

Cormac points to his own skull, bisecting in mime, and explains further. A belief that, like, early or primitive man had a brain that wasn't unified. Or linked or something. So, basically, one part of the mind spoke to the other.

One part, the man repeats, spoke to the other.

Left side to the right, say, or right to left. Man heard his own ideas as a voice in his head. Exactly like, I suppose, schizophrenia – or forms of it.

The book is clear about the link to schizophrenia, but Cormac presents it as if it has occurred to him. He does this because he wants to avoid seeming didactic: by showing openness, comprehension might become collaboration with the bookseller. It's a trick he's cultivated through teaching, but it works to defuse hostility generally.

It occurs to him now how proletarian a virtue it is. I am still, he thinks warmly, apologising.

Are you looking for this book about the mind? the bookseller asks.

No. It's just I've never met anyone else who's read it. It's like I hallucinated it so I could learn this weird thing about the bicameral mind.

The bookseller moves off to serve someone else.

Oh, I'm not schizophrenic or anything, Cormac says after him.

He leaves. He walks to a café and sits at one of the tables outside, wrought iron wrapping agitatedly around itself to support a disc reading PERONI, and sits dazzled by the sun but clear-headed in this moment of leisure. He shouldn't have missed the opening of Nina's show. He was careless about dates, but that was a mistake. To have been careless with her. She would see it that way.

The man who comes to take his cup away gives Cormac a curious smile.


That evening, he eats alone when Senan is sound-checking. He opens the PDF Patrick sent and tries at last to read, finding his eyes wandering in a wince from the screen to the air above the screen. His brother's emotional register – arcane, gesticulating – is moving and embarrassing in equal degrees. Cormac scrolls down hastily to take in the gist, another trick he's learned, for grading essays economically. When he does, the document springs to life with meta-devices that offer to bring him to segments and subsections with titles and tabulations: Our Lives At Home, The Death, The Aftermath, My Wife, When You Are Old.

Sliding back to the top, Cormac takes in an extraordinary and completely extraneous potted history of their great-grandfather, dead before they were born, who topped socks at the hosiery factory to acclaim because his hands were long, and thin, and mechanically talented. There is a delinquent *fig.* and Cormac thinks, Oh god, he's going to include photographs.

He remembers, with an abruptness that feels loaded, even mystical, in its specificity, kissing his brother, drunk, on Patrick's wedding day: pulling the other man close and smelling the sweat that is always so oddly, so emphatically, different from his own. The vigour of this intimacy. It was a dance floor and a small child, some cousin, in a dress like an upturned tulip, dipped and swatted at balloons. The memory retains the little girl hopping concentratedly and framed by the wide panel of a woman's skirt behind. His brother is red-faced and sweating and raises a hand to slap Cormac lovingly on the cheek.

He shuts the laptop down. He dresses and leaves for Brogan's at seven thirty. He is drinking a pint by the bar when Caroline arrives, her hair tamped down by a felt beret. She romps towards him with a welcoming expression so different from the aloofness of their first encounter at the laundry show. Several other men turn to watch her pass them with longing because she's like a little shower in a drought.

He kisses her and feels little to nothing.

Oh, he thinks.


In the apartment that morning, Senan said, You never did anything with this place.

What would I do with it? Cormac asked.

You could decorate it.

It isn't mine.

Yes, but you could still decorate it. You know I wouldn't mind.

Senan is backstage now. Onstage: roadies stooping moodily. They've left the pub and sit, now, in the stalls, watching people file in and bang out the fold-up cinema seats.

Caroline begins to tell him something. She tells him about a show at Sadler's Wells. It was a *Rite of Spring* in red dust, the stage entirely covered in red dust, cabbage dye or dry sand – or dry paint – poured out across the entire stage. My friends and I were in the cheap seats, she explains. We were in the balcony wing on bar stools. We were early and we saw the stagehands come in a gang to rake the dust – comb it – into fans, really carefully and organised, like they'd practised a hundred times, and then the dancers came on in red satin slips and red satin, sort of, *loincloths* – they were an English troupe, I can't remember who – and did the *Rite of Spring*, which is very violent and all about dashing and really, you know, *raw*, all over this dust, so it was kicked up and messed up and all up their legs.

She holds out a calf in sheer tights and runs her fingers over it. Then, she says, when it was over and the lights came up, the stagehands came back – the roadies – to sweep the dust, all of it, into a kind of gutter, and get rid of it.

She says, It was one of the nicest things I've ever seen. She says: The clay we are using in *Bridget Cleary* – I suppose I am thinking of it. Dust and dirt.

There is something he wants to ask her, but he can't remember now.

I had to give up ballet, she tells him, because I am too tall.

Were you sorry?

No. You need to be, like, a functioning anorexic.

Oh wow, he remembers. Ballet – that's what I wanted to say. It's mentioned in this book I am looking at, *The Bicameral Mind*.

Yeah, that one about schizophrenia.

You know it? He is surprised.

It came into my hands weirdly. Ritual studies. It says ballet originated with dancing in temples to pagan gods.

Yes! He looks at her. I've never met anyone else who's read it, he says.

Oh, I don't know if I'd say *read* exactly. I just know about it – unnatural contortions, worship or, well, I suppose, *summoning*: kind of demonic.

So you were like a priestess, he teases.

In my previous life.

You look like a priestess now. You have presence.

She laughs, slightly orgasmically, flattered. He doesn't understand why the erotic impulse towards her has gone away. She is beautiful, but in this hungry, queenly way; her little fists grip the curling rail; they are at the edge of the first slope of seats and divided from the next by an iron rail. Perhaps it's Senan. But he's always been able to go between men and women easily. He's always been dominant either way.

There is movement now onstage. A woman with hair in Heidi braids, long dress, and a cello moves into place with the other musicians, one of whom is Senan playing, this time, an acoustic guitar, attending plainly to something being discussed in the wings. When they begin, the singer struts into view. He is thin and tall and young and his regional accent remains conspicuously intact throughout every song, which is a strange thing to hear, since after the layered Clannad Celtic steam of panpipe pop that was the sound of Ireland in the nineties there was a long time without accents. Accents were pared back.

The lyrics are florid. He sings about old men and poetry in the backroom of a bar in the Liberties, then the back-room of a bar in Paris.

It's the waif-goes-to-Montmartre thing, Cormac shouts at Caroline.

What? She widens her eyes, cocks an ear, shakes her head.

When Cormac was a teenager, there were no computers and nothing beyond terrestrial TV, illegal radio stations, local authority libraries. Nonetheless he creamed off the top of high culture and squirrelled away facts with the intensity of aspiration; social climbing, but slantwise. Early on, for example, he saw Catholic imagery for the kitschly pitiful copy it was. He made his father tramp through empty fields and rutted lanes – passing the ostrich farm, a random innovation near Courtlough, none of the absurd birds in sight – to locate the rag-tree with calcified scraps still tied to it. Cormac photographed this and developed the images in the town chemist. He knew they were haunting but also contrived.

And noy, the singer shouts, I want you to turn to the person next to you, and introduce yourselves! It strikes me, he says, how, these days, when we know so much, we have become so separated. Have ye noticed that?

Instead of introducing herself, Caroline kisses Cormac on the lips. Music pauses after a while and the musicians begin to clear out. He can see Senan drinking from a water bottle and helping others push an amplifier to the side. The woman with braids lingers, staring at her feet, until Senan inclines his head and says something that makes her laugh. The roadies suspend a circle so a girl-acrobat can perform: she turns and tumbles in ribbons, part Shibari, part circus. Throughout this Caroline frowns and leans forward and tries to work out who the acrobat is. After this the musicians return. It gets hammier and harder to endure.

Cormac feels grateful for the interval. The bar is crowded and loud of course. Caroline finds a table, a free-standing disc draped in velvet and secured – the velvet is secured – around its single plinth with another ribbon. It has the waiting shape of a folded parasol. Someone has opened a fire door. Everything feels familiar as genre in a slightly sea-sick way. The loneliness of this girl's company is a known loneliness, but to think of someone this way – to find them dull because they are complete – seems a disturbing way to think. If she got to know him, her disgust would surely turn to boredom too. It happens in the end.

Like a controlled freefall, this, to feel: *failure*, like a carnival ride. Vertigo with finish line, without fatal risk. To fail socially is to fade into privacy.

Cormac carries this new clarity with him, smiling.

How are you finding it? he asks.

Corny, she reports, but I try to be tolerant.

Would you like to bounce?

She laughs. I would, she says.

A bar in a side-street is anachronistically empty, as if waiting for something.

It's eleven, the barman calls. We're closing soon.

Already?

Half eleven is closing time. He drills this ironically.

They slide into a booth. The table is a beautiful puce-wood mahogany, dug and scratched, but the chairs are all a terrible idea, surplus Queen Anne knock-offs with deflated pouffes and ragefully crooked rivets. Every chair with a short leg. The lights are all up and the box-fresh vintage kitsch of the place is entirely wrong washed by white light and smelling of pine-scented bleach.

This is it now, Cormac says gravely. Pubs closing at closing time like the pubs of the dreaded Sassenach.

See, we can talk here, Caroline explains, because it's quiet.

Oh god, he thinks.

There is a unity of culture between this pub interior – which ought to be dingily lit by tasselled lamps – and the strained folk of the show they've just seen, and all of it emanates from a structure of feeling somewhere between the port wine forest chamber above Parnell Square and Mrs O'Mara's living room. It remembers copperwork coal boxes with shepherds dozing in shallow relief as the coal boxes in turn remember the Last of the Gaelic Elite. Cormac feels only compassion and fatigue to recognise this and grieve something. Lit flatly it is maliciously stripped of mystique, with the barman crashing chairs together angrily.

I worked with this guy years ago, Cormac finds himself saying. JP Devlin. He was a runner – for booking agents, I mean – and then, I suppose, an entrepreneur. He was one of those guys really shafted after the crash.

Caroline nods, blinking receptively. She begins the process of removing her many-buttoned duffel coat, scrunching the beret out of sight.

There was this time in Dublin, when I was at college, say, when you were part of an underground kind of culture, like a broad one, if you were weird, if you looked weird at all, if you dressed arty, say, if you looked – queer. They'd call you that, I mean, queer. Anyone strange stuck together. The pubs were full of oul lads and establishment and you wouldn't really – socialise, you know? In the same way.

How old *are* you? Caroline asks.

He laughs. Older than you. What I'm saying is JP was one of these Celtic Tiger people, you know, who saw opportunity in this and bought up cheap venues and changed them up. He was the beginning of this culture.

Gentrification.

Exactly! Cormac holds up his hands to her. There you have it. Gentrification. Then there were suddenly gay bars and a kind of *outsider aesthetic* and it felt fresh then, really new. But in the crash the banks went after all of them.

How tragic.

You joke, but it kind of was. All of this fun and then all of this – shit. I don't think it's the same any more. Dublin is not a good place to make art. He finds himself recognising this. It's too commercial, it has to make money.

He says: There were so many suicides. Really a lot of suicides.

And then, out of nowhere, Caroline asks him, Are you seeing anyone else?

Cormac smiles at her on a reflex, as a stalling device. No, he says carefully. She is relieved but assumes a look of modest puzzlement to cover it.

Me neither, she says.

Only I— They have both removed their coats. It's

248

actually still quite cold. The doors are open and the ancient laneway dipping – oozing – by outside. He halts. He tries again. Only I, I'm not, like, sure. I'm not sure.

Caroline blinks expectantly again. After another moment, she says: Sure of what?

I'm not sure if, well, if I want a relationship.

Caroline's tongue has extended beyond her bottom lip in concentration. It sits pinkly there, the mere tip of it. She looks down at the table and raises her eyebrows and seems to think fiercely, for a moment, to herself. At length, she says: Ah.

I – so. Cormac is not sure if an apology would be the right thing just now.

Why not? she asks, raising her face. You mean not with me, or not at all?

Well, I mean like—

Yes, it would be early to say *with me*, but do you mean *at all*?

I guess I mean at all.

But why did you ask me out then?

I like you.

Here lads, last orders if you want to sit, the barman calls.

Caroline turns on the barman sharply. Table service? she asks. He shrugs. Well, all right then a Shiraz, please, she says, pronouncing it correctly. It's either careless or vindictive to order something too slow to consume and Cormac enjoys it, even though he is also, opposite her, petrified.

The barman volleys back with, I can only give you a plastic glass.

Wow, says Caroline. That is all. That's all she answers: Wow.

She returns her attention to Cormac. The barman delivers her drink almost contritely. They remain the only people in the bar.

Sorry – say again, why did you ask me out in the first place?

I like you. He swallows hard. He sees himself watching and watching the watching, pathetically unformed and callous and conscious of it but at a loss.

I am sorry, he says. I like you – I thought that—

She waits. She unscrews her quarter-bottle and fills the plastic glass. The plastic glass has a stem and everything.

Listen, I thought that maybe I'd feel different because – I find you – I mean, really radiant and great.

Caroline looks up at this. I'm not going to forgive you, she says archly, just because you called me radiant.

No? Damnit. He shakes his head. They laugh: his nervous, hers hollow.

You wanted to have sex with me, she says.

I wanted to get to know you. But there is this thing about me. I – it just, like, it never works. With my friends I can be very happy. As he is saying it, the fact of this matter, of this quirk, becomes visible to him. Becomes abstract and, as a result, defensible.

With my friends I am happy and easy and I can't do any harm, he says. With you – with a relationship. You see, I can do harm. I end up doing harm.

She closes her eyes. He is surprised as seconds tick by.

It's better this way, I know it is, Cormac affirms. Panic puts a note of harshness in his tone. He feels cruelty coming on.

Yeah. She speaks spikily back. I don't want to be the kind of person who's like – Oh I can change him! Oh, I can wait for him! But, I mean, the way you put it tempts a girl. Pretty typical ambivalence.

Oh yes? He shifts in his seat.

Yeah. You put it like that and it seems to say, *test me.* If you don't want a relationship you can't go asking women out.

OK.

You go trawling for, like, casual sex on an app like everyone else.

Right.

This kind of carry-on makes it look like you *do* want something.

I don't, Caroline.

But you want the other person to, like, take responsibility for it.

He's annoyed. He is trying to be honest with her, but what she is projecting feels, to him, gratuitously complex. I know how I feel, he says firmly, that's all. It's a feeling. No matter how much I might like you. I know it won't work.

So defeatist, Caroline concludes. She sips. Oh well, she sighs. He can see her anger emerging now that her efforts are still for naught. Jesus, how embarrassing, she says. I am sorry for you. I would never want to be like you.

She stands to leave, slipping on her coat quietly, and his heart races as he sits still in humiliation and waits for her to depart.

I would never want to be dead like that, she stabs. I would never want my life to be a joke of – what is it, no harm?

She gets no response.

No meaning, Cormac, is what that really is.

251

He doesn't look up. She leaves her wine glass two-thirds full, a print of lipstick on the rim. He wants to get up and run and flip the table or thump through the streets. The shame is coloured white and ear-splitting in its intensity, but he is alone and safe now, he knows – it's over, it's no longer happening. Sounds that have been waiting rise in a chorus of mundanity: chairs stacking and freezers droning and a drunk in the street shrieking joyfully yoo-hoo, yoo-hoo, c'mere to me.

Four hours altogether, down, and a stopover in Caher-siveen, where Mass on a tannoy echoes in a frosty market street. Cold mist from the mountains closing in so that Cahersiveen is an interspace, a hovering place, in the clouds, between heaven and earth. Nina waits on a bench by a bank for Ned, who is coming to drop her out and then returning to Dingle again.

The bus from Killarney wound around the metallic peninsula, lined with hardy bungalows and rockeries of coloured stones. She kept thinking of the Will Oldham song: Shall I play ball with the dogs, or walk away? It was brutely beautiful. The architecture was execrable: hacien-das, wagon wheels.

Extracted a card from the tarot pack: seven of wands, toil and steep incline. Fighting off haters and the evil eye.

In Cahersiveen, she is cold. She feels herself to be the city person that she is, underdressed and melancholy at the first weak sight of sun through the mountain mist on a January day. Should I play ball with the dogs, or walk away?

Over the tannoy, a priest coughs or drops something.

A man has parked in an alleyway and is waving to her, wearing a deerstalker hat.

Ned. She greets him.

Put that in the back. He helps her lift the suitcase and place it next to a spare wheel. How's the form? he asks. The interior of the old, long car is hairy with tassels and scapulars. It belongs, he explains, to his father.

Thank you for helping out, Nina says.

I think you're crazy, girl. You know there'll be no boats going out at all.

I can see it though. I'll just look at it.

I hope you ordered fuel.

I didn't. Should I?

Jesus. He laughs.

Poor amadán, she says. Pity the poor Dublin amadán.

Yes you should order some, but we can stop at the petrol station. I'll wait for the call. I will wait for you begging me to come and get you down.

I'm terrible at lighting fires.

Everyone has to learn sometime.

I'll get drunk and stay drunk instead.

Sounds like a plan, says Ned.

The roads ease into boreens with a green dorsal of grass. They wind empty under the leaden afternoon, marshy but ruptured the whole way up – from coast to peak – with rocks so specific, so complicated, they seem godly and deliberate. As if a magnet works on them, these rocks form walls and gulleys, plumb lines dropping from a hillside to an inlet of white waves, and everywhere divide the landscape up with eerie accuracy.

Daubed rams and cattle track the car. The immense skelligs stand, mist-smudged, offshore, like dinosaurs.

Nina left Heuston hours before, constipated. She sat waiting and scalded inside by coffee. Someone took a seat at the painted piano to sing 'Jingle Bells': Christmas is gone and everything austerely purposeful, so this was antisocial ragging on the piano really. Now she looks at the mountains, mustard and green with gorse and grass and plaqued at every point with rocks, and thinks, I will fast and stare out to sea. I will either feel worse than I do, as bad as it gets, or be healed.

She feels, always, able to be playful with Ned; he is easy company and doesn't intimidate her. He makes sculptures in a turf shed. He knows how to drive a tractor and jump over electric fences for fun. He has so many brothers and sisters, Nina pictures them cuffing him over the head as they pass: some bonny, mindless, clannish kind of life. Not she: suburban, nervy.

Climbing the mountain now, nervily.

How is Ciara? she asks.

His girlfriend is angry with him because they're not married. Nina struggles to understand why Ned, who seems so wounded by this and is back in his family home, doesn't just propose to her. Nobody has proposed to Nina in a long time. Nobody has wanted to treat her as anything other than fun. She too, were she in sight of a long, quiet rest, would desire this and feel pain if it was withheld.

I don't know, Ned answers simply.

Climbing the mountain, out of Wi-Fi range. Holiday homes in fits and harbours, white fleets: their gambrels and their gable ends like sails. Ned swings the car into the forecourt of the petrol station and store she remembers from last time. There are two young girls working behind the counter. She buys some groceries, a bottle

255

of wine, and a bale of briquettes Ned carries to the car.

Toilet roll, she says. Remember last time, we forgot?

Driving on, the boreens narrow around pens of sheep, a fold, a fell, until they are right against a cliff collapsing into the sea. The great Skellig, grazing, fills the sky.

The house is as it was before, bitty gingham blinds, and the key underneath a stone by the door. There are stones everywhere. There are more stones than anything else. You walk everywhere over a moving, rolling, road of stones.

Do you want to come in?

No, to be honest I should get back. It's a good hour.

All right. Thank you. It won't be the same, she says, without you. Last time he spent a lot of the residency on the phone to Ciara; when he was not on the phone to Ciara, he was walking blank-eyed in the mountain pass. She waves him off warmly. She is alone, now, with the peace. Not even the sound of waves, because the waves are too far away – the sea just sits there, rocking quietly.

The house is freezing and the tapers tickle out. She cannot get the fire going at all. Boils eggs; eats, dumbly and miserably, rolls of bread. Goes to bed early, because it's so cold, in the loft. There is nothing to be seen through the window now: rain on the pane and fathomless black without. The wind whinnies rather than roars off the sea. She doesn't feel threatened, only lonely, with a purity born of alignment between heart and environment: she feels racked, entirely, by lack.

Remembers something Cormac said. When I stayed there – talking about the mountain house, the artists' colony – I almost hanged myself from the beams. Nina stares at the beams meeting in a hood of cobwebs over her head.

In the night it gets wild, with a gale breaking on the gable and engulfing it. The stones of the house have been there for three hundred years and withstand it implacably: you don't worry, despite the chill you don't feel actual draughts. The stones are stacked and sealed as regularly as undressed stones can be, and the mismatches between them reveal secret recesses, like shelves, into which guests have placed seashells, beads, the claw of a crab, matchsticks, a painted pumice face.

The rest of the hamlet is ruins, a church and guttered huts, with hearths intact and window frames standing dramatically in stone. During the eighteen-forties everyone left, but some of them died here before they could. Ned has told her that, outside Dingle, a field is left alone because the district knows it as a grave: people set off on the winding mountain roads to the port but died midway. Because the village was built of stone, it lasted after the final wagon had departed. She thinks of crevassed faces boring out of shawls beyond the grave, watching her incuriously – the toughness of the place and people, their sufferings, make it hard to slide into. She never spoke Irish after school.

I stand before my nation's miseries, she writes, like an aid worker.

She sends a photograph of the workspace, paint-splattered stone under the grey gleam of a skylight, to Cormac. He answers after some time with a thumbs-up. She wants to write, Lately you are nothing but a supercilious prick.

The dead are baffled. He has always been a supercilious prick. So few of the artists who stay here are interesting, they think. But at least the Americans who make calls all day to tell people they are on the blasted precipice of

Europe bother to eat. Nina does nothing but boil two more eggs and scroll Twitter and feel sorry for herself. She'll get hungry and bring this bleak energy of scarcity to the entire day.

Nina thinks of painting the non-consenting dead.

Ha-ha, she says. She de-shells eggs over oilcloth. In the suitcase are two canvases she spent happy days stretching in Dublin; in the corner of the workspace is an easel so old it looks unsteady, but holds up. There are drawings. She sits and draws underneath the white light of the workspace, the stones with tinctures of red, clay or memories of the cooled volcano aeons ago. It's cold. She has to try the stove again and fail. She has to walk to Ballinskelligs to get closer to the sea.

On the road, in raw, overlapping moments, there is a sideways drill of rain, followed by a twist of painful sunlight and then more rain. Down the mountain pass and stepping into a verge of dripping honeysuckle to avoid passing cars, Nina finds four standing stones flocked by yard-wide, jungle-looking leaves. Walking through this part of the road is texturally different to the rest of the route and it must, she thinks, be the standing stones: they were a shrine or a site of punishment once.

Ned knows everything about the mountain farm where he grew up and although she's never seen it, she believes it must be like this, fierce and steep. The ease people feel with place moves her: they always have somewhere to return to. She feels she belongs nowhere, which is absurd for an Irish person, but it's true – since college, she berates herself, I've failed to be taken in by any kind of circle in Dublin. There are art people, but she's only invited along to things as somebody's guest. It is her shyness, maybe. It's the way people don't take a young woman seriously and then, suddenly, she is not so young and even less of a candidate.

Anyone with power has married and increased. Think of Garrett, for example. Think of Garrett painfully. He proposed to write up her show and she knew it was sexual interest, but that didn't matter, it was welcome even, after everything.

A lot of opportunities squandered, Nina thinks.

Here is Ballinskelligs, not even a town. Not even the coffee shop open. The strand is screaming with scarf-trailing breezes and she walks unsteadily along it, aiming for the ruined tower on a mudflat within reach. Raking, mentally, over the faintest ember of consolation and harming herself compulsively.

She couldn't help loving him. It was the purest of accidents. It happened at a moment of openness, when she was dying of shame and grief over an abortion she had to travel to England for. In the days afterwards, she'd wandered a church in Oxford, where she was staying in the borrowed flat of a friend: it had a war chapel and a raft of poppy wreathes that gave the place the pleasant watery smell of a garden centre.

Art she made about it, and considered discreet, was reviewed by a critic:

It is dismaying that a young artist like MacLeod should focus on squalid or unfortunate experiences with men.

And Nina had written *Bitch* seven times on the cover of a paperback before realising she had done it at all: raising her writing hand, she looked curiously at *Bitch*, capitalised each time, as if it were automatic writing. What comes out of it, by extrapolation? Bit, itch, tsk, bitcoin, coin-of-entry, tic.

Drinking later at a really bad gig in the Liquor Rooms. Must have been other people there, but she remembers, now, only a lonely table and the slush of finished gins. Cormac was standing over her, handsome as he had been when he'd taught her, and she thought: That's it. The sex was excellent. Her heart was open as the throat of a baby bird. She wanted to be made new. At that time, every pregnancy she saw was like a slap, so she went backwards, into a marshmallow childhood; she painted humanoid Ribena stains and made playhouses. She found exuberance and immensity. She borrowed a flat in London for a month and avoided all the acquaintances there. The man who'd jacked her life sent missives sometimes: whore, slut, whore, slut, forgive me, whore. She told Cormac once and he looked away, then stirred his coffee, then said: Well, you got away.

Exactly, waft the dead in Ballinskelligs. Just a prick.

There were days of silence, she tells them in defence. I couldn't talk about this with anybody. It was

squalid and unfortunate.

You let it happen, the dead insist.

She tramps back. At various points she wonders if the turn was wrong, but it comes to rights, and she reaches the house just as a car humps over the road of stone and crunches further up the mountain out of sight.

An hour later she is drawing at the table when there

comes, singularly, a knock at the door. A man in a duffel coat who looks familiar stands outside.

Heya, he says. I was staying here last week – you didn't happen to find a yoga mat left behind anywhere, did you?

No. Nina leans on the door frame, folding her arms. She's pleased, she realises, to see someone. I didn't, I'm afraid.

The caretaker must have cleaned it out. He laughs. Sounds stupid, he says, but I've had it for years. I got it in India.

You're a musician, she says, I recognise you. Cian.

Ha, yes.

I am a fan!

He laughs. You are? Are you sure?

I'm sorry that I don't have your yoga mat.

Here it's grand. It's probably gone to the arts centre. She notices, for the first time, a car humming behind him on the stones. She notices his large brown eyes. So how is it going for you? he asks. The residency?

Oh, I was here before. She catches herself. I mean: I am finishing something. I am drawing a lot of rocks.

Lot of rocks around here, he agrees.

Could you get the stove thing working, she asks with a shot of inspiration, when you were here?

Oh sure. If you like, I can do it for you.

Inside, she is conscious of the room as she has spread it out, the canvas on the lumber easel and the drawing paper scattered everywhere. He makes a taper from newspaper and lights it tentatively, shutting the screen afterwards.

Those small briquettes are better, he says, than the peat. He is tall, much longer in here than outdoors or on TV.

Lovely, she flirts. It's not a lot of craic up here. Do you enjoy it?

261

I come a good bit, and I'm staying locally. There are a few of us around. He looks at her.

Anything fun, she asks, going down?

Well, a gig in Dingle, you know, next week. It's recording a bit mostly. If you'd like, I can let you know – you know, if anything's happening?

Take my number, she suggests. I am called Nina.

When he leaves she sits around thinking of sex and feeling sulky, then depressed. The night comes on again and the mountain's edge is a sinister fringe of grass and sedge. She records the time of a sudden, late sputter of birdsong – nineteen-thirty-eight exactly – in case this is significant.

Draws a card. The hanged man, naturally. Looks again at the beams.

She starts on the canvas the next afternoon, engrossed for hours in applying outlines to the cells of the stretch, which is tight enough to show fibres in warp and weft. All begins with drawing for Nina. The idea of advancing without proportion, pure abstraction, is mystifying to her, like speaking in tongues.

She celebrates herself with a glass of Shiraz that is kitchen-cold. After this, she feels antic and antsy because the musician hasn't contacted her. Nobody wants to see me, she thinks. She feels sadness again and has wine on the brain and so every awful possibility – life forever in the dilated moment, walking around Oxford in a state of horror still without a full descriptive sentence, not a one – stretches anguishing ahead. Nina on one glass of wine thinks, Were it not for my loved ones I too would hang myself. Cormac has explained some of it to her: In London, he says, I just rotted inside and I had to keep running away.

Why?

I couldn't, you know. He became inarticulate at this. Like, the responsibility. I don't know. I got so bored. I mean, I couldn't concentrate: I thought my life was passing, I was stuck. I don't know how to explain this, he said.

You weren't ready.

I couldn't marry her, he conceded. But afterwards I was like, pure mad. All over the place. He tried to laugh.

What changed?

Meditation. I learned to be by myself, he claimed.

Nina meditates. The night is seaside-peaceful, so dark it's like the world has fallen away. She dreams there are berries growing from the tips of her hair and when she picks and eats them they taste, nauseatingly, like grapes.

She wakes and thinks: I've never enjoyed grapes.

Today, the sky is blue. As she is sloping down the mountain road and coming to the spooky palms with their creeping, feed-me-Seymour vibrancy, a little car peaks on the nearby hill, but when Nina steps into the hedge to let it pass, it slows instead and the window is rolled – manually, vigorously – down.

I thought you might be the Nina all right.

Oh wow, Senan, she says. Oh wow!

Do you want a lift into Ballinskelligs?

Although she's enjoying the walk, she says, Yes, that would be great. As she climbs into the passenger seat, he apologises for the smell of cigarettes and explains, We have this bass player staying with us and he smokes like a chimney. I don't even let him smoke in the car; this is how he smells *generally*.

Wow, she says redundantly. She recovers herself. How are you here?

There are a few of us, we are working. I know. He laughs. You go into the wilds and start running into people. I used to come to the Gaeltacht down here, actually, when I was at school.

Senan doesn't seem to spot an oncoming car until it is perilously close, albeit extremely slow: when he sees it, he says, Oh! lightly, almost delightedly, and hits the brake. Both drivers slide tightly by one another with waves. I saw your beautiful show, he tells her, before it closed.

Oh wow! Thank you.

Cormac sent me. I mean, he said I had to see it. It was wonderful.

Thank you, she repeats. His earnestness makes her glow. The mention of Cormac makes her glow. She has to stop herself asking for more. She has been intensely intrigued by Senan ever since Cormac told her about the dynamic between them at school, which he told in a moment of moving openness when he was unhappy and had invited her, randomly, out, and walked around the hoop of Merrion Square – which was closed in the dark – explaining that he missed her and would like to see more of her. This was when she came back from London.

Oh, of course, she told him softly at Merrion Square. Carefully, remedially, because he was hopping with nerves and seemed slightly out of his mind.

When he'd recovered, weeks later, he reverted to supercilious prick, and this pattern re-enacted itself with semi-regularity for nearly a year until he swept into her studio before Christmas and asked for it – the energy – again, a final time. She didn't hear from him after that. The silence of her phone was a viral load. She was sick, skittering, full of rage, alienated from everyone else over

Christmas: Nina was Done With This. On New Year's Day there came a desultory message – Happy NY – and she'd answered, Thanks! Have such a head on me.

She says to Senan now, blandly, So, have you seen Cormac?

Ah, says Senan. Well, just before Christmas, yes.

Me too.

Where did you want to go?

I don't know, I'm just walking.

Would you like to come up to the house and meet everyone?

I would. Nina turns to him archly. She spreads her hands. I would. I would love nothing more than to procrastinate.

Thought so. It's intense, isn't it?

Every time I go on residency, I think: Oh, great idea. But it's not. It's hang-yourself-from-the-roof-beams.

Cormac always says that, Senan nods. Hang yourself.

The house is a farmhouse on a slope. A sheepdog bounds from the woodshed; Nina lets it push its face into her hands.

Good doggy-dog, she says.

A woman with a headscarf crosses from the washing line. Long dresses in Liberty and Orla Kiely print jerking on the constant, caustic breeze. Hey, hey! She waves. Nina recognises her from somewhere. Probably an actress or a singer.

This is Nina, I found her on the road. She's a stray.

Hey. The woman lifts her skirt to reveal wellies and tips over a cavity dashed in the cobblestones; over a puddle.

Nina MacLeod the artist, Senan says.

Oh, we were at your wonderful show.

Nina covers her face with hands in a pretend gesture

of humility. She smells the hand cream from her floral washbag: a scent like Earl Grey tea.

Senan. The woman changes tack immediately. Her voice drops. She says: Your bassist is drunk again.

I'll take him for a walk.

Nina stands before the farmhouse and looks up. Each window gazes glazedly over the dark green slope, the ropy rocks emerging from the slope, the distant strip of dismal sea. It's lonely and cruel, the place, like everywhere in the area, stripped of pretension and civility. Not for the first time she thinks, I should really just *move* to London. Or Berlin.

She is glad to be here – surely – but she has no way back alone. The woman's energy has changed. The darkness of her voice: Bassist drunk. She folds her arms. Her accent is RP.

She doesn't want me here, Nina realises. She feels little and bitchy underneath her coat. I will, she thinks, go in.

Come on, Senan sighs.

There is a butty hallway and a big kitchen with a range in a shade of duck-egg, linoleum blistered near the range. Wine bottles with candles staggering out of them. A dark-haired man at the table, bent to explaining something to a lithe man – the musician from yesterday, she realises – with the ringing vehemence of inebriation.

So you are boring everyone again, Senan lilts. The dark man, who must be the bassist, glances up.

Indeed, he says.

We have a guest. This is Nina.

Nina knows she will disappoint these people. That is what is happening. They are bored, but she will disappoint them. She looks at the space: there are mandala hangings and a wicker rack of briquettes interspersed with pizza delivery boxes. The musician, Cian, spreads his arms. We met!

We did. I still don't have your yoga mat.

What? Oh yeah, no worries at all.

The woman crosses the room and puts her hands on Cian's shoulders. Nina thinks: Oh god. She wants to go back suddenly. She thinks of her lumber easel standing sagely underneath the skylight. She thinks of the webby beams. The dog bangs into the kitchen and settles on a rug before the range.

Will you stay for dinner? the woman asks.

If it's not too much trouble, Nina says.

Dinner is stew, ladled generously as Nina – tipsy on wine against her empty stomach – closes her fists sentimentally.

Oh my goodness *thank you*, she says.

The entire situation has become ridiculous. The woman hardly speaks – she ladles, with a vicious intent that is slightly pathetic, and slaps plates before everyone. The dark-haired bassist rolls a cigarette and watches her with a smile.

Kerry, he says, brings out the worst in everyone.

We are writing, Cian explains.

Do you get like this, I mean, when you write? Nina asks.

Cian shrugs with what seems like anger. This anger has nothing to do with her. Nina is hygienically grateful for the wisdom – wisdom earned with age and acclimatisation to men – that this has nothing to do with her and, indeed, she might be anyone. Anyone female. His shrug is faintly enraged.

You have to go into it, he explains.

Nina wants to laugh. Instead, she eats. Breaking to use the toilet scattered with manly shrapnel, with shaving bowls and a scummy lather-brush upturned in a dish of soap slivers, she messages Cormac: Hanging with friends of yours.

Some nights we've been doing mushrooms, Senan tells her when she returns to the table. They grow in the foresty bit. You know where the palms are?

Yes! Nina cries. Yes! Those freaky palms.

Yeah, there's a house there. They're cool with it. They have access to some woods – a small one – and there are lots of little psilocybin mushrooms. You have to pick a lot.

You need eighty or so, the bassist weighs in at once.

Eighty? Nina pretends to be surprised.

We brew them as tea, reports the woman.

I will buy some from you, Nina says.

Don't be silly, says Senan. You can do them with us after this. Just eat. They take about forty minutes.

Are you sure?

Nature's bounty.

The bassist laughs. Ireland, he says. This magical place.

There are shrooms in the UK. Tarquin makes chocolates, the woman points out. She actually points a fork.

Those are incredible, the bassist agrees.

Hold on. Nina puts down her own fork. There are shrooms in the stew? Everyone begins laughing somewhat gratefully: she has broken the emotional omerta.

Oh goodness no, the woman says.

Nina's phone grinds in her coat pocket. Cormac: Oh my, oh who? he asks. The next message says: Aren't you in Blnskg? She frowns and then thinks, Oh right, Ballinskelligs.

Yes, a few people here. Senan and everything. She sets the phone aside then, regally. She pours wine.

I'm so glad I ran into you, Senan, she says. She says this camply and feels confident finally.

Garrett met her in the Lord Edward on a white-cold, pipingly frigid night. The world was under the strict spell of promised snow. She'd spent New Year's Eve with her housemates making sigils from their wishes, abbreviating these, screwing the paper up and burning it in the flame of a church candle.

There are feelings I am trying to have for you, he began.

It's OK, she told him. I never expected.

Alice and I go back a long time.

I don't even know why you are telling me this.

She walked to the bus past Cormac's place but didn't knock. The next day, she went to a housing crisis meeting in City Hall with her housemate, who was campaigning: three anxious architects stood up and shouted over each other. One was a woman with a long, grey and distrait braid. Nina was learning that most people on the Left had money under them like gravity and their passion was elastically egotistical. She left early and passed Cormac's place, but didn't knock.

I might move completely to Berlin, she told a housemate.

Yeah, deadly idea, the woman said.

She helps the woman with the Liberty print dresses, now, wash plates. It is a warmly satisfying job, shaking each brisk disc above a trench-deep Belfast sink. She sees the wise lines in the woman's face and learns the woman is an actress who has been with Cian – caring, Nina thinks, for him – for some time. Until this year she's been the real one, or the one with a career.

Nina looks at her and wonders if she would like this life for herself: sponsor, mother, enlightened one. She is drunk now and philosophical. She accepts a mug of mushroom tea, spiced so stingingly with ginger it opens the pores, and washes it back before taking position cross-legged on a tumbledown couch.

Watch for the Protestant cushions, Cian remarks.

The – what?

Duck-down. It comes out everywhere.

There is no difference, Senan claims sonorously, between Protestants and Catholics.

There are a number of differences, Cian says.

Her attention roves over the room as she thinks, I won't be here again, I don't want to be, so take it in. Wall hanging with spirals winding out from one another furiously; a wooden cupboard with a half-moon carved above like the entrance to a souk. Padded peace comes over her. It is as safe and sealed and static as an airproof booth. She will be paired with the woman, she knows. The boys will want to talk to each other. They will prefer the women to make vacant small talk – the posh woman, her accent knowing nasal: *Well*, I mean we all know what he's like.

Cormac. Of course.

Just lost, the bassist suggests.

Before I left Dublin, the woman explains, I was walking in the Phoenix Park and he fell over himself crossing to me to say hello. He's just lovely, you know? Fell over himself.

He likes performers, Nina agrees.

They laugh. Their eyes light up with greed. Performers! All but Senan, who looks at his knees.

Cormac has answered her message. She is placidly aware that she may be hallucinating, but it seems to read: Enjoy.

These are strong, Cian says. Are we ready to go out? He shuffles a large camper's backpack onto his shoulders.

It's dark, Nina points out with surprise when the door is opened. The door is wobbled wood with many coats and cardigans hooked to it: these look like flower bulbs and taproots through the soft screen of the high.

Wrap up, the woman advises. She stands next to Nina now, buttoning a coat and smiling coldly.

Nina still feels peaceful and somewhat stuffed up, as if her ears have been blocked with cotton wool. She hears her own pulse and the rustle of her hair in the hood of her coat closer and more intactly than the noises of the room. In the yard of cobblestones she looks at the stars. Orion, obvious Orion, breadcrumbed overhead. The woman has no interest in being paired with her, which is a relief.

Come, Senan says to the bassist, who is lying on the couch.

Can't we stay?

No. Come.

My legs are jelly.

Walk! The trees await.

Together, shining torches, they make their way down the rutted slope, carefully over larger stones. At the bottom of a laneway, a gate swings thinly open and leads to another laneway.

This goes up and around, the woman explains. She points to where the landscape rolls up blackly over them.

Nina still feels the air to be cotton-wool close and her body alert, sinuous, as a cat, responding to her inclinations fluidly. She swings her hips and lets her hands open in front of her. The trees either side are indifferent, the countryside still, polished by starlight or with odd winking houselights in the mountainside. It seems like everyone else is higher than her. The woman is dancing, the bassist hunched and moving stiffly on the rim of the ditch, and Cian repeats *These are strong* again.

They are not so strong, she thinks. They are perfectly all right. But suddenly the incline opens on a height and, between trees staggered it seems for the very purpose, the skellig is there: the skellig is prehistoric, basking like a whale.

Oh, she says, stopping. The others stop.

Here?

Further on, commands someone.

Nina. Senan extends his hand smilingly. She takes it, dry and warm, as they advance up the end of the incline together. At the top, wind zips across the rock face until they step into a hollow between some alien-looking trees – fir trees. There is a huge stone here, as big as a small sofa. It was a Mass rock, Senan says. He points to a well in the centre of the rock. If there was Mass, he explains, this would be filled up with water to let people know.

What if it rained? Nina refutes this: No, I don't think that makes sense. It would be always full of water, all the time.

She says: There are people over there.

No people.

None? I can see them, a little group.

Hallucination.

OK. The people are speaking to one another in ordinary tones. She hears the burry buzz of their speech but no actual words. Yes, this is indeed a hallucination. There are no other people here. These are the dead – of course, the dead.

Breeze tears across the landscape vividly. The skellig sits there, dark and hulking but, with time and attention, emerging from the dark behind – the little white razoring waves – as distinct, dusty shimmering, matte with a gloomy glowing gloss. It is utterly, mutely, happy with itself. It has the private, patient permanence of a Galápagos tortoise. The common shape and energy strikes Nina warmly as significant, appropriate, and she is telling them all this candidly – telling them, rock is island is monk's cell is thousand-year-old tortoise.

Memory of Encarta interactive CD-ROM. She yelps with laughter. Oh dear. Calm down. *Galápagos*.

The dead hush and look at her judgingly.

I could roll in the grass, Senan confides. He still has her hand. Cian walks in front of them, standing in silhouette against the skellig, and lets out a long, happy, doggish howl.

Now punch, shouts the bassist. Cian swivels and starts to unpack the camper's bag. There is a large thermos and several chipped mugs carried from the house.

Oh that was it! Nina says. Rattling in your bag. All the way up. I thought it might be money or something.

Cups. It's rum punch, Cian repeats. The drink is hot and, like the mushroom tea, simmered strongly with ginger. It will bring you down, Cian says. He seems almost sober now, doling the drink out carefully. Not a drop spilled. The woman has sat herself solidly on the Mass

273

rock, wellies hovering a foot above the ground, and Nina says, I don't want to come down!

In a bit you will. Makes it nicer this way.

They are all making such a fuss, Nina thinks. She decides to climb onto the Mass rock too.

Are the people still there? Senan asks. She shakes her head. Will I roll in the grass? Senan asks.

I'll join you.

But he doesn't. He climbs onto the Mass rock.

Thank you for this, Nina says to them all. Thank you for this experience. She looks up. A satellite skids briskly between layered veils of stars. You don't see skies in the city. You only see them at the edge of the solid world. She still feels most sober and most knowing and separate from them all. In this state of arousal, she feels the different tensions between them, loose and visible, like buoys bobbing on a cord submerged: the actress losing her musician, her boy-lover; the bassist defensively attached to Senan; Senan blandly passive as a saint.

And me, she thinks, outside everything.

Turning to Senan, she says, We are bound by Cormac.

Yes. Senan smiles.

I think I was in love with him for a while.

Oh, that never works.

No.

You love him with a kind of space.

Senan holds out his long fingers as he speaks. They are exceptionally elegant. A torch is lit: a torch spikes a clean white line into the trees. You love him, he continues, with a kind of – membrane around him, you know? A no-go zone.

I know what you mean, Nina says.

It is good for personal growth.

They both laugh. Nina feels the clean, sheer outline of the night: the night cut from life, as exemplary.

It takes a day to shake off the hangover, the shakes themselves, the rocky deposit where appetite should be. Cormac, piqued by her uncharacteristic silence, calls in the evening.

Think I'll go wandering, he declares. Thinking of subletting or something or giving it up. Get out of town.

Where would you go? she asks smoothly. He has threatened this before. He sometimes does when he's dissatisfied.

I mean there are lots of places. Berlin. Bucharest.

You'd have to come back. She hears herself sounding short.

Yeah maybe. Maybe not.

You'd give up Senan's apartment.

Senan! he says. Let me tell you a story about Senan. Senan's uncle is an undertaker, right? Yes, I mean he's from Offaly: there is nothing to do there except die. Anyway when Senan was a teenager he worked with the apprentice undertakers one night putting a coffin together and they got wasted drunk, in the shed in Offaly you must imagine – in the shed – and set, like, the nail gun to maximum strength. I don't know, they were shooting holes in the wall or something. Anyway, they forgot to set the nail gun back to average strength or whatever. So the head undertaker, Senan's uncle, comes in in the morning to nail whatever dead person into the coffin with too much strength. The nails shot right through, too forcefully.

Anyway, you know what happens next: at the altar the strapping sons lift the coffin and the bottom falls out of it.

275

Did this – really happen?

Yes it did. We were at school. He felt terrible about it.

I can imagine.

I thought it was hilarious. I had to carry my brother's coffin, you know; you have to do that when you're a man.

Nina is standing at the easel. In the time since he's called, she has moved away from the easel and boiled the basic, short-corded kettle in the freezing kitchen space; she has stewed a cup of tea. Now she is back at the easel, eyeing anguished a blister in the seventh lucky layer of a flower-rotting mauve.

You don't bring your brother into things, she says with sudden boldness, unless you're annoyed.

Don't I?

Cormac simply loves hearing about himself. But it is vulnerable, suddenly: he sounds vulnerable. Nina steps back from the canvas and sits on the collapsed couch. The stove is cold and empty. Maybe that was rude of me to say, she tells him in a gentler tone. I apologise.

No worries.

The spell – in a moment, it breaks.

So you'd leave, she says. You'd go all over the place.

Probably not, he shoots perversely. Petulantly. So what, he changes, did you do with the gang last night?

Oh, we got high.

You did! He sounds happy for her. She wants to make him angry again. It felt promising just then.

Senan has a boyfriend.

Does he indeed. Senan has terrible taste. I know that actress, he continues cheerfully, she has a house near Hampstead Heath. Alva and I, when we were going out, had dinner with her – she used to host these dinner parties,

276

put you next to someone from the Royal Court or whatever, a Redgrave, that toff actress who seduced the wife of
a diplomat or whatever—

I don't, Nina says stiffly, know these people.

Well it's no great loss. Aristocrats tend to be messed up.
Boo-hoo.

Boo-hoo! Ah but she's nice, that woman.

No doubt they are all nice to you. Now, Nina thinks, I
am the one who is irritated. She asks, So how *are* you? She
blows roughly over the top of her tea.

Re-reading your notes on my work. I have it open here.

Oh ignore that! I was harsh. Nina pauses. Or, she says,
absorb it. I might have said some interesting things.

Oh sure, absolutely. I've also got this manuscript from
my brother. My brother wrote a memoir.

He did?

It's a little – tender.

It's nice that you read it.

I was kind of moved that he gave it to me.

I have to go, she tells him suddenly. I have to work.
You are confusing my muses – I am running out of time.

My apologies, of course. I might go back to my own
shit and populist photographs.

You do that, she says smiling. You go back to your
populist photographs. And if, her voice lifts, you go travelling, you can lend me your apartment for the duration.

What?

If you leave Dublin, like you said.

Ah no, Cormac yawns. I will stay.

Well then, we'll get coffee when I come back up.

That we will, he tells her in a higher voice. I look forward to it. I look forward to you.

Ha! Nina says. I'm sorry, what?

Ringing off, she puts the hot phone on the arm of the couch and finishes her mug of tea.

Senan, doughtily stoned, drove her back in the small hours of the morning, singing together, *Sé mo laoch, mo ghille mear / Sé mo Shaesar, ghille mear*. The fields, the peninsula, the mountains around them were effaced entirely by a suspended blend of darknesses, shadows and recesses, blank acres of heavy ash, and all that lay ahead was the road springing forth in the stems of the headlamps.

I am following the road, Senan said. Is all I am doing.

It must go somewhere. Here!

He parked on a platform under Bolus Head. The houses of the colony withstood wind rushing around them as always. Overhead, a long slice of moon was finally visible. She became concerned just then, through the fog of benignity, that he might die on the way back – veer into the sea.

Do you want to stay, she asked, and wait a bit?

Are there instruments?

Oh – no.

OK. We'll use the voices only, then.

He sang 'The Parting Glass'. He sang 'Daffodil Mulligan'. At her urging, he sang 'Panis Angelicus'. He was a weird, solemn stamp on the creeping dawn. When it was bright, he said, I feel pretty sober now. I will go.

At the car she embraced him intensely, crushingly. Senan, she said, you are a little gift from God.

Come back again, he told her, and hang out.

Yeah! Nina knew she would not. There were five days left on the residency and she had too much work to do.

# Acknowledgements

I am grateful to the Arts Council of Ireland, who supported this book financially, and to University College Dublin for hosting me as Writer in Residence in 2021. Warm thanks are due, once again, to my editor Lettice Franklin, without whom I couldn't have finished this novel, and to my agent Matthew Turner. Love to my family and friends, especially my sister Aoife Frances. Sydney Weinberg and Ronan Cassidy read early drafts and I am grateful for their feedback. Some of the creative works in this novel are based on art by Laura Fitzgerald, Aileen Murphy, David Timmons, Fiona Reilly, Jonathan Mayhew, and ANU Productions: for the purpose of scene-setting I have riffed off surfaces but the real work is excellent and I encourage you to check it out. Thanks, finally, to the Irish Writer's Centre for sending me to Cill Rialaig in 2020.

# About the Author

Niamh Campbell's debut novel, *This Happy* (2020), was shortlisted for the An Post Irish Book Awards, the Kerry Group Irish Novel of the Year Award, the John McGahern Book Prize and the Kate O'Brien Award. In 2020, she also won the Sunday Times Audible Short Story Award for her story 'Love Many'. She lives and works in Dublin.